"IT COULDN'T HAVE BEEN SELF-INFLICTED?" ASKED JEAN.

"No weapon yet," Doug Niven said briefly. "But we need your guesstimate as to the time of death."

Jean put her hand under the sheet and on the chest. It was cool but still well above room temperature, and when she bent the elbow it moved without any resistance. "Not long," she said. "A couple of hours at most.

"It's odd to find the body still tucked up in bed," Jean mused. "You'd think that if somebody came with a lethal weapon there would be some movement of self-defense."

"Probably asleep, don't you think?"

But Jean was not con...
cotton pillow and ...
weapon accomplishe...

A BONNY CASE
OF MURDER

A BONNY CASE OF MURDER

A Dr. Jean Montrose Mystery

by

C. F. ROE

Ⓢ

A SIGNET BOOK

SIGNET
Published by the Penguin Group
Penguin Books USA Inc., 375 Hudson Street,
New York, New York 10014, U.S.A.
Penguin Books Ltd, 27 Wrights Lane,
London W8 5TZ, England
Penguin Books Australia Ltd, Ringwood,
Victoria, Australia
Penguin Books Canada Ltd, 10 Alcorn Avenue,
Toronto, Ontario, Canada M4V 3B2
Penguin Books (N.Z.) Ltd, 182–190 Wairau Road,
Auckland 10, New Zealand

Penguin Books Ltd, Registered Offices:
Harmondsworth, Middlesex, England

First published in the United States by Signet,
an imprint of Dutton Signet,
a division of Penguin Books USA Inc.
Previously published in Great Britain by Headline Book
Publishing PLC under the title *Deadly Partnership*.

First Signet Printing, June, 1994
10 9 8 7 6 5 4 3 2 1

PART ONE

Chapter 1

Donald Tarland seemed preoccupied all through dinner, and his wife, Teresa, was very aware of it, although she was reasonably sure it didn't have anything directly to do with her. Maybe he'd tell her about it over coffee; usually he loosened up a bit after a meal. Tonight, they finished their espresso in silence.

Donald called for the bill. He was about forty, solidly built, good-looking in a rather square-faced, prim kind of way, and wore glasses with round lenses that gave him a slightly surprised expression. To his annoyance, because he took quite a pride in his appearance, Donald's black hair had recently started to go thin on top, although there was no gray in it yet. They had gone out to dinner to celebrate his birthday, a few days late because things had been quite hectic at the office. The Kinross was a smallish restaurant with a nice ambiance, red plush upholstery and excellent food, located in a cul-de-sac off South Street in Perth. It was run by Bob and Louise Fraser, a pleasant middle-aged couple who'd come to Perth about the same time as Donald and Teresa. With them had come their daughter, Caroline, who presently worked as a secretary in Donald's office and sometimes helped out in the restaurant, and their son, Mark, usually called Marco. Tonight the service had not been up to the usual; Louise, a big-boned, strong woman, had been rushing around doing most of the serving, helped only by one waitress. Now it was quieter, and most of the customers had left.

"Isn't Marco working tonight?" asked Donald when Louise presented the bill. "You look as if you could have used a bit of extra help."

Louise, not normally a smiler, smiled; to Teresa it seemed forced. "He took the evening off, Mr. Tarland. You know how boys are, they like to run around. A restaurant is well, restrictive, you know, for a young man his age." She took Donald's gold American Express card and went off toward the cash register.

"She seems upset," said Teresa, watching Louise's receding back. "I hear he's a bit wild, that Marco."

"So I believe. From the sounds of it, I wonder if he has the kind of temperament to work in a restaurant," agreed Donald, but Teresa still had the impression that his mind was occupied with other matters.

She sat back, watching him. Teresa was an attractive woman, elegantly outfitted in a red chiffon dress, and had an air of calm, almost of serenity, about her, which she always seemed to maintain even under adverse circumstances. Her features were picture perfect, her skin flawless. Teresa had high cheekbones and big, dark slightly almond-shaped eyes, which she always encircled, and with devastating effect, with a faint but skillfully drawn line of eye pencil. Her nose, slight retroussé, was so prettily shaped that some of her friends had been known to wonder aloud whether nature had been given a helping hand with it. Over Donald's shoulder, Teresa saw Louise coming back from the desk.

"How's Caroline doing?" Louise asked Donald, putting the tray with the receipt on the table. "I hope she's behaving herself." Caroline had been working in Donald's office for almost a year now.

"She's doing splendidly, Louise," replied Donald, carefully putting his card back in his wallet. "She's a hard worker, gets along with everybody. We're very pleased with her."

Louise gave him a long look, as if she were quite surprised that her daughter could be earning such compliments. Teresa noted the look, and wondered.

"I'm glad she's settling down," said Louise, but her voice was cold, and Teresa got the strong impression that Louise's daughter, Caroline, was not her favorite child, by any means.

Donald signed the American Express form, took his copy, folded it and carefully put it in his wallet with the card, then he and Teresa got up, and Louise helped them on with their coats. Bob, her husband, who did all the cooking for the restaurant, appeared from the kitchen, wiping his hands on his white apron. He came over to the desk and shook hands with Donald and Teresa. Bob was a big man, overweight, with a poorly shaven double chin that came over the high collar of his chef's jacket, and big, kindly brown eyes, which now had a concerned look about them.

After the usual greetings, Bob took Donald aside for a moment. "Look, Donald," he said rather hesitantly, and Donald thought he was having some difficulty keeping his gaze level. "I'm having a real problem with Marco. He's wild, angry all the time, and he's getting worse. I don't know what to do. Tonight, for no reason, he just stormed out, when he was supposed to be working here. Just before that, he threw a plate at his mother. Marco doesn't listen to me or Louise, and he's so violent. I'm afraid he's going to do something really bad, get himself into trouble so serious we won't be able to get him out of it.

Donald put a hand on Bob's arm. "What can I do? I'll be happy to help, any way I can."

"I don't know . . . Maybe you could just talk to him. He likes you and Teresa, and of course with her being a psychologist maybe he'd listen. He needs somebody to talk to, and he doesn't seem able to talk to us. I don't know why. He just gets angry." Bob spread his hands helplessly. "And, of course, he doesn't ever talk to his wife." He glanced quickly at Donald. "You know about that situation."

Donald nodded, deliberately noncommittal. He knew that Marco had married an Italian girl called Francesca, two weeks after meeting her on a holiday in Ibiza, but that was the extent of his knowledge.

"Marco's basically a good kid, Donald, and just needs some guidance. . . ." Bob sounded as if he were trying to convince himself of his son's worth.

"Of course he is," said Donald. "Why don't we have him over to the house tomorrow? It's Saturday, and maybe he'd like to bring Francesca with him. She could chat with Teresa while we talked."

"Well, there's a problem with that too, you know." Bob's gaze went to the floor. "He . . . well, he says he can't stand being around her. It's a shame, because she's pregnant, you know."

"Right, of course," said Donald hurriedly. "Well, he can come over by himself, if that's what he'd prefer. We both like him, you know. Maybe he'd like to give us a hand in the garden. It's planting time, and I'd pay him, of course."

"Whatever you think. Donald, I really appreciate your help."

"Our pleasure, Bob. Really. Right, Teresa?" He turned back to his wife.

"Whatever you say, dear," she said. "Actually I didn't hear a word the two of you were saying."

"I'll tell you all about it in the car," he said, taking her arm firmly and leading her toward the door.

Outside, it was dark, and chilly for late April, and Teresa turned up the astrakhan collar of her black woolen coat. She took Donald's arm, and the clip of her heels rang loud in the deserted cul-de-sac. A cat leaped down from the top of a dustbin, and the lid crashed on the ground, startling Teresa. Feeling unaccountably nervous, she gripped Donald's arm more firmly. Maybe it was because the cul-de-sac was dark, as the one streetlight attached to the high wall on their left wasn't working. The orange lights of South Street glowed about fifty yards ahead of them; once there, they had to cross the street, then cut across over the car park where Donald had left the car.

From the street they heard the sound of rapid footsteps, and a man came running around the corner, heading directly toward them. Almost immediately, another figure, slighter, but faster, came after him, running with the quicksilvery speed of a stoat. Donald and Teresa stopped, surprised, and Teresa gave a little gasp and clung to his arm. A few yards into the cul-de-sac, the second man caught up with the first, leaped on him and pulled him to the ground. Both Donald and Teresa heard the dull thud of his fists slamming repeatedly into the prone figure. Then he sprang to his feet and started kicking his victim in the ribs with a viciousness that made Donald's blood run cold. The only sounds from the man on the ground were grunts as the air was repeatedly kicked out of his chest.

After a few seconds of paralysis, Donald started to move forward, shouting, "Hey! Hey you! Stop that!"

Teresa, frightened for him, tried to hold him back. The attacker paused, looked up, put in a final boot, and shouted something at the still figure before running swiftly back into South Street.

Donald and Teresa hurried forward to help the victim. Donald put a hand under his armpit and helped him to a sitting position, but the man scrambled up to his feet and stood swaying, unable to do more than gasp for breath. In the dim light from the mercury arc lamps they could see he was young, in his early twenties, disheveled, and with blood on his face.

"I'll go and call the police," said Teresa, starting to go back to the restaurant entrance.

"No! Don't!" The young man staggered forward, then almost fell again. His breath came in loud, painful wheezes. "I'll be all right."

"Shouldn't you go to the hospital to get checked? He may have really hurt you." Donald peered at him in the gloom. "Isn't your name Brian? Brian Wooley?" The young man didn't answer, maybe because he was having trouble breathing; he certainly seemed to be in a lot of pain. Donald was concerned, and looked apprehensively up the alley, wondering if the attacker might return to finish the job.

The young man pulled away from him. "I'll be all right," he repeated, then pulled his coat around himself before hobbling away as fast as he could, back toward the street, his body twisted painfully to the side he'd been kicked on.

"My God," muttered Donald, putting a protective arm around Teresa. "A person's not safe even in Perth nowadays."

They found their car where they had left it, and drove home very subdued. As Donald pulled into the garage, Teresa said quietly, "Who did you say it was? Didn't you ask him if he was Brian something?"

"Brian Wooley. I think it was him. He used to be Caroline Fraser's boyfriend but she dumped him a few weeks ago."

"Did you get a good look at the other man? The one who attacked him?"

Donald shook his head. "No, I didn't. It all happened so fast."

"He looked a bit like Marco Fraser, the same kind of slim, athletic build, didn't you think?"

Donald didn't answer for a moment, but in the dark, his expression was very thoughtful indeed. "I feel sorry for Louise and Bob," he said. "It's a shame. They're really good people."

"Not to mention Francesca," said Teresa. "I hear she's having quite a bit of trouble with her pregnancy, and Marco doesn't even sleep there. He's apparently moved back in with his parents. Anyway he seems to be there all the time."

"Or else hanging around his sister Caroline," said Donald with an off inflection to his voice.

"So you're going to talk to him?" asked Teresa, remembering what Donald had told her in the car. "A fat lot of good that'll do."

"You never know," replied Donald, pulling down the garage door. The odd timbre was still in his voice. "You never know."

That night, after they were in bed, Teresa lay awake for a long time. Donald hadn't discussed whatever it was that had been troubling him throughout the evening, and now although he had fallen asleep, he kept tossing and turning and making occasional little gasping and grunting noises.

Maybe the attack they had witnessed was influencing the way Teresa was thinking, but it came to her that Donald was acting guilty about something. About what? Teresa couldn't imagine, but as she fell uneasily asleep, she realized that in addition, Donald was seriously afraid. But of whom or of what, Teresa hadn't the faintest idea.

Chapter 2

Two weeks later, on a fine morning that seemed to contain within it all the spirit of spring, Caroline Fraser was busy at her desk, perhaps experiencing it more than most, and certainly full of cheerfulness and enthusiasm. Macandon Industries was on the first floor of new office premises above a bookseller's shop, part of the shopping mall opposite St. John's kirk. The office had been laid out in an open plan style for the three of them, Aileen Farquar, the administrative assistant to both partners, Peter Duggan, the bookkeeper, who came in three times a week, and herself. They were separated only by low, frosted-glass partitions, topped with bright green plastic ferns. Only Donald Tarland and "Mac" MacFadyen had separate offices, and each had a door that opened into the common secretarial area.

If there was any tension in the office, Caroline certainly didn't seem to notice it, although Aileen's occasional glances from her desk next to the window were far from friendly. She had been angry with Caroline for at least a couple of weeks although, when Peter Duggan was there, Aileen made her hostility less obvious.

Mac MacFadyen's door opened, and he came out into the office. Aileen suddenly sat up straight, became very attentive and smiling, but Mac ignored her and came over to Caroline's desk. He was well dressed in a navy-blue blazer with a carefully knotted dark red tie over a shirt with broad red and white stripes. The crease in his gray slacks was razor-sharp. Mac was good-looking in a rather military way, with a bristly moustache and bright blue eyes, and a twinkling, easy, friendly manner. He also had a limp, which became more obvious when he was tired.

"I don't remember if I told you," he said, putting both hands on her desk and looking directly at Caroline, "when we buy a new mailing list, we use a disk with a secondary program that automatically eliminates duplicate names and addresses. I can show you how to use it, if you like."

"I know about that program, thanks, Mac," replied Caroline, smiling up at him and feeling Aileen Farquar's furious eyes boring into her from across the room. "Actually, Aileen showed me how to use it."

Mac seemed jittery about something; his eyes were restless, and his hand movements were nervous and jerky. After going over to the filing cabinets and aimlessly opening and closing one of them, he went back into his office. Apparently he'd only come out for that brief conversation with Caroline, and not once did he acknowledge Aileen's presence in the office.

Caroline had joined Macandon Industries when the company relocated in Perth about a year before. It was a small but fast-growing mail-order firm that sold high quality china, cutlery, kitchenware and ornaments of various kinds. She'd replied to the ad in the *Courier*, and duly appeared when summoned to their new offices in the St. John's Mall. The two owners had interviewed her together. At first Caroline felt intimidated by Mr. Tarland, who sat strict and businesslike in a dark formal suit and had an unsmiling expression, but she quickly warmed to the other one, whom Mr. Tarland called Mac. Mac had been very relaxed that first morning, sitting comfortably back in his chair, with his tie loose and shirtsleeves rolled part-way up over his thick, muscular arms. He'd grinned at her as if they were old friends, tilted his chair back and asked what kind of work she'd done, where she'd gone to school, and what she liked doing when she wasn't working her fingers to the bone for her employer. Caroline told them that she'd spent a year in secretarial college in Dunfermline, had done some temporary work for a big department store in Perth, and she felt sure they would have nothing but good things to say about her. She smiled when she said that, and even Mr. Tarland seemed to thaw a bit as a result, because he almost smiled back at her.

Mac went on to explain what they wanted. "Aside from typing, filing, and all that general secretarial kind of work," he told her, "we need someone with computer training to manage and update our mailing lists and help to prepare the catalogue." He sounded very friendly, but Caroline got a strong impression that the two of them knew exactly what they wanted and anybody who wasn't prepared to work hard and enthusiastically wouldn't last long with them. "We put out three color catalogues a year," Mac went on, "Spring, Summer and the Christmas one, which is the biggie, because that's when we do over forty per cent of our business."

He glanced over at Mr. Tarland with an air of friendly respect. "Mr. Tarland and I do the buying, and if you join us, we might let you help with some of the items, if you show the right kind of initiative."

While Mac asked the questions and Caroline answered, Mr. Tarland watched her with a kind of silent intensity which made her nervous when she glanced over at him, because she couldn't tell whether he liked her or not.

Two days later, Aileen Farquar, the administrative assistant, who had interviewed her briefly after Donald and Mac had finished with her, phoned to tell her she had the job.

Caroline was the only new full-time person Macandon hired; Aileen had worked for them since the company started in Glasgow two years before, and she moved up to

Perth with them. Aileen was a little above average height, a woman with strong features and slightly prominent teeth which she hid by keeping her upper lip down over them when she smiled. There was something about her wide gray eyes that gave her a look of vulnerability, but that could change as quickly as the North Sea in a storm. When Aileen was feeling resentful or hostile, those same gray eyes would narrow and flash fire, and her lips would tighten with an expression that would shock the people who only saw the benign side of her personality. Aileen's best feature was her shoulder-length golden blond hair, luxurious and straight except for a slight curling in at the ends. She had a habit of drawing attention to it by tossing the hair out of her eyes with a sharp and rather theatrical movement of her head. Sometimes Caroline, when she happened to be feeling mischievous, was hard put not to mimic her, but her hair, although just as blond, was curly and not as amenable to tossing.

When Caroline first came to work, Aileen had been very nice to her, showing her the ropes and pointing out some of the bosses' quirks and preferences. They had even got to be quite good friends, not close, because Aileen was quite a bit older, about thirty-five, some twelve years Caroline's senior, and didn't like to go dancing or listen to rock music or do the things Caroline enjoyed.

And Aileen had a good sense of humor, although it could be a bit acid. She had a way of taking the mickey out of people without their ever knowing it that could put Caroline in stitches. The only thing she had absolutely no sense of humor about was anything that had to do with Mac. She was desperately in love with him, and to hear her talk about it, he was equally smitten with her. But, judging from the amount of time Aileen spent by herself in the first floor flat she rented in Ainslie Place, Caroline decided the woman was dreaming, until she saw the two of them out together a couple of times. Once, to Caroline's astonishment, Aileen had shouted across the busy High Street at her and, later when she thought about it, Caroline decided that Aileen was just drawing attention to the fact that Mac was actually with her.

Aileen didn't like Perth, she confided to Caroline, nor did she seem particularly to enjoy her job as administrative assistant to Mac and Mr. Tarland, although there was no question that she did it conscientiously and well. Until her mother died a year before, Aileen had lived with her in a big house in Kelvinside, she told Caroline, so when Donald and Mac decided for various financial reasons to move the company up to Perth, she came with them. It was just about that time, she told Caroline, keeping her lip firmly lowered, that she and Mac had Come to An Agreement. Poor Aileen, thought Caroline, with a mixture of amusement and pity, the woman's entire life seemed to revolve around Mac, and she'd go on about how wonderful he was, what a great dresser, and, as she repeatedly hinted, a spectacular lover.

And now, although the whole thing had started almost two months ago, for the last couple of weeks Mac had been making his play for Caroline very obvious, and it was driving Aileen wild.

The door to Mac's office opened and he came out again, this time more his jolly, bright-eyed and smiling self. He looked at Caroline, winked, and went over to the filing cabinet with a handful of papers.

Aileen got up from her chair and went over to him. "You and Mr. Tarland have a luncheon appointment," she told him in her precise way, and Caroline suppressed a broad grin as Aileen gazed at him with that sickening expression of dog-like devotion. "Twelve-thirty, Mac," said Aileen, "at the Theater restaurant, with Mr. Montrose."

"Right. Are we going with him, or is he going with us?"

"He made the appointment," said Aileen, picking up a

highlight pen and drawing a thick yellow line through
the notation in the desk diary. "He wants to talk to you
about a new product they're planning."

"Fine. Does Mr. Tarland know?"

"Mr. Tarland knows *everything*, Mac, you know that,"
replied Aileen. Caroline, half listening, thought that
Aileen, although she'd spoken lightly and smiled, had
said the words with more than necessary emphasis, and
maybe she also glanced momentarily over at her.

Mac looked over at Caroline. "How are Steven Montrose's glass paperweights selling?"

"I don't know," replied Caroline tartly. "You're in
charge of sales, not me."

Not at all put out, Mac grinned at her.

"I put last month's sales figures on your desk, Mac,"
Aileen purred at him. "Including everything on the
Scone Glass works." But Mac wasn't listening to her,
and with a smile aimed exclusively at Caroline he went
back into his office, leaving the door open.

Aileen shut the desk diary with a smack.

"It's twenty past, Mac," she called out to him, a note
of desperation in her voice. "It's time you got going, or
you'll be late."

"God, you are a nag, Aileen," he said, coming out of
the office and putting on his coat. He was smiling, but
even Caroline could feel his antipathy for Aileen. Mac
had become much ruder to her in the last couple of
weeks, ever since he started to pay such marked attention to Caroline. In spite of herself, Caroline couldn't
help enjoying the situation. She hadn't consciously done
anything to lead Mac on, although she knew that Aileen
would violently disagree with that.

Caroline was dimly aware that she was at least partly
at fault in having let the situation reach such proportions.
She knew that she wasn't the most secure of persons,
and wanted everybody, or at least every man who came
across her path, to like her. Often enough she would fin-

ish up going to bed with a man, even if she didn't particularly like him, for no better reason than that she needed his approval and attention. But now that things were different, she wouldn't need to do that kind of thing any more.

Mac opened the door to Donald's office.

"Ready for lunch, Donald? We're eating with Steven Montrose in ten minutes."

A moment later Donald Tarland came out, nodded at Caroline in a preoccupied way, but ignored Aileen. After the two men left the office, Aileen put the cover on her electric typewriter. "What are you doing for lunch?" she asked. Her voice sounded shrill, although she seemed to be making an effort to keep it under control.

"Nothing," replied Caroline. "I brought a sandwich."

"Good," said Aileen, her long lips tightening with anticipation. "Because right now you and I are going to have a little talk, Caroline Fraser, just the two of us."

Steven Montrose was already sitting at a table when Mac and Donald Tarland came into the restaurant. He got up when they came up to his table, and shook hands with both men.

"You two don't look as if you're worried about any recession," he said, smiling. Steven was the principal supplier of handmade glassware for their mail-order business.

"What recession?" asked Mac, sitting down. "This is going to be the best year we ever had." Steven happened to glance at Donald at that moment and thought he saw a flicker of something, perhaps annoyance at Mac's words, although Mac didn't sound as if he were trying to be boastful.

"You deserve it," said Steven, holding the menu card at arm's length and peering at it. "It's because you sell such good-quality merchandise." With a sigh he reached into his pocket and pulled out a pair of reading glasses, and put them on.

"Oh, the miseries of advancing age," he said. "What are you gentlemen having?"

The waitress came and took their orders, and Steven watched the different styles of his guests; after a quick glance at the list of daily specials pinned to the menu, Mac ordered the businessman's lunch, which consisted of green pea soup, pot roast, cabinet pudding and coffee. Donald Tarland, on the other hand, looked carefully through the entire menu before making his selection. He looked up and saw Steven watching him.

"Calories," he said, "vitamins and minerals, that's what I look for. Here . . ." Donald took a plastic card out of his breast pocket and passed it to Steven. "That shows the minimum daily requirements of every vitamin and mineral, and how much there is in most commonly used foods. For instance, I'd guess that Mac's cabinet pudding would have about three hundred calories, half of that from fat, and maybe a quarter of his requirements of thiamine."

"It's always fun going out with Donald," said Mac, shaking his head. "If ever there's a lull in the conversation we can always get on to the mysteries of vitamin metabolism."

They all laughed, but Donald's laughter sounded forced. Steven was momentarily surprised at that, because the two of them always had this line of banter where Mac gently teased Donald, who usually would say something clever back. It was part of the way they did business. Steven had often wondered why they got on so well. Their attitudes to most things seemed to be diametrically opposed, but they seemed to have a good partnership, and their business results certainly appeared to bear that out.

Steven had brought a sample of a new glass paperweight on which different Scottish clan emblems could be fused using a new process, and as usual, Mac was enthusiastic, and Donald cautious. They talked about prices, discounts, delivery times, packaging and similar matters for a while, then Donald looked at his watch. There was no doubt about it, thought Steven, there's a lot of tension between them, although they're both trying to hide it.

"We'll get back to you with a definite answer before the end of the week," Donald promised Steven, getting to his feet at the end of the meal. "If we have any more questions, we'll get them to you before then."

"Good," said Steven.

"By the way," said Donald, "Teresa and I are having a few people over for Sunday brunch, not this coming Sunday but the next. We're hoping you and Jean can come."

"I'm sure we'd love to. I'll have to check with her, of course. She's in charge of our social calendar, such as it is."

"How is Jean? Still as busy?"

"Fine. You know how she is, running all the time."

"Teresa would love to see her, you know, for coffee or something, but she doesn't like to call, knowing how busy Jean is."

"I'll get Jean to phone her," promised Steven.

It was on the tip of his tongue to say he'd prefer that they paid their bills rather than invite him to Sunday brunch. Some of these bills were more than sixty days overdue, and he couldn't afford to extend credit to them forever.

Mac got to his feet, dropped his napkin on the table, said goodbye and followed Donald. Thoughtfully, Steven watched them thread their way between the tables toward the door. There was something wrong between the two men, he was now quite certain. Just as long as it wasn't serious, he thought. In just a few months, their mail-order company had become his biggest wholesale customer and he didn't want anything to upset the situation.

Aileen Farquar came over to Caroline's desk, leaned over and glowered at her. She couldn't avoid acknowledging that Caroline Fraser was a very attractive young woman, but of course, she thought sourly, no one knew it better than she did. Twenty-three years old, straight-backed, with a splendid figure. Caroline looked back at Aileen with an amused, even impish expression. She wore her hair in big, blond curls framing her rounded face. Her eyes were large, dark and assured, her complexion creamy and regular. Watching her with a jealous and predatory look, Aileen could see why Caroline attracted so much attention in Perth, already noted for the vigorous, healthy appearance of its young women long before Walter Scott made it public knowledge.

Aileen put her hands on the desk and leaned toward her just as Mac had done, but there was nothing of Mac's friendliness about Aileen. For a moment Caroline thought she was going to strike her, and, astonished by the degree of hostility in Aileen's eyes, she slid her chair back on its wheels as far as it would go, and surveyed her coolly from just outside her range.

Aileen's lips were set in a tight, straight, scarlet line. She must have been a really pretty woman maybe five years ago, thought Caroline, staring calmly back at her, but she'd really gone off a lot, even in the last few months.

"You seem to have taken a very strong liking to Mac," she said. Her voice was sharp, and Caroline's quick instinct sensed the fear in it. Again, an unexpected but enjoyable sense of power came over Caroline. She raised her eyebrows fractionally, and shrugged her shoulders just enough, knowing that her every look and movement was being scrutinized and measured for meaning by Aileen's seagull-sharp eyes.

Caroline knew that at this point she should be careful.

There was no point in further antagonizing the person she worked most closely with. "He's always been very nice to me," Caroline said, her voice neutral. At the same time, she brought her chair back to its original position. She wasn't going to let this sad old creature intimidate her.

"Mac is a very wonderful person," went on Aileen, enunciating her words carefully. Caroline wondered how often she'd rehearsed the speech. "And just because he is friendly and nice to everyone, some people have been known to take him up wrong, and think he's really interested in them."

Caroline opened her lower desk drawer and took out a box of floppy disks and put it beside her computer. She was only trying to appear cool and uninvolved, but to Aileen it must have looked as if she wasn't paying attention to her, because her voice became louder. "Caroline, what I'm saying is, lay off him, all right? We have a strong relationship, him and me, don't you understand that? Don't you . . ."

"Don't shout at me," interrupted Caroline. She reached into her bag at the foot of her chair and pulled out her lipstick. "Who the hell do you think you are, telling me what to do?" Her mouth gave a teasing twitch, and little devils danced around the corners of her eyes.

"Listen, Aileen," she said, deliberately holding the lipstick in front of her and turning the base to make the pink tip slowly emerge and retreat. "I know what your problem is with Mac, just don't involve me if you can't hang on to your man. He's not a child, and he doesn't belong to anyone. He decided what he wants to do, and who he wants to do it with."

Caroline stood up and adjusted her skirt. "And now, if you don't mind, I'm going off to the park to eat my sandwich in peace."

Caroline picked up her bag and left the office without looking back. If she had, she would have seen a very unpleasant and calculating expression on Aileen's face.

Chapter 3

Caroline emerged from the main entrance to the Mall, and turned left, crinkling her eyes up against the sun which was shining full in her face. She crossed the road opposite the solid beige sandstone facade of St. John's kirk, and headed for the North Inch, her heart still beating fast after that brief encounter with Aileen. She walked quickly along George Street, looking from sheer habit in the shop windows, and passed under some scaffolding where workmen were restoring a building. There were a few wolf whistles from the men taking their lunchbreak in the street outside, but she barely noticed them, and hurried across Charlotte Street to the green grass of the North Inch, looking for a vacant bench.

The weather was warm, windless with only a few high strands of cirrus in the blue sky. Near the foot of the statue of Prince Albert, Caroline found a bench, one of the new ones they'd installed when that corner of the park was recently refurbished. She sat down with her back to the old bridge, pulled a transparent container with a prawn sandwich out of her bag, and looked at it for a moment. She didn't feel very hungry, in fact even a little nauseated, but she knew that she'd get a headache in the afternoon if she didn't eat anything. She could feel a wave of anger which arose against Aileen for upsetting her like that, but at the same time she knew she was at fault too; she could certainly have handled the situation in a more diplomatic way, and she hadn't needed to do that little byplay with the lipstick. Poor Aileen, she was more to be pitied than blamed. Caroline fished in her bag, took out a small square milk carton and put it on the bench beside her. A blue and brown pigeon flew down from Albert's white-streaked bronze shoulder and landed on the path in front of her, and strutted up and down, watching her with his aggressive, little golden beady-round eyes. His confident walk reminded her a bit of Mac. Damn him too, she thought, as she pulled open the triangular plastic sandwich pack. How obvious and indiscreet he was! And there had been no need for him to upset Aileen so unkindly. But to think that she had actually moved to Perth just to be with him! How dumb could the woman get? Caroline laughed out loud at the thought of Aileen's expression when she found out what was really going on.

Another pigeon flew down. They ignored each other, and each strutted to and fro as if he were the only pigeon in the world. Caroline threw each of them a corner of her sandwich bread, just as, from time to time, she'd thrown men a corner of her life.

In retrospect, Caroline recognized that she'd been very vulnerable at the time it happened, a few weeks ago, when she had got rid of Brian. Well, she'd *tried* to get rid of Brian. What an unnecessary fuss that had been! Even now, Caroline flushed with annoyance at the recollection.

She'd contrived an argument with him, not an easy thing to do, because Brian was a meek, gentle person who disliked rows of any kind. And he was so very much in love with her. But Caroline was thoroughly bored with him, and stirred up a quarrel on some ridiculous pretext. Once the argument really got going, she took the opportunity to tell him she didn't want to ever see him again. And that was true, because she already had someone else firmly in her sights, someone who could satisfy her need for wealth and security. And that was something Brian would never have been able to do.

But Brian stubbornly refused to accept the fact that he had been ditched. He kept phoning, waited for her when she came out of work, and generally made a nuisance of himself. After a week of this, Caroline had mentioned it while having dinner with Marco and her parents at their home. Marco hadn't said much at the time, but she knew him, and was only too well aware of how he felt about her. That evening, a Thursday, Marco had gone as usual to his drama group, but come home late. Caroline didn't see Brian for another three days, and when she did, he was sporting a dark blue eye, a puffed up cheek, and a split lip. That day the police came around to talk to Marco, but they couldn't prove anything against him. He told them that Brian had been drunk, picked a quarrel with him, and he'd hit him in self-defense. Marco was lucky not to have ended up in jail, but the worst part was that he'd threatened to go after Brian again if he didn't leave her strictly alone.

After Brian, though, she'd spent a wonderful peaceful week during which she'd had time to catch up with her reading, spend some deliciously illicit time with her new man, play the guitar again, and see the friends she hadn't seen for a while. On a couple of occasions she thought she saw Brian skulking around her flat, but she might easily have been mistaken. But at the back of her mind was a continuing serious concern about her brother Marco, and she knew that by enlisting his help she might have stirred up a fire that could consume her. Marco was a couple of years younger than she was, but very possessive and aggressive about her. Every time she happened to go anywhere with him Caroline had the feeling that he was looking around with those dark, arrogant eyes of his, daring people to look at her so he could pick a fight with them.

Caroline dropped the sandwich wrappers in the wire rubbish bin on the opposite side of the path, and looked at her watch. She still had twenty minutes of her lunch-hour left, and she decided to take a brisk walk around the Inch. Usually there were lots of people around at lunchtime on a fine day like this, but today there were only a few joggers pounding around the path, a couple of salmon fishermen up to their waists in the river, and two elderly men swinging putters as they headed toward the golf course.

Caroline slung her purse over her shoulder and started to walk down the tiled part of the path toward the river, thinking about her own problems, and feeling a bit scared about the things going on in her life. Of course she wasn't quite certain about everything yet, and a knot formed and tightened in her stomach as she considered the possibilities, and her options. Her head was in a whirl, although anyone seeing her firm, confident step would never have guessed it, certainly not the rather plump, middle-aged woman coming in the other direction, pushing an old lady around the park in a wheel-chair.

Caroline watched them approach, then recognized the woman pushing the chair. It was her doctor, Jean Montrose.

"Well, Caroline," said Jean, coming to a halt. "Isn't it a wonderful day? Mother, I'd like you to meet Caroline Fraser."

"Nice to meet you," said Caroline, smiling, and stretching out her hand. Mrs. Findlay watched her with sharp, uncompromising eyes, growled something unintelligible and kept her hands under the blanket.

"We're just taking a wee walk, Caroline," said Jean hurriedly, embarrassed at her mother's lack of courtesy. "It was just too fine a day to stay indoors."

A thought came to Caroline. "Could I come to see you, Dr. Montrose?" she asked. "I mean at the surgery." She sounded flustered.

"Yes, of course." Jean looked at Caroline, wondering what was the matter. People often came to discuss their problems with her even when there was nothing physically wrong with them. "How about tomorrow? I'm off this afternoon." There was something in Caroline's expression that she couldn't fathom, but it rang an alarm. "Unless it's urgent, of course. . . ."

"Oh no. Tomorrow will be just fine," replied Caroline. "Can I come after work, a bit before five?"

Mrs. Findlay didn't take her eyes off Caroline all the time they were talking, and her lips only tightened when Caroline politely said goodbye and continued her walk around the park. But during that brief conversation, everything had come together in Caroline's mind, and now she knew exactly what she was going to do.

"Really, Mother," said Jean, after Caroline was out of earshot. "You didn't have to be so impolite. Caroline's a very nice person." Jean felt really annoyed by her mother's rudeness and pushed the wheelchair forward with more vigor than before.

"I didn't say she wasn't," replied Mrs. Findlay. "Who is she? Is she married? And do you have to push this thing so fast? Who do you think you are? Manuel Fangio?"

On the way back around the Inch, Jean patiently did her best to answer the string of questions her mother asked about Caroline. At least it showed that she was still interested in other people, and Jean knew that was something to encourage in persons of her mother's age.

It was a hard push up the ramp to the nursing home on Barossa Place, but Jean made it without assistance, then turned and backed through the door, pulling the wheelchair in behind her. Bess, a rheumatic old golden spaniel that belonged to the matron, came and sniffed at the wheelchair. A swift foot shot out from under the blanket, and Bess retreated. Jean sighed internally but said nothing; for all she knew, she might behave like that too when she was eighty. Her mother's room, clean and airy, had a big window that looked out over the garden but, at this point, Mrs. Findlay refused adamantly to walk further than to the bathroom.

"Do you want me to break the other hip, or what?" she had asked earlier when Jean suggested they take a walk around and look at the flowers. "That way you'd get rid of me faster, I suppose, and give some business to your colleagues into the bargain."

With the help of a nurse, Jean got her mother back into bed. When she got her breath back, Mrs. Findlay stared at Jean and said, "That girl, the one we met in the park—well, she's *trouble*, I can tell you that just from looking at her."

Jean knew better than to argue. Certainly to her mother's generation, the way Caroline walked and the confident way in which she behaved would have branded her as a hussy or worse.

Jean fluffed up her mother's pillows, kissed her on the forehead and left. On the way out, she met Mrs. Kimball, the matron, coming out of her office.

"She's looking real well today, Mrs. Findlay is," said Mrs. Kimball. She was a large, capable, maternal-looking woman with gray hair that straggled from under her old-fashioned nurse's cap, and whose blue uniform bulged roundly in every direction.

"We went all the way around the Inch," said Jean. "She's a bit tired now, I think."

Mrs. Kimball pushed a strand of hair out of her eyes. "That's fine with us, Dr. Montrose," she said. "She hasn't been in the best of moods for the last two days, so I hope the wee outing made her feel better." She hesitated for a moment. "The girls are telling me she's about ready to get up to something again."

"Oh dear," sighed Jean. "I hope she doesn't."

Mrs. Kimball gave her uniform a hitch, and a different set of buttons took up the strain. "Well, to tell you the truth, Doctor, we like her. She keeps everybody on their toes. I certainly prefer her to a lot of *them*. . . ." She waved a pudgy hand in the direction of the other patients' rooms. "Those that just sit, you know, that could but won't, because there's no life or spirit left in them."

After leaving the nursing home, Jean got into her car, fastened her seat belt, and sat back for a moment, thinking about the things she still had to do that day. She had to get food for dinner, and even though it was her afternoon off, she'd promised to visit little Francesca Fraser, Marco's wife, whose baby was due in a couple of months but who was developing some fluid retention and a worryingly high blood pressure. But even as she went methodically through the list of her tasks, at the back of Jean's mind there was something worrying her, something she had not even identified, except that it had something to do with Caroline Fraser.

Chapter 4

After leaving Steven at the Theater restaurant, Donald Tarland and Mac drove back to their office in Donald's car. Mac chatted on cheerfully, but was very much aware of Donald's silent, almost hostile manner.

When they reached the office, Donald said, "Mac, I need to talk to you about a couple of things. Let's go into my office because most of the papers are there."

Half an hour later, after Donald had shown him the proof, Mac, ashen faced, sat back in his chair. "I just borrowed the money, Donald, I'm sure you understand that. I never had any intention of keeping it. I had some extraordinary expenses, and needed it immediately. I hoped to have it back in the till before you even became aware of it."

"Why didn't you just ask me?" Donald's face was cold, unforgiving.

"Because you'd have said no, that's why," replied Mac. "Look, I thought I could pay it all back before the end of the month, but I'll pay it back over the next six, OK?"

"No, it's not OK," said Donald, after a pause. "For one thing, the auditors are coming in this month, as you very well know, and they'll pick it up instantly."

"We don't *need* to have the auditors in now," said Mac. "We have only two shareholders, you and me, and we can simply put it through on the books as a loan."

"That won't work. Mac, I don't care how you do it,

but the money has to be back by the end of the week. You can ask your bank for a loan. . . ."

Mac was already shaking his head. "I've already borrowed all I can get," he said.

Suddenly Donald thumped his hand on the desk. "What in God's name are you doing with it?" he asked. "You already make a good salary, and you're not married. Where does all that money go?"

Mac hesitated, and his face quivered for a second as he tried to make up his mind. Then, very deliberately, he rolled up the sleeve of his shirt, and Donald saw the red needle tracks going into the veins of his arm.

After a long silence, Mac looked up and said, in a barely audible voice, "That's where it goes, Don."

"My God," breathed Donald. "How long . . ."

"It doesn't matter," cut in Mac, rolling down his sleeve. "I'm about at the end of my rope, Donald. I'm out of money, the habit's catching up with me, it's costing me a hundred pounds a day, and at this point I don't know what to do. I'm going down to see Dr. Montrose tomorrow. Maybe she can do something to help.

When Donald left the office it was 4:30 in the afternoon, much earlier than when he usually went home. He nodded absently to Aileen and Caroline; they were both getting ready to leave. It was his stiff posture and quick movements they noticed; his face was impassive as always, but they both instantly knew he was furious, and both simultaneously wondered if they could have done anything to upset him.

Donald sped down the stairs, his mind working at top speed in spite of his anger. Mac had embezzled a substantial amount of money, at the worst possible time, when every penny in the business was being stretched to the limit. But it was more the fact that he'd done it, and confessed about his drug addiction on top of everything that had shaken Donald to his very core. He shook his head, feeling for the car keys in his pocket. He'd had no idea. None at all, even though his sources of information were now better than they'd ever been. What sho}ld he do? He'd always known, of course, that Mac didn't have the same kind of high ethical standards as he did, that he didn't take the business as seriously as he, Donald, did. But Mac was a wonderful salesman, or had been until recently. Donald went over the figures in his mind, and realized that some of their big accounts had been very quiet recently, and others had dropped out completely.

Donald got into his BMW and slammed the door closed with a force that would have made him furious if someone else had done it. He had to think about this; the last thing he wanted to do was call the police, but maybe he should. He sat back in his gray leather seat and headed for home.

Teresa was in the kitchen of their big, immaculately kept riverside house. She heard the angry crunch of tires as Donald came to an abrupt halt, and she watched him come through the back door into the kitchen.

"A bad day at the office, dear?"

Donald's lips were in a tight straight line, and he obviously didn't take in Teresa's tone of voice.

"Yes, it *was* bad, Teresa." He sat down heavily at the kitchen counter and pushed a bowl of fresh flowers out of the way. The bowl tipped, and Teresa caught it just in time and replaced it gently just out of his reach. "A really nasty problem came up today." Donald told her about Mac, the proof of his embezzlement, and the shocking sight of his scarred, needletracked arms.

Donald put his head between his hands. He could feel his heart pounding with anger, fear and frustration. "Teresa, right now, I just don't know what to do about it."

"How long has he been doing this, do you think? I mean the drugs?"

"Teresa, I don't know, but probably as long as he's been with us. That's over a year."

"At a hundred pounds a day! My God!" Teresa's eyes opened wide. "You know, Donald," she went on, "I always told you there was something odd about him. He was too . . . I don't know, too spruced up, as if external appearances were the only thing he worried about."

"That's important for a salesman," replied Donald. He grinned faintly at her. "Here I am, married to a trained psychologist . . . Maybe I should get you to do profiles on all our employees from now on."

"I've heard worse ideas, my dear."

"Not only that, but Mac's got my whole office in a turmoil," went on Donald, his words coming out faster than he wanted them to. "You know he's been going out with Aileen Farquar ever since we came up here, and now he's got something going with Caroline. You can imagine how Aileen's reacting. She looks as if she'd like to gouge Caroline's eyes out."

"Well, I suppose I would too, in her position," replied Teresa. "After all, Caroline is pretty hot stuff, from what I've heard."

Donald opened his mouth as if he were about to say something, but changed his mind. "I don't want to call in the police about the embezzlement," said Donald, turning from a subject which was so obviously distasteful to him.

"I agree," answered Teresa after a moment's pause. "They'd stir up trouble, get your name in the papers, and ultimately do us no good."

Donald shivered at the thought. He really was looking the picture of misery, thought Teresa, and she came around the counter to put an affectionate hand on his shoulder.

"He's turned out to be a complete loser," Donald went on. He reached out and idly started to pull the lower leaves off the small irises in the vase. "I wish he'd go and get a job somewhere else, but he owns half the stock in Macandon."

"Could you buy it off him?"

Donald snorted. "What with? I don't even know how I'm going to pay next month's bills, let alone buy him out."

Teresa sighed. "Well, I'm sure it'll work out somehow. Maybe he can get off his heroin. Other people manage to, and it's not as if he was a down and outer. There are treatment centers for people like him."

"He said he's going down to see Jean Montrose tomorrow. Maybe she can get him straightened out."

"Well, if anyone can . . . Meanwhile, maybe you should just tell the bank that all checks need both your signatures. At least that'll stop the leak."

"I did that already. Obviously."

Teresa seemed to be mulling over something, and Donald watched her. She moved the flower vase out of his reach again. "I'm a bit scared," she said.

"Why? I'm sure we can get everything straightened out, eventually." But Donald didn't look as if he had any real hope of that ever happening.

"It's not that, Donald. I'm a bit scared of him. Of Mac." She paused, her eyes still fixed thoughtfully on Donald.

Donald raised his head and his mouth opened slightly. "You think he's dangerous? Mac? Come on, Teresa. Mac isn't any more dangerous than Rudolph." Rudolph, their Skye terrier, looked up from his basket when he heard his name, and wagged his tail.

Teresa put two spotless glasses on the counter, reached into a cupboard and took out a big crystal decanter, then poured a glass of pale dry sherry for each of them.

"For a start, Donald, drug addicts are dangerous, by definition," she said, taking a slow sip from her glass. "Secondly, you are now officially aware of his addiction, and he may regret having told you." Teresa ticked off the points on her elegant, carefully manicured fingers. "And third, you've found out about his embezzlement. Have you told anybody else about it?

"No, of course not," he retorted. "I just found out about it today. And anyway, who would I tell?"

They heard the noise of footsteps on the gravel outside, then a quick ring on the back-door bell. Donald started up, but Teresa said, "Relax, that's just Marco."

Marco let himself in. He was slightly built, wiry and muscular, with an easily recognizable walk, slightly shambling but with an unmistakably macho swagger. He sat down on one of the kitchen stools.

"One day I'm going to kill that kid," he muttered.

"Which one this time, Marco?" Teresa smiled at him. "Would you like a cup of tea?"

"Thanks. Do you have any of that good fruitcake left? It's that creep Brian. He still won't leave Caroline alone. I've told him . . ."

"I think we may have seen you telling him, a couple of weeks ago, outside your parents' restaurant," said Donald. "Was that you?"

Marco shrugged.

"You won't believe this," he said. "I saw him last night," he went on, "he'd climbed up on the roof outside Caroline's flat. I yelled at him, and he vanished." Marco grinned. "I bet I scared him enough so he almost fell off that roof."

"Marco, you're always looking for trouble. What were *you* doing there?" Teresa put a cup of tea on the counter in front of him, then reached for the fruitcake tin high up in the cupboard to her right. "You should have been home taking care of Francesca." Somehow, Teresa managed to make her tone friendly and not censorious. Marco ignored her last comment.

"I was just keeping an eye on things," he said.

"Why didn't you tell the police?" asked Donald. "It's their job to deal with Peeping Toms."

"Me? Tell the police?" Marco gave a short laugh. "Huh! Do you think they'd listen to me? Not likely. They'd be more likely to put *me* behind bars."

"That's what happens when you get a reputation around this town, Marco. Here. There's more in the tin if you want it."

"Marco, at some point, you're going to have to learn that there are better ways of dealing with situations than hitting people over the head," said Donald earnestly. "Have you *talked* to Brian?"

"Yeah, I talked to him," grinned Marco, wolfing up his thick slice of fruitcake. "Two weeks ago, I talked to him."

Donald and Teresa glanced briefly at each other. They'd done as Bob Fraser had asked them, but so far Marco hadn't shown much sign of changing his attitude, although he visited often enough and was obviously relaxed and comfortable with them.

"Do you want to stay for supper?" asked Teresa.

"No, thanks." Marco looked at his watch. "I have my drama group. I missed last week, so I'd better go tonight."

"What play are you doing?" asked Donald.

"*The Importance of Being Earnest*," replied Marco.

"Do you play Ernest?" Teresa took Marco's cup and saucer and rinsed them.

"No. I'm Lane, the manservant. There aren't too many lines to remember, and he's the only one in the whole play with any sense."

"And he's the best-looking one there, too, I'm sure," Teresa turned her head to smile at him.

Marco blushed, mumbled something and a few minutes later went out.

After Marco left, Teresa and Donald got back to talking about Mac. Donald grew very despondent, in spite of Teresa's efforts to cheer him up.

"I just don't know what to do," he said. "The bills are coming in like locusts, and unless something really good happens, and soon, we may be out of business in a couple of months."

Teresa thought about what that would mean. The social position they'd taken so much trouble to build up would be gone forever, Donald's cherished Rotary Club, his eldership at the church . . . But the thought of losing her lovely house and possessions was what made Teresa quiver internally. No, she thought, as she tidied up before turning out the lights and going to bed, that could not be allowed to happen.

When Jean got home after a brief visit to Francesca Fraser, both Fiona and Lisbie were home. Fiona heard the car pull in to the short driveway, and came out to meet her mother. Jean, struggling to get out of the car, watched her daughter's slim figure coming toward her. Fiona was so pretty and assured and unselfconscious, it always made Jean smile with pride and a little wonder.

"I don't know how you do it," she said. "I know you worked all day, but there you are, looking like a Fabergé model."

"Fabergé's dead, Mum. Do you think he has all the angels in designer dresses by now? Here, give me the groceries." Fiona reached in the back and took out two bulging shopping bags. She wrinkled her nose. "Plastic," she said. "It's not recyclable. We should be using paper bags."

"Yes, dear," said Jean. "Is your father home?"

"He phoned a wee while ago. He'll be about half an hour late, he said."

They went through the front garden into the house. As they went, Jean noticed that the new rosebuds looked in good shape although there had been a touch of frost the night before. Alley, their big marmalade cat, met them at the door, gazing calmly at them in his aristocratic way.

"Look at him sitting there," said Fiona. "He reminds me of Cole, the butler up at Strathalmond castle." She grinned back over her shoulder. "Do you remember him?"

"Yes, I most certainly do," said Jean, her lips tightening at the recollection. "Except Alley's hair isn't gray. Don't let him get near the food. I got some salmon for dinner."

"Great. Caroline told me last week how to make a quick Hollandaise sauce that never separates, so let's try that, OK?"

Lisbie was watching television, lying on the floor of what Steven called the morning room, but which, next to the kitchen, was the room they all used most. There, in the evenings, Jean would go through her patient cards and check laboratory reports. The girls read or watched television, and Steven napped or read his trade journals and financial reports.

"Hi, Mum." Lisbie didn't turn her head. "When's dinner?"

"When your father gets home, dear. Now you go and put on some proper clothes this minute. You're not decent, in the . . . whatever it is."

"I just had a bath," replied Lisbie, sitting up and grinning. "And I bet Daddy'd like it."

"I can tell you he would *not*," said Jean sternly. "Upstairs, right now!"

Slowly, Lisbie got to her feet. She was like a junior version of her mother, pretty, more rounded than Fiona, and with Jean's open smile.

"Mum, if you ever want to borrow it . . ." Lisbie grinned suggestively and touched the skimpy black nylon lace. She squealed when Jean landed a brisk smack on her bottom as she passed in the doorway.

Dinner that evening was quiet; Steven served the

salmon, looking askance at the Hollandaise sauce. He preferred his salmon simply grilled, without any foreign frills, but knew better than to mention it. As usual, Jean was preoccupied with a lot of things, but her ears perked up when she heard Fiona say that she was going out after dinner for a drink with Caroline.

"Where will you go?" she asked.

"We're going first to the Isle of Skye lounge," replied Fiona, referring to the hotel overlooking the old bridge across the River Tay. She rather ostentatiously pulled some long, transparent salmon bones out of her mouth, and glanced at Steven, hoping to irritate him. "Then we'll maybe go on from there."

"They say she's quite a girl, that Caroline," said Lisbie, watching her sister.

"She is," retorted Fiona. "Don't you wish you looked as good as her?"

"Yes," said Lisbie, quick as a flash. "I wish I did. But it must be so embarrassing for you when you're out with her, looking the way *you* do."

Before Jean could stop her, Fiona had thrown a hard roll and caught Lisbie on the chest with it. Steven slammed down his knife and fork, but nobody paid any attention.

"She hit me on the boob!" said Lisbie, aggrieved, clutching her chest. Steven went pink with annoyance. He didn't like that kind of language at the table.

"It's such a big target," Fiona shouted back. "I couldn't miss."

"That's enough from you two," said Jean calmly. "Steven, would you like a bit more of the sauce?"

The rest of the meal passed in comparative peace, although a few *sub rosa* comments were heard from time to time from the girls. "Better than those two gooseberries *you* have," muttered Lisbie, and after a while Fiona said something about starting a dairy farm, but by that time nobody was paying any attention.

They were just finishing the meal when there was the sound of a car horn outside. "That's her," said Fiona, jumping up. She dropped her napkin on the table and ran out.

Steven raised his eyebrows at Jean. "Who's she going out with?"

"Caroline Fraser. Her parents have that nice restaurant down by the station," she said. "The Kinross. Remember? We went there a couple of months ago with the Tarlands."

"I had lunch today with Donald and Mac," said Steven. "Do you ever see Teresa?"

"Not much," said Jean. "In fact I haven't seen her since that time at the Kinross."

"I'm sure she'd love to see more of you," said Steven. "In fact, Donald mentioned it today. He said Teresa didn't like to phone because you're so busy."

"All right," promised Jean, feeling guilty, and wondering where she would find the time. "I'll phone her. Maybe I'll have lunch with her next week."

"Good."

They heard Caroline's car drive away. Steven was sounding irritable. "Wasn't it the Fraser's boy who got himself into some kind of trouble? Marco Fraser?"

"Yes, it was," interrupted Lisbie. "He's in our drama group. He's very good. Maybe a bit too macho, but very sexy."

"He sounds like somebody you should steer very clear of, from what I've heard about him," said Steven, sounding stern.

"Well, he can put his shoes under my bed any time he likes," said Lisbie, forgetting that Fiona wasn't there to pick up the ball and help her out. Under her parents' astonished gaze, she blushed deeply, jumped to her feet and hastily started to clear the dishes.

Chapter 5

"What are you for?" asked Fiona. They had found an empty table by the window which looked out over the bridge.

"Campari," replied Caroline, her eyes moving automatically around the room, checking out the talent, although she certainly wasn't at all interested in picking anybody up. It was just that old habits died hard.

Fiona walked over to the bar. "Hi, Joan, how's it going?" She chatted for a moment. "A lager and lime for me and a Campari for Caroline, please." Joan, an attractive brunette, had been at school with Fiona until she left to have a baby.

Fiona got back to her table, put Caroline's Campari down in front of her, and sank down into a chair opposite her.

"You know, we used to envy her," she said, nodding in Joan's direction. "She was in the same class as me at school. She left to have a baby, can you imagine? And she left school early, too. It made her so much more grown-up than the rest of us."

"She never got married, though, did she?" asked Caroline, who had met Joan before.

"No. She didn't want to. He went off and joined the Navy, or something. But Joan said she didn't care, she could manage. I hope she still feels the same way."

Caroline shook her head emphatically. "I can't imagine how any girl would want to do that. I'd have made damn sure he married me, or else he'd be paying for me and that baby for the rest of his natural life."

Fiona smiled at Caroline's forcefulness.

"Joan looks sort of tired, don't you think?"

Caroline shrugged. "Anybody'd look tired, doing bartending all evening. Still, it might be more fun than what I'm doing."

Fiona sipped her lager, and watched Caroline over the rim of her glass. "I thought you liked it. It must be better than when you worked with us."

"It has its advantages. . . ." Caroline grinned. "How's things back at the store? Sometimes I miss the gang."

"You remember Mr. Pratt? The one who was always putting his hand up the girls' skirts? Well, he's stopped. Two of the new trainees put in a complaint about sexual harassment, and management hauled him over the coals. He was really indignant. He'd been doing it so long he thought it was part of his job."

They laughed, having both been at one time or another at the receiving end of Mr. Pratt's roving hands.

"So what's happening with your love life?" asked Fiona. "The last I heard was about the tour guide in Bangkok, and that was weeks and weeks ago."

"Oh, he was *dreamy*," replied Caroline. "I never heard a word from him since I got home, though, the rat."

"Was he what put you off Brian?"

"Yes, partly, I suppose." Caroline didn't seem to want to pursue the subject.

"You'd never have settled for him anyway," said Fiona, watching her friend carefully. "You're far too ambitious."

"Right. He was nice enough, poor old Brian, but he'd about as much get-up-and-go as a jellyfish."

"So what's happening now? Who do you have in the net?"

To Fiona's surprise, two spots of color came into Caroline's cheeks, and she leaned forward confidentially over the table. "I may be getting married, Fiona."

Fiona looked at Caroline with utter astonishment.

"Married! My God, Caroline! Congratulations . . .who to?"

"Well, I can't tell you right now, because, well, he's not entirely free, for one thing."

"Not *entirely* free? Is he married?"

Caroline refused to be drawn into any further discussion.

"Let's talk about you, for a change," she said, sounding a little flustered. She looked at their empty glasses. "Same again?" she asked, getting up. Fiona nodded. Fiona suddenly wondered if she hadn't had a couple of drinks before they went out.

Caroline's step was not quite steady as she went over to the bar, and Fiona worried momentarily about the drive home. The bar had filled up quite rapidly, mostly with men, and Fiona was aware of the sexual interest that Caroline aroused, nothing more overt than turning of heads and stares, but one could almost feel the intensity of it. Fiona, who could turn a few heads herself, sensed that Caroline was in a different league; there was something feral and exotic about what she exuded, something quite different from the home-grown Perth variety of charm.

When she came back, Caroline carried the drinks very steadily. She sat down, looked hard at Fiona, took a deep breath and started to say something, then changed her mind and shook her head. "It doesn't matter," she said. "It's something I have to sort out myself."

Fiona knew Caroline well enough not to ask any more questions. Caroline had a low flashpoint, and like her brother Marco, whom she resembled strongly, she could flare up without much provocation, but Fiona felt concerned all the same. She could sense that a major change had come over Caroline, but she couldn't tell if it was good or bad. One moment her eyes flashed with excitement, and the next something came and clouded them.

Half an hour later, Caroline got up, ready to go home. Fiona, who had expected they would go on elsewhere, maybe dancing, was surprised but not put out. There was something strange about the way Caroline was acting, but she obviously wasn't about to discuss whatever or whoever it was that had arisen in her life.

On the drive back to the Montroses' house, Caroline was completely silent, and as Fiona was undoing her seat belt, she noticed that Caroline was shivering.

"What's the matter?" she asked. "Are you cold?"

"No," said Caroline, trying to smile. "I'm not cold."

"What is it, then?"

"I'm scared, Fiona, that's all." And she refused to say another word, and drove off with Fiona staring after the car as it disappeared down the hill.

Chapter 6

Jean Montrose pulled up outside one of the council houses in Nimmo Terrace and stepped out, locking the car door after her. In this neighborhood, it wasn't unusual for strange cars to get broken into or stolen, and a doctor's car was even more valuable because there always might be drugs in it. Louise Fraser, Francesca's mother-in-law, had called the surgery and asked Jean to call in.

A curtain moved on the second floor, and when Jean got up there, puffing a bit after going up four flights of concrete steps, the door was opened by Louise before she even had time to knock.

"I saw you coming, Doctor," she said. "Francesca's not feeling at all well today. She's in her bed, in here."

The bedroom was stuffy, the window was closed, and a two-bar electric radiator was emitting a close, unhealthy heat. A large blue-and-gold Madonna stood on the narrow mantelpiece, looking serene in spite of her precarious position. There was no sign that Marco had ever been there, no male clothes, shoes, anything. From her bed, Francesca watched Jean come in. She was a tiny woman, so small that she looked like a child lost in the double bed, propped up by two pillows, and covered only by one thin sheet. She was pale, her nostrils dilated with each breath, and indeed she looked ill. The great mound of her pregnancy bulging up under the sheet looked far too big for her.

"Well, Francesca, what's been happening since I saw you?" Jean felt concerned; Francesca's blood pressure had been going up steadily for the last two weeks.

"I'm very breathless, Dr. Montrose," said Francesca, taking the sentence in two bites. "I think the baby's just . . .taking up too much room." She finished the words in a rush, then lay back, her thin chest heaving. Jean could see the blue veins standing out on the upper part of Francesca's breasts.

"You're probably right," said Jean, smiling. "Let's take a look." Jean put her black bag on the chair and took out her blood pressure equipment and a stethoscope. "We'll see how the baby's doing first." Jean's voice was calm and reassuring, and the tension in the two other women seemed to relax, as if they were handing their activities over to the capable Dr. Montrose.

Jean pulled back the sheet. Francesca's belly-button was projecting at the dome of her belly, and a number of veins coursed around it, through the white, puffy-looking tight shiny skin of her abdomen. Jean listened; the rapid tap-tap-tap of the baby's heart was clearly audible through the stethoscope. "Would you like to listen?" she asked Francesca, but Francesca shook her head, too breathless and tired to speak.

Jean covered her belly, then lifted up the bottom of the sheet to look at her legs. They were slightly swollen, as were both her ankles. Jean pressed with her fingers for a moment; the indentations in the puffy flesh remained after she removed her hand.

"All right, Francesca, let's check your blood pressure." Francesca lay back, apathetic, her head turned away from Jean, then made a grimace and Jean, her hand against Francesca's belly, felt the baby move. "He kicked you, didn't he?"

Francesca nodded.

"Well, maybe he'll be a goalie for the Rangers one day," said Jean, smiling. She wasn't feeing at all reassured by what she was finding. Louise laughed, a loud, nervous laugh; her eyes didn't leave her daughter-in-law's face for an instant. Jean pulled the sleeve of Francesca's nightie up, and wrapped the cuff around her tiny arm.

"It's like trying to take blood pressure on a pencil," she said, holding Francesca's hand for a moment. It was hot, dry, and felt lifeless. Jean put the bell of her stethoscope on the inside of Francesca's elbow, and pumped the rubber bulb until the cuff tightened, and the mercury went near the top of the scale. Then she gradually let the air out, and the mercury came slowly down the glass tubing, until Jean suddenly heard the hard thump of Francesca's heartbeat through the stethoscope. She repeated the process to be sure, then unwrapped Francesca's arm.

"It's high isn't it?" said Francesca. "I can feel it beating in my head when it gets really high."

"I think we're going to have to put you in the hospital," said Jean, putting her equipment in her black bag.

Francesca said nothing, but Louise's lip trembled, and she bent down to hug her daughter-in-law, but Francesca became breathless again, and Mrs. Fraser stood up, tears running down both sides of her face.

"Does she have to go in?" asked Mrs. Fraser. "I'll take real good care of her, and I'll do whatever . . ."

"No, Louise," said Francesca, her voice so faint it was barely audible. "I have to go. I've known it for days, because everything's been getting worse. Now, I cannot even get out of my bed."

There was no phone in the house, so Jean sent Mrs. Fraser over to a neighbor to call an ambulance.

"I'm scared, Dr. Montrose," whispered Francesca after her mother-in-law had put on her coat and gone out.

"Everything's going to be all right," replied Jean. "You'll see. They'll probably induce you as soon as they

get your blood pressure down, then you'll come home
with a fine baby, just what you wanted.

Francesca shook her head. The tears were still running
out of her eyes although she didn't seem to be weeping.

"I don't think I'm going to get through this, Dr. Montrose. I don't know why, I just have this feeling."

"Nonsense, Francesca. They'll take good care of you,
don't worry." Jean only wished she felt as confident as
she tried to sound.

"Hey, Brian, have you finished that Bentley? The customer's coming for it in half an hour."

Brian Wooley shouted back from under the folding
hood of the car. "I still have the carburetors to tune," he
said. He leaned back, away from the blanket protecting
the side of the vehicle.

"Jesus, Brian, you've been at it all morning. What's
the problem?" Mike Chivas was upset. Brian, whose
work had until recently been very competent, had been
slacking off for a while now, always sloping off to hide
in the bathroom, or just taking far too long to do even
simple jobs.

"The carbs on the S2s are a bitch," replied Brian, his
voice flat and expressionless. Mike shook his head and
went back into the office. He knew as well as Brian that
the twin carburetors on this model were actually not difficult to tune, and many owner-enthusiasts did it themselves.

Brian made a slight adjustment to the spring-loaded
screw that controlled the amount of air coming through
the throttle, and the Bentley's deep exhaust note changed
slightly, but it still wasn't right. The tension in Brian's
body increased, and he was aware that his hands were
shaking. He couldn't get it right; he couldn't get anything right, not since Caroline had given him the heave-
ho only a few weeks ago, but now it seemed like a
lifetime away, a lifetime of unending misery. With a

greasy hand Brian rubbed the sore place on his jaw where Marco had hit him. It still ached, even though the bruises were gone.

There was nothing he could do about the situation, he knew that, but he couldn't get her out of his mind, not for a moment. And he couldn't help hoping that she would come back to him, that she would realize nobody could ever love her the way he did. Brian couldn't sleep at night; he kept waking up, then he'd try to read for a while, smoke a cigarette, or make himself a cup of coffee, then walk around his room until it was time to get up and go to work. Sometimes he'd go out in the middle of the night and just roam around, usually going past Caroline's house at some point in his travels. He was beginning to think he was going mad, and his work was suffering, because he just couldn't keep his mind off Caroline long enough to do a job properly.

Everything had been fine with him and Caroline until about a couple of months before, when she had started acting different, not as loving, and sometimes she didn't show up when they had a date. That was after she'd come back from a two week vacation in Thailand, of all places, having won the trip with a ticket in a Christmas raffle. Brian knew Caroline had been around, had known men before him, but it was different with him, or so she'd said. But he worried about it, because he had fallen for her in a way he'd never done before, and knew he never could again. Caroline, with her liveliness, her unpredictability, her beauty, had swept him into a different dimension. She was the love of his life. It had never occurred to him until one of his friends told him that Caroline had just been playing with him, and had much bigger fish in her sights.

At that point, Brian clenched his fists until the nails bit into his palms. He couldn't think about the Bentley, about the carburetors, about anything except Caroline, and for the next half hour he poked around ineffectually at the car, changing the settings, turning them back, unable to keep his mind on what he was doing. When he saw Colonel Strathdee arriving to pick up his car, he quickly closed the bonnet and disappeared in the direction of the garage toilets. He simply could not bear the thought of talking to anyone.

Jean Montrose was expecting Mac MacFadyen the next afternoon in the surgery, and peeked in the waiting room at the time he was due. He was there, sitting very upright; his immaculate, military, freshly laundered appearance contrasting markedly with the other less formally dressed patients.

But when he came into her examining room, she quickly saw that all was not well with him. His limp was pronounced, his eyes had no expression, and his skin seemed gray and loose on his face. Momentarily he made Jean think of a once-fine, well-upholstered piece of furniture that had lost half its stuffing.

"Well, Mac, what brings you here?" she asked after the brief civilities. "I see you're having some pain in your left hip." Mac had got on the practice's list when he came to Perth, but he had never actually been in the surgery to see either Helen or Jean.

Mac hesitated for only a moment, then faced her squarely. "I am, but it's not that. You know I was in the Army, and fought in the Falklands War, don't you?" he said, and Jean nodded, wondering what he was leading up to. "Well, I got through that all right," he went on, "but a couple of years ago I was with a friend of mine who's in the Household Cavalry, exercising a couple of horses on Rotten Row. There was a demonstration going on near Marble Arch, and somebody let off a firecracker right next to us. My horse reared and fell." Mac paused, and his hand went unconsciously to his left hip. "Unfortunately, I couldn't get my foot out of the stirrups in time and he fell on me, and I was hurt. Actually quite badly."

He tried to sound nonchalant, but it didn't come off. "I had a fractured pelvis and a broken hip that kept me in the hospital for months, and I had four operations." Mac pulled himself together and sat up very straight. "I was in pain for nearly all that time, and needed a lot of pain medicine, codeine, pethidine, morphine. They tried every kind known to man, even some experimental ones. Then I got out of the hospital, but they wouldn't give me any more drugs; they said I might get addicted." Mac laughed, but there was no humor in it. "Sometimes the pain was so bad I just wept, because it never let up, and just went on and on."

Jean's sympathetic heart went out to him; she knew Mac socially, having met him with Steven, and hadn't thought much of this fashion-plate man who seemed more concerned about his appearance than anything else. Now she was beginning to understand why; his fine clothes were just camouflage for the damaged body beneath.

"But of course I didn't come here for True Confessions, Jean. . . ." Mac tried to smile. He felt very unsure of himself at that moment, unsure of whether he was doing the right thing in coming to talk to Jean Montrose, and unsure of whether he could once again bare his soul and scars. And the old fears were creeping up on him again, and gaining ground. If he gave himself up for treatment, they'd make him go through withdrawal, and he knew what the screaming horrors of that experience would be like. The thought sent a chill through his entire body, or was that because he would be needing a hit within thirty minutes? Mac took a deep breath, stood up and took off his blazer. The brass buttons glinted in the light and he put it carefully on the back of the chair. He rolled up one sleeve of his snowy-white shirt, and Jean caught her breath when she saw the red, scarred needle tracks in the crook of his arm. Several of them were infected, and the tissues around were inflamed and swollen.

Mac smiled, but there was no trace of his old confidence. "The best feeling in my entire life was my first hit of heroin," he said. "I was in Glasgow looking for a job, actually the one I have now. I had an appointment to meet Donald Tarland, who wanted to start up a mail-order company, but I was having such pain that I hadn't slept the night before, although I'd taken handfuls of aspirins and codeine. I didn't know how I was going to get through the day, let alone get through an interview, and I finally decided to go out and buy something, anything to get rid of my pain. I know my way around Glasgow, and I knew where to go. I'll never forget it. There was this old wizened man on the fifth floor of one of the old Gorbals tenements that had somehow escaped being pulled down; he had thin, wiry gray arms with a tattoo of a girl and a snake on the right one. He watched my eyes every second he was pushing that plunger, as if he could *taste* it himself."

Mac paused for a moment, remembering, and Jean looked at him and tried to visualize him as a confident young Army officer whose life had been shattered in an unlucky moment, and how, with more and more difficulty, he continued to maintain an outer shell of appearances to preserve his own self-respect.

Mac's voice had a faraway tone, as if he were back in the tenements of Glasgow, reliving the episode. "Nothing happened for a moment, then there was this *unbelievable* flush, a *hit* of . . . I don't even know what to call it, joy, pleasure, almost like, well, an orgasm, except a hundred times better. . . ." He glanced at Jean, not wanting to embarrass her, but he needn't have worried. "For a couple of minutes I didn't even realize that the pain had gone completely, the first time for months."

Mac's entire face lit up with the recollection, and Jean felt a lump rise in her throat. Poor Mac, she thought; what agonies he must have suffered.

"After that," went on Mac quietly, "there was no going back. Not even morphine was half as good."

Mac sat down in the chair. "My habit costs me a hundred pounds a day now," he said quietly. "Although it's the only thing that ever helped me, it's destroying my life. I'm in trouble with my partner, and my social life . . . well, it's taken a different turn and I don't want to compromise things." He started to roll his sleeve down and fastened the button. "I hate to admit it, Jean, but at this point, I really need help."

"I'll certainly try," said Jean, but her heart was somewhere in her boots. She knew only too well that the chances of getting Mac off heroin were small, particularly if it was the only thing that could take away his pain. "There's a methadone program we can get you into," she said, trying to sound upbeat and reassuring. "But you're going to need inpatient care first." She looked at Mac thoughtfully. "When did you have your last . . . dose?"

Mac looked at his watch. "About four and a half hours ago," he replied. He smiled. "Actually, I didn't need to look at my watch at all. All the time, I know almost to the minute how long it was, and how much longer I can last till I have to have the next hit."

"Have you ever shared needles?" asked Jean. "I'm sure you know the risk of AIDS, hepatitis and so on."

"Never. I have my own little store of them. I bought them all new, but I must say, they're getting a bit blunt." He stared at Jean, and she suddenly realized that he was asking her not only for needles but for a supply of drugs too.

"You know I can't prescribe heroin," she said. "And even if I could, it would only make things worse for you in the long run."

"How about some MS or some pethidine, just to tide me over?" With a sinking heart, Mac realized that he had chickened out. He just couldn't face the reality of going into a place to be forcibly detoxified. Although his voice was strong, his eyes were pleading and tiny droplets of sweat had appeared on his forehead, just under the hairline.

Jean shook her head. "Mac, you know I can't." She reached for the phone. "I'll try to get you in one of the clinics," she said, but Mac was already on his feet, fastening the bright brass buttons of his blazer.

"Thanks anyway, doc," he said with an artificial cheerfulness. "Maybe I'll come back and turn myself in next week, maybe not."

Chapter 7

Caroline Fraser was feeling rather pleased with herself when she left work that day. She had got permission to leave early, and had bumped into Mac who was coming back into the office, but he seemed in a hurry and they hadn't had a chance to talk. There was a crisp taste of Spring in the afternoon air. She decided to walk over to Jean Montrose's office, and take a small detour to see the trees around the edge of the South Inch. They were a bright new-leaf green, and to Caroline's eyes seemed full of promise, full of fresh, succulent new life. She needed to feel the clean air circulate in her lungs after spending all day in the stuffy office. Aileen was always cold, and liked to have the heating on all the time.

The walk only took ten minutes, and when she got to Jean's surgery at the corner of William Street, she was feeling full of life and energy. Helen Inkster's green Ford was parked outside the surgery, but Jean Montrose's white Renault was nowhere to be seen.

Caroline negotiated the puddle just inside the gate, left from a heavy shower a couple of hours before, and walked the short distance to the door. Eleanor, the secretary, smiled at her with that knowing, disapproving smile that Caroline was so familiar with. Everybody in Perth seemed to know her, even people she didn't remember ever seeing before.

"If you'll just have a seat in the waiting room, it should be about twenty minutes. Dr. Montrose had to go to the hospital a few minutes ago, and I'm not sure when she'll be back." Caroline was very aware that Eleanor was staring covertly at her as she spoke, but Caroline was used to that too. Women stared just as much as the men, usually in an equally intrusive but different way; they seemed more interested in her clothes, her jewelry, and how she wore them.

Helen Inkster, Jean's partner, came out of the tiny lab where they did urine and blood tests. "Well, Caroline!" She gave her a swift, appraising glance. "You look in pretty good trim."

"I'm doing all right, Dr. Inkster." Caroline felt a rush of annoyance, directed mostly at the nosy Eleanor. Helen was all right, in her tough masculine way, but Caroline was beginning to regret her decision to talk to Jean Montrose. She knew Eleanor; in no time flat, she'd have the word around town that Caroline Fraser had been in to see the doctor.

Fifteen minutes later, Eleanor came into the waiting room. "Dr. Montrose isn't back yet, but Dr. Inkster can see you now." Caroline followed her into Helen's office, wondering how she was going to say what she had to say.

Helen was sitting at her desk, a big old-fashioned dark oak monster with lots of drawers, each with a small ornate brass handle.

"Well, you're a nice change from my usual bunch of old folks," said Helen in her gruff, booming voice. "What's the matter?"

"Not much," said Caroline, feeling suddenly nervous. She liked Helen all right, but Jean was the one she wanted to talk to. "I mean, it's not bothering me much." Her mind was racing. She had to say something, or Helen would think she was out of her head.

"What isn't?"

Caroline remembered some symptoms she'd had a few weeks ago, after coming back from Thailand. "I have some burning when I pee," she said. "It's not that bad, but I thought I'd better get it checked."

"Not uncommon," said Helen. "Anything else?" Her sharp eyes watched Caroline's.

"No," replied Caroline. "That's it."

Helen hesitated for a second, sensing that there was more to Caroline's visit than that. "OK," she said, getting up. "Let's take a look at you."

A few minutes later, after giving a urine sample and being examined, Caroline put her clothes back on.

"Nothing the miracles of modern science can't cure," said Helen. She scribbled on the prescription pad and tore off the top copy. "This is ampicillin," she said. "Take one every eight hours for ten days, Caroline. If it's not a lot better, come back in early next week, OK?"

Caroline left a couple of minutes later, feeling disappointed that Jean Montrose hadn't been there. Helen was fine, a nice woman, but not a person to whom a girl could talk about her real problems.

Caroline walked back toward South Street, feeling irritable and aimless, and tried to decide what she would do that evening. She stopped at the wine shop because they had a special Australian white on sale, then at the chemist on the corner opposite, and finally she went over to Marks and Spencer's to get something for dinner. When she got home, Caroline put the vegetable casserole and the wine in the refrigerator, and went into the bathroom to do the test. The phone rang, startling her, and after the conversation she put on a coat because it was beginning to get chilly, and went out again, feeling very cheerful indeed.

Donald Tarland's office was not fancy, although it contained everything he needed to run his business. The walls were painted white, with a couple of reproduction Constables on the wall, one of them hanging behind his chair. On the plain wooden desk was a telephone con-

sole, a row of filing cabinets stood opposite the door,
and under the window which looked out over the street,
a small table with a modern computer terminal and
printer.

Donald sat at his desk trying to straighten out his
thoughts. How had he managed to get himself into such
a mess? He'd known Mac for well over a year; at the
time they met he'd been looking for somebody to help
him start up a mail-order business, someone with a
cheerful, outgoing personality who could handle the
salesmen and clients, close deals with suppliers, and
who could put some capital into the business. Donald
knew his own limitations; he tended to be introspective,
quiet and soft-spoken, and was uncomfortable with other
people, and knew that just as often he made them uncomfortable too. His strong points were in finance, and
in addition he had an undeniable flair for knowing what
people wanted to buy, and how much they were willing
to pay. Mac had answered the advertisement he'd put in
a trade paper, and they met in Glasgow, where Donald
had been working for a few weeks out of a small rented
office.

The two men had got on immediately.

"Take a look at this," Donald had said, pulling a catalogue out of his desk drawer. "Tell me what you think."

The catalogue was about thirty pages long, with
black-and-white photos of a variety of articles from
power saws to scuba tanks.

"Do you want me to say it's wonderful, or do you
want the truth?" asked Mac, flipping over the pages. He
was feeling so great, so full of energy and life after that
first hit that he couldn't believe it.

"I was hoping you could do both," replied Donald,
smiling, and astonished at his own quickness of wit.

Mac put his hands on the desk. "The truth is, Donald,
it won't work."

Donald closed the catalogue, momentarily annoyed.

He'd worked for months to find the different items, negotiating the best prices, and producing the catalogue. He was actually rather proud of it.

"Nowadays you need color, for a start," said Mac. "Secondly, you're trying to cover too wide a field. If consumers want this kind of thing by mail, from refrigerators to carpets, they'll buy them from one of the big, well-known mail-order houses. They know they can get a better price because the biggies buy by the truckload."

Donald had to admit the logic of Mac's criticism, and after an afternoon of discussion, they went out to dinner and talked about working together. Donald had a substantial amount to invest, Mac had his discharge bounty from the Army plus money from an insurance policy. Between them they had enough to set up in business, and had done so. They had agreed to specialize in high-quality merchandise such as cookware, china, glass and silverware, unusual items with a substantial markup, where they could make money and develop a reputation for quality at the same time.

At that time, Donald remembered, Mac had a very nice girlfriend whom he was planning to marry, but soon after she went off with someone else after a big row with Mac. Mac had been tight-lipped about it, and Donald never found out what had happened.

Donald switched on his computer, then took out a thick file from the cabinet and put it on his desk. He leafed through it, checking items with his usual thoroughness. The premiums for the various insurance policies were coming due in a couple of weeks, and Donald wondered how he was going to pay them. Business had dropped off markedly over the last several months; Mac had said it was because of the recession, but in retrospect Donald wondered if that was the whole story. Maybe Mac was too consumed with his addiction and hadn't been doing his job.

Donald reached for the phone and put a call through

to a company in Sheffield that supplied them with high-quality steel kitchenware.

"Well," said Donald's opposite number there, "where have you been? We have a new line we wanted you people to see. I called Mac, he said he was coming, but that was four weeks ago. Is he still working with you?"

It was the same story with two other suppliers, and the printers were waiting to get the copy on the new items for the Christmas catalogue. "Sorry," the foreman said, "I told him it had to be in this time last week or we'd have to put him off for five weeks. We have other customers to take care of."

Donald replaced the phone and put his head between his hands. This had started as a mere disaster, but was now turning into a catastrophe. No wonder business was down. Maybe Caroline had some idea what was going on; Donald suspected that she had had something going at one time with Mac, but he wasn't sure. He *was* pretty sure it wasn't going on now.

The door opened and Caroline came in, taking off her coat. He smiled at her and thought that she was like a breath of Spring air, and felt very fortunate that they'd employed her. She stood in front of the desk, waiting.

"Come and take a look at this," he said. "I want to show you these numbers." He indicated the comxuter printout in front of him. "These are last month's figures, and the two months before. Over here . . ." He pointed to three columns of numbers. "These are the corresponding figures for last year. We're slipping, Caroline, slipping badly."

From the tension on Donald's face and the way his shoulders were hunched up, it was clear to Caroline that what the poor man needed was a good massage. She smiled briefly to herself; she knew just how to do that, and had had plenty of compliments on the different ways she could make a man relax.

She looked over his shoulder at the figures. "I was

meaning to talk to you about that," she said quietly. "Of course, I probably don't know everything that's going on, but from what I can see, the business is in deep trouble."

After they had discussed the possible solutions to the problem and Donald had partially calmed down, Caroline took a deep breath, and decided to tell him what was going on in *her* life. There really wasn't anybody else with whom she could discuss it frankly, and Donald was a really good and understanding person. Caroline felt reasonably certain he would see her point of view, but she still felt a quiver of apprehension in her stomach when she went back around the desk and sat down in the visitor's chair.

Donald was busy adding up a column of figures with a pencil and his calculator, and it wasn't until Caroline had cleared her throat a couple of times that he paid attention. He put down the pencil, sat back and smiled at her.

"Caroline, I can always tell when you have something on your mind," he said. "I'm listening."

Chapter 8

Mac's third-floor flat was comfortable enough, if one didn't mind the untidy austerity of a bachelor pad. His bedroom was deliberately stark, reminding him of Army life. There was a single bed in the far corner, with a square wooden table next to it, surmounted by an anglepoise lamp for reading in bed. Opposite the unvarnished chest of drawers was a small bookshelf containing several military publications, a book on mass marketing, and some journals. As usual, Mac was in the second bedroom, where he had set up an elaborate model of the Falkland Islands; his hobby was to re-fight the war. On the blue sheet that represented the South Atlantic Ocean, small models of the opposing warships headed for the disputed waters, with the British aircraft carriers still too far away to be effective. Mac sat on a chair overlooking the Islands. How would the Americans have done it? There was little question in his mind; air power would have been the key. They would have mounted a fast and deadly assault with a really large force of parachutists, brought in by transports which would have been refuelled in mid-air. Air-to-sea missiles would have taken care of the Argentinian Navy as soon as they got outside the thirty mile limit, and by the time the Royal Navy came up it would have been all over, with no casualties beyond a few fractured ankles among the parachutists. Mac dimmed the lights to represent nightfall, and the various installations glowed with the light from tiny bulbs fitted inside them. Immersed in his strategic exercise, he didn't hear the door buzzer until the second ring. Donald Tarland was at the door, looking as grim as he'd ever seen him.

"Come in, Donald," said Mac affably. "I'm fighting the Falklands War all over again. Let me go and switch it off. Please, get yourself a drink; everything's on the kitchen counter."

Silently, Donald went into the kitchen and looked around, his nose wrinkling at the untidiness of Mac's kitchen; it was more or less as he remembered it from previous visits. Pots on the counter, a set of kitchen knives in a wooden block, a coffee machine with a half-full pot of cold coffee still underneath it. Donald wondered how long Teresa would take to get the place sparkling and tidy, reached into the cupboard for a glass and poured himself a stiff whisky. When Mac came back in, Donald put his glass down.

"Mac," he said, "I really need an explanation from you. I called some of our suppliers and customers. . . ." Tight-lipped, Donald told him about his conversations, and their complaints about never hearing from Mac. ". . . We're going to go out of business unless we mend these fences, Mac. I'm going to call them all again next week, and if everything isn't shipshape, you and I are going to have to part company. I'm sorry, Mac, but you haven't left me any other option."

After Donald left, holding his folded coat over his arm and feeling angry and faintly larcenous, Mac went back to his war, and lost himself again in the exhilarating memories of when he was healthy and confident and full of the joy and excitement of life.

Fiona sat up suddenly at the dinner table. "That's my boyfriend!" she said, her head on one side.

"How can she tell?" Steven asked Jean across the table. "I didn't hear anything."

"Sexual vibrations," said Lisbie, solemnly. "She told me. She feels them. I don't know how, but she actually *feels* them in her . . ."

"Lisbie! That's quite enough of that," said Steven loudly. If there was one thing he wouldn't tolerate it was crude or suggestive language. "Please eat your dinner and spare us your coarse observations."

"I was just going to say she feels them in . . ."

"LISBIE!"

The doorbell rang and Fiona ran to answer it.

"In her *heart*," said Lisbie quickly. "Dad, you have a dirty mind." They could hear the indistinct conversation as Fiona let the visitor in.

"Bring him into the dining room," called Jean.

A moment later, Inspector Douglas Niven came in, smiling in a bemused way, as he always did when Fiona was around. He was taking his raincoat off as he walked in to the dining room, and Fiona took it and went back into the hall to hang it up.

"Well," said Steven, without marked enthusiasm. "We haven't seen you here for a while."

"Right. I've been pretty busy, with one thing and another."

Fiona came back in. "Would you like a cup of coffee?" she asked.

"Yes, thanks, Fiona," he said, smiling at her.

"I know how you like it," she announced, coffee pot in hand, and sounding a bit possessive. "Black with a wee bit of sugar, right?"

"Don't think you're special," said Lisbie, grinning. "She knows how all her boyfriends like their coffee."

"What's new in the battle against crime?" Steven passed his empty plate back to Jean, who put it on top before transferring the stack to the sideboard.

"Not much." Douglas took the cup Fiona proffered. "But I do have some news." He looked at Jean. "That's really why I came over. Cathie's going to have a baby."

"Wonderful!" said Jean.

There was a crash behind her as a coffee cup was slammed into its saucer. Jean looked around for a second at Fiona, who had made the disturbance, then smiled bemusedly at Douglas. "When is the great event?"

"Not till the end of December," replied Doug, a grin threatening to split his face in two. "She'll be coming to see you soon," he went on. "She used one of those pregnancy tests from the chemists."

"I hope it'll be all right," said Fiona darkly. She came around the table and sat down next to Lisbie, far away from Douglas. "I was thinking of that baby that Mum took care of, the one with Forth-Sachs disease, who died."

"Tay-Sachs, dear," said Jean. "Now if you girls wouldn't mind clearing up the dishes, the rest of us'll go into the living room."

"I'll just go upstairs in a minute to watch the news," said Steven. "I'll see you later."

Jean and Douglas went through to the living room and Doug installed himself in Steven's green high-backed chair.

"How's Cathie doing?" asked Jean. "She must be really pleased. She's waited long enough."

"Aye, she's happy a' right," said Douglas. He looked slender and professional, with his glasses and serious expression, but maybe because of a recent haircut which had left his gray-blond hair almost crewcut, he seemed younger and more innocent-looking. "It's amazing," he said, "she's starting to collect baby clothes already, a cot, toys, God knows what all."

They chatted on about Cathie for a little while, but at the back of her mind, Jean worried. Maybe it was because several of the recent pregnancies she'd taken care of had been difficult, like poor little Francesca's. That reminded her to call the hospital, which she did as soon as Doug had left. There, the news was not good. They were trying a new kind of medication on Francesca, but according to the nurse, she was accumulating fluid and they were all very worried about her. Jean promised to come in to see her the next day, although she really didn't know when she'd find the time, as she'd promised to visit her mother during the lunch-hour.

After leaving the office for the second time, Caroline went home and ate her dinner in front of the TV. That was one of the nice things about living by oneself, she thought. When you're at home, you can do what you like, eat what you like when you like. Still, when everything was all straightened out, things would be a lot different, and her life would be more regulated, perhaps, but so, so much better. A little after ten, Caroline decided to stop in to see her parents. Marco would be there too, probably. She wondered how he would take the news when she decided to make it public. The restaurant wasn't far enough to take her car, so Caroline walked, after putting on a raincoat. It was chilly and starting to rain, a thin, foggy drizzle that put tiny beads of moisture on her hair. By the time she got there, the restaurant was just closing, and Caroline met the last customers coming out of the door.

"You're just in time for a nice dinner, huh?" said Bob, grinning happily and holding the door open while she slipped inside. He pulled off his apron and gave her a big hug. Bob Fraser loved his family, his food and his restaurant in that order. "Here, let me get you something. You look as if you haven't eaten in a week." Bob put his arm around her and they walked into the kitchen together. "Look who I found wandering around in the rain outside," he announced. Louise poked her head around the door of the big freezer, both hands full of plastic containers of food.

"Caroline! Here, come and give me a hand. I thought you'd forgotten us."

Caroline slipped off her coat, and came over to kiss her mother's damp forehead and started to pass her the containers which she placed on the freezer shelves. Bob hurried around, taking food from an assortment of glass dishes and putting it on a plate, a few slices of pepperoni, some black olives, green pepper and aubergine salad, some paper-thin slices of Parma ham, half a hard-boiled egg, then poured a generous amount of thick greenish olive oil over it, then a little vinegar. "Here," he said, handing Caroline the loaded plate, "a little antipasto. Eat it while I fix you a nice omelette with some ratatouille."

"No, thanks, Pa, this'll be plenty. It looks delicious." Caroline was not feeling at all hungry, but she washed a fork at the sink, put the plate on the draining board and obediently started to eat.

"So what's new?" asked her father, hovering around. "What have you been doing that's interesting?"

"Let her eat in peace," said her mother. "In a minute we'll go upstairs and she can talk then."

"Where's Marco?" asked Caroline.

Bob's expression clouded. "He got mad again, and went out. Luckily Rose could come in, otherwise, your mother and me, we'd still be serving dinners now. What a temper he has, that boy. It'll get him into serious trouble one day."

"It already has," said Louise in her deep voice, glancing at Caroline.

Half an hour later, after all the food had been put away and everything was tidied up, Bob turned off the lights and they all went up through the back stairs to the Frasers' large, comfortable flat.

Marco came in a few moments later. His rages didn't usually last long, but while they lasted, they were fearsome. He went over to his father, eyes downcast. "Dad, I'm sorry. It was my fault. I'll make up the time in the restaurant this weekend, OK?"

Bob shrugged his big shoulders. "You can't take back what you've done, Marco. Tonight, your mother and me, we had to work like dogs because of your temper. When we're dead, what will you do when somebody makes you angry? Beat them up? Kill them? You can't live like that, son."

"Look, I said I was sorry. . . ." Marco turned quickly to his sister, smiled broadly, put his arms around her and swung her around in a circle. Caroline could feel the strength of him, and it scared and reassured her at the same time. "Caroline, baby, where have you been? You never come home these days."

"I'm surprised she comes home at all, after what you did to that Brian," said Louise.

"I did the right thing," said Marco, turning fast as a snake to face his mother. Strong as she was, Louise moved back in her chair when she saw his expression. "He was following her around, being a nuisance. He won't give her no more trouble," he said. "And if he does . . . Well, I can take care of that too." He grinned confidently around at his family. "Brothers were put here by God to protect their big sisters."

"Violence never does nobody any good," said Bob, uneasy with his son's attitude.

"Francesca's in the hospital," said Louise. "Dr. Montrose put her in today. Marco, it's a disgrace that you don't take better care of her."

Marco shrugged; it was obvious that he hadn't the slightest interest in Francesca, sick or well. All the time, he didn't take his eyes off Caroline. As usual, that made her feel nervous, and she looked at her watch.

"I have to go home now," she said. "I have work to go to in the morning."

Louise watched her daughter's expression and wondered. Caroline seemed anxious and excited at the same time, and it crossed her mind that she might be going out to meet someone.

"I can come in to help tomorrow night, if you like," said Caroline. "I'm not doing anything else."

"Great," said Marco quickly, although Caroline was not talking to him but to their father. His eyes were glistening.

"You keep quiet," said Bob angrily. "And you're to leave her alone tomorrow, d'you hear?"

Marco grinned at him, but there was no humor in his expression.

Caroline, tying the belt around her raincoat, stared at Marco for a second, then put her hand on Bob's arm.

"Don't worry, Dad, he doesn't scare me. I can take care of myself," she said."

"No you can't," said Marco, in a jibing voice. "You still need your brother to take care of you."

Caroline shrugged. Her father said nothing, but accompanied her downstairs, gave her a big hug then closed the front door behind her. Outside, it was still drizzling, and the wind was picking up.

Chapter 9

"I'm terribly sorry, Colonel Strathdee. If you can possibly leave the car for a couple of hours, I'll personally see that the Bentley's fixed properly. I can let you have a temporary replacement, of course, but I'm afraid I only have a Jaguar."

"Well, all right," said the Colonel, but he was visibly irritated. He slapped one leather glove into the one he was wearing. "But, dammit, I want you to realize that this is a great nuisance to me. I've had to come back into town, and I have a board meeting in Edinburgh in an hour."

He glowered at Mike Chivas. "This is the first time I've ever had bad service from you people." He sounded disappointed and surprised, and Mike felt his whole body tighten up with anger at Brian. Colonel Strathdee was an important and influential customer, and the last person Mike wanted to antagonize.

"You can have it back this afternoon, sir," he said. "I'll have it going so smoothly you'll have to get out to see if the motor's still running."

Five minutes later, after he had sent the Colonel off in an almost new Jaguar, Mike walked over to the repair shop.

"Brian!" he called out through the doorway. "Come through to the office a minute, please."

Brian was on his back, changing the silencer on a Silver Shadow. He came out from under the car, put down his wrench and wiped his hands on a piece of rag. He'd seen the Colonel's Bentley come back in, and guessed what Mike's summons was about.

"What the hell is the matter with you?" asked Mike as soon as Brian had come in and closed the door. "Colonel Strathdee's Bentley sounds like a delivery lorry, and he's really steaming."

"Sorry, Mike," mumbled Brian. "I don't seem to be able to concentrate, or something."

"Brian, do you remember what I told you last Thursday, when you forgot to replace the oil you'd drained out of that Aston-Martin? Well, I wasn't kidding. You're costing us too much money and too much good will." Mike took a deep breath and gripped the edge of the desk with both hands. "Brian, I'm sorry to have to do this, but you're fired. I'll send your check in the post. Don't even go back into the shop. Just go."

Brian walked down the road, dazed and angry, his head in a whirl. Everything was scrambling and shoving around in his head, the Bentley, the carburetors, Mike's angry, disappointed expression. Now he had no job, and he could imagine what kind of references he'd get from the garage. A vision of Marco came to him, and again he saw the way Marco's face had twisted when he booted him in the ribs, and of course that led him back to thinking about Caroline, and that was like having slivers of glass pushed into his soul. His step quickened, as if he were trying to escape from his thoughts, and in the overheated climate of his brain a nucleus of hatred started to grow. By the time he reached home, he knew what he was going to have to do. He felt suddenly detached, as if a new person had budded somewhere out of him, a quiet unflustered separate person who took it all as calmly as if it were happening to someone else. And whoever or whatever it was had taken command and was telling him exactly what to do in a soft voice which came from deep within him.

* * *

On her way home, Jean stopped at the hospital to see Francesca. The maternity unit was on the third floor, and rather than wait for the lift, Jean started to go up the stairs which coiled around the wire-enclosed shaft. By the second floor she was sorry she hadn't waited, and sat down for a moment on the bench at the top of the stairs.

"Well, if it isn't Jean Montrose," said a deep voice. It was Dr. Peter Macintosh, the head of Obstetrics and Gynecology, who had been at medical school with Jean in Aberdeen. "What brings you up here?"

"Peter, it's nice to see you," said Jean, still puffing a bit. "I'm on my way up to your ward. I sent a patient, Francesca Fraser, in earlier today."

Peter sat down on the bench beside Jean. "I'm really worried about that girl," he said. "Her blood pressure's way up, and . . . I don't know, there's something about her attitude that troubles me. She doesn't speak much English, but it's not that."

"It's a rather sad story." Jean glanced at Peter. Some hospital doctors she knew didn't want to know anything about their patients except the diagnosis, but Peter was one of the good ones. "She's married to a chap by the name of Marco Fraser. You've probably heard of him— his folks own the Kinross restaurant."

Peter shook his head.

"Anyway, Marco was on a holiday in Ibiza two years ago, met this nice little Italian girl who didn't speak a word of English, brought her back and married her within a couple of weeks." Jean was silent for a moment, thinking about the rather strange timing of that apparently spontaneous love affair. Marco had gone on holiday a couple of weeks after his sister Caroline had started on what seemed to be a serious romance.

"He's neglected her completely, from the day they were married." Jean's voice betrayed her indignation. "He leaves her alone for days at a time, and I suspect that he got rough with her on a couple of occasions. And the poor girl, she has no friends, no relatives, except for her parents-in-law, who more or less take care of her." Jean stood up. "If he hasn't been in to see her, I'm going to call him in and give him a piece of my mind."

"Well, Jean, I hope you never have to do that to me for any reason," said Peter smiling. "Anyway, as I was saying, Francesca's in quite a bit of trouble. She has a tiny pelvis, but it's too early to do a Caesarean unless we're absolutely forced to, because the baby's chances would be no better than marginal."

Jean sighed. "Good luck, Peter. I know you'll do your best for her."

"Aye, we'll do that all right," he said. "I'll let you know if we get into an emergency situation."

Up on the third floor, Jean pushed one of the double doors that led into the maternity unit and walked in. The nurse looked up from the desk. "Oh, hello, Dr. Montrose. The woman in 302, Mrs. Fraser, was asking for you."

Jean returned her greeting and started to walk down the corridor, then turned back. "Pat, do you happen to know if her husband was in?"

"No, Dr. Montrose." She hesitated. "Actually, she said she didn't want to see him."

Jean took a deep breath before going into room 302 and got her most encouraging smile ready.

"Well, yesterday I finally had it out with Caroline," said Aileen, leaning over the table to hold on to Mac's wrist. She was wearing an electric blue silk dress with a high flounced hem which might have looked good on her when she was twenty, but now seemed slightly ridiculous. Two pink splashes of blusher illuminated her cheekbones, and her eyes, glowing with an obsessive intensity, stared out of caverns of mascara. Aileen looked at Mac as if she were contemplating eating him raw. "At lunchtime. I told her that you and I were a unit, and not to mess with us."

Mac's eyes didn't leave the menu. Now he felt fully recovered from his visit to Jean's surgery, but just afterward he'd felt so shaky he'd hurried back to the office, given himself an extra jolt of heroin and almost passed out. "What did she say?"

"I had to explain to her that we had a very strong relationship, you and I, and that although you sometimes take her out, it was because it's a nice thing to do in a small office, but that you weren't at all impressed by her seductive tricks."

Mac put the menu down and looked at Aileen over the single candle. For some time now, he had worn an expression of bored irritation when he was with her, but either she didn't notice or was so infatuated with him that she didn't care.

"I don't give a damn what you said." Mac's voice was ominously quiet. "I asked what did SHE say."

Aileen hesitated, and stared at him, trying to understand his mood.

"She . . . Well, she more or less told me to mind my own business."

"Good for her. So why *don't* you mind your own business?"

Oh dear, thought Aileen, I've got him annoyed again. I never seem to be able to say things in a way that doesn't upset him. And now he was looking at her with that awful expression, the way he might look at a piece of decaying fish.

"Oh Mac, I'm sorry, let's talk about something else. Tell me what happened yesterday in the office, between you and Donald? I could hear him—he has no right to talk to you in that tone of voice." Aileen sounded indignant.

Mac shrugged. The waiter came and they ordered. Mac ordered a bottle of claret which duly came, and

Mac swirled it around the glass, sniffed, then tasted it. After a pause that lasted several seconds, Mac nodded, and the waiter filled the glasses.

"Partners in a business always fight," he said, taking a sip of wine. "We have a few disagreements from time to time, but basically we get along all right together."

"I know, but this time it was different. It didn't sound like one of your usual arguments." Aileen was watching Mac, admiring his starched white cuffs, the elegant gold cuff-links (which she had given him), the snowy white of his shirt, the perfection of his regimental tie with the little gold cannons on it, but she was concerned about what was going on between the two partners. Mac had come out of Donald's office looking as if he'd been whipped, and Donald, well, he never looked exactly as if he were bubbling over with joy, but when he came out he was like lightning looking for something to strike.

"Was it about the catalogue?" asked Aileen. "The printers have been calling, and they're upset. Maybe they called him directly."

"No, it wasn't," said Mac. His tone would have told anybody but Aileen that the subject was now closed.

"The bank?" persisted Aileen. "Mr. Simon, the Manager, talked to Donald a couple of days ago, and it wasn't good, from the sound of it. I'd have thought . . ."

"What with?" Mac's voice was suddenly louder, angry. Something in the conversation seemed to have annoyed him, and Aileen couldn't think what it might have been.

At the end of the meal, Mac got up and went to the gents', carefully timing it to coincide with the waiter coming with the bill. As usual, Aileen paid.

They were both silent as Mac drove Aileen home. She lived in a rented flat in one of the big houses in Ainslie Place that had been converted into flats. As usual, Aileen asked Mac if he'd like to come in for coffee and a night-cap.

No sooner had Mac sat down in one of the two big easy chairs than Aileen came over and sat in his lap, and after a few moments started to breathe hard, and her fingers reached to unbutton his shirt. It always made her feel wild and unprincipled to initiate things, but she'd stopped worrying about that long ago.

They made love, in the dark as he always insisted, then Mac sat up in bed, and after a moment Aileen could just distinguish him in the gloom, putting his shirt on. He seemed to have a thing about that; although he didn't mind leaving his shirt open, he seemed to hate having it off. Now she knew why that was.

"Are you leaving?" Aileen reached over and clung to him with both arms. "You haven't been here for ages, and already you're going? Can't you stay for a little while? Or stay the night, if you like."

Mac gently detached her hands and got out of the bed, quietly getting into his clothes.

"What's the matter, Mac? Aren't you even speaking to me now?" Aileen's voice rose to a nervous whine, and Mac's lip curled with annoyance in the darkness. He felt disgusted at himself, using this woman the way he did, but there was nothing else he could do; he was coming to the end of his options. He cleared his throat, and pulled up the zip on his trousers.

"Aileen," he said, trying to keep his voice normal, "I'm sorry, but I need some money."

In the dark he heard Aileen's sudden, distressed intake of breath. "I gave you a hundred pounds last week," she said after a moment. Her voice was low, and he could tell she was afraid of annoying him.

"This is *this* week," he replied brusquely, knowing that she would do anything, pay anything, to push away the fear of losing him.

"I don't know how much I have . . . Can I put on the light?"

"All right." Mac buttoned his sleeves.

Aileen put the bedside light on and crept out of bed, holding her arms crossed over her chest. A strange woman, thought Mac. In the dark, she had a tigerish, sex-starved abandon and a vocabulary which had astounded him at first, but the passion dissipated instantly in the light, like a cinema screen when the house lights go on.

She was going through her purse, a large, serviceable leather container, and Mac felt his impatience rising like the mercury in a thermometer, but he said nothing. His eyes didn't leave her; he tied his shoelaces by feel.

Finally she took some money out of it, reluctantly, it seemed to him.

"I only have five pounds," she said. "I don't get paid until the end of the week."

"Can you borrow some?" Once again his voice was harsh, unyielding. "I have to have it."

"Oh, Mac . . ." Aileen got to her feet and came over to put her thin arms around him. He resisted the impulse to push her away violently. "I can't. Two days ago the bank manager called me about my overdraft."

"Well, I'll just have to get it elsewhere, then." Mac made an effort to sound calm, but Aileen perceived the clear threat in his voice.

"Mac, is that all you want me for? Is all of this just because I give you money? Don't you love me any more?" Her voice was full of tears, and again Mac felt an insane urge to throw the whining bitch against the wall, to . . . He shook himself, almost frightened at the violence of his thoughts.

"I don't have any more." Aileen paused, gathering her courage. "Mac," she said in a faint voice, "you're using that money to buy drugs, aren't you?"

There was a long, long silence, that gathered in the darkness like a thunderhead. Then Mac spoke, his voice soft and menacing. "Just how did you come to that conclusion, Aileen?"

"I watch you, Mac." Aileen's voice was high, frightened at what she'd done. She'd been pretty sure for weeks about what was going on, but never had the courage to confront him until now. "I see when you're in high spirits, then after a time you get all nervous and withdrawn and you go off somewhere, like to the bathroom, and you come out all bright and sparkly again. And the money—you never have any, but you always need it urgently. What else could it be?"

"So you've been spying on me, eh?" There was a sudden menace in his tone.

"God, no, Mac! I love you, and people notice things in the person they love . . ."

Suddenly he loomed up in the darkness in front of her, and she felt him catch her by the hair on the back of her head.

"You're sure you don't have any more money, Aileen? Tucked away in a sock, or under the bed?" His voice had a strange, hissing quality that terrified her. "Are you sure? Sure?" With every word, he jerked her head back until she thought he was going to break her neck, and she whimpered with fear and pain.

"Please, Mac! I love you. . . ."

"Don't ever think you're my last resort, you bitch," he said, but it was the tone of his voice more than what he said that horrified Aileen.

He pushed her hard, and she fell back on the dresser. A couple of seconds later she heard the door slam and he was gone.

Aileen threw herself on the bed, clutching the pillow and wetting it with her angry tears. She was sure she knew where he was going. He'd probably told Caroline he would be coming over, and at this moment she was probably waiting for him, dressed in some seductive transparent underwear so that when he came in he'd be able to see those big breasts of hers, thrusting up at him through the thin nylon. . . . In her pain, Aileen clasped her own thin breasts; her imagination became so vivid that it was as if she were there, standing alongside Caroline, watching from the window for Mac's car to pull up outside her flat.

Of course Caroline had egged him on with her sexy tricks, just the way she egged on every man who'd ever looked at her, or Mac would never have succumbed. Aileen sat bolt upright, clenching her fists in the dark. Right from the moment that girl walked into the office, she knew that she was going to cause trouble. Just the way she walked, that sexy swing of her hips, that was enough to tell anybody what she was like. And those two men, Donald and Mac, usually sensible enough about most things, they'd fallen for her like ripe fruit, and hired her on the spot. Aileen had to admit that Caroline had done a good job, that the transfer of the customer and supplier files on to the computer had been carried out faster and more efficiently than anybody had expected, and that Caroline had been entirely responsible for that.

She had stolen their hearts, all right. Donald's she couldn't care less about, but Mac, he was hers, hers, hers. Aileen slid down the bed and started to weep again, a soft, hopeless flood of tears. Mac wasn't hers any more, and there was no use kidding herself about it. Here she was in Perth, a town she didn't like and where she knew nobody, had no family or friends. Not that she'd had many in Glasgow either, she reminded herself, but Glasgow was her town, and even being along there wasn't so bad.

The darkness seemed to close in on her as she lay there, her eyes open but seeing nothing. Mac had been draining her money for over a year now, and he'd gone through almost all she had made when she sold her mother's house. His story wasn't always the same; sometimes he'd just temporarily run out of cash, other times he was investing it in shares in a pharmaceutical company. The strange thing was that she'd never understood the reason behind Mac's sudden rages, his equally sudden transformation to a funny, charming and lovable person, courteous and full of the joy of life. Maybe it was because she loved him so hopelessly that she had ignored all the warning signs, and in addition had allowed him to strip her of all the money she possessed. But she wouldn't have cared if she could be sure that he was hers, and only hers. For that she'd have dressed in rags and done housework, made any kind of sacrifice, but he wasn't hers, and she would have to face up to it, or do something about it.

It was all Caroline Fraser's fault, that was clear. If it hadn't been for her, she might have been married to Mac by now. A wave of hatred caught Aileen up so powerfully that she bit her own arm until it bled, wishing it was Caroline's neck she had between her teeth.

She lay in bed, tense as a poised hawk, thought for a while, then switched on the light and got dressed.

Chapter 10

Earlier that evening, Caroline walked over to her parents' restaurant as she had promised. When she helped out in the restaurant, it was always good for business, because she was not only very attractive to look at, but had a nice manner, and the customers, especially the male ones, loved her.

Half an hour before they opened for dinner, Marco stood by the big wine rack and watched his sister put out the place settings, while he fiddled idly with his tie. He went over to the table she was arranging and put his hand flat on the middle of her bottom when she leaned forward to position a glass.

Caroline jumped back. "Get your hands off me!" She was angry, but hardly surprised; he never stopped pawing her when he had the chance.

"Remember you're my *brother*, not my boyfriend." She picked up a pepper mill and a salt shaker in one hand and slammed them on the table. "And what about Francesca?" Caroline's voice was loud enough to be heard in the kitchen. "Why don't you go and paw her? I bet you haven't even been up to the hospital to see her, let alone give her a hug, the poor little thing!"

"I don't think you *are* my sister," replied Marco, his eyes not leaving her face. "You may look like me, but you don't think like me. . . ."

"Or feel like you, either, I'd like to remind you," said Caroline, trying to move around the table away from him. He put out both hands and held her arms in a hard, tight grip and stared at her with lust written all over his face.

"Let me go or I'll scream," said Caroline loudly. Sometimes she was really afraid of him. "This time, Dad'll half kill you. Remember what he said last time you touched me." With a sharp jolt, Caroline shook herself free and went back to the kitchen, and all the way she could feel his look burning into the back of her.

Marco went back to the wine rack when the swing door to the kitchen closed after her. He felt the heat in his groin and it was getting unbearable. He knew that one day he would do something, something he'd certainly regret, but he knew he was going to do it, because it was already getting too strong for him and he wouldn't be able to resist the impulse. And if she resisted, if she fought? Marco shrugged to himself. He'd dealt before with women who'd struggled and fought, and he knew exactly what to do to get the better of them. You scared them with a knife until they were too afraid to move.

He took a bottle of Valpolicella from the rack and idly wiped the neck with a cloth. He still hadn't got over his brief but unpleasant interview with Dr. Montrose earlier that day. She'd phoned and asked him to come to the surgery, there and then, and as it was only a couple of minutes away, it was hard to refuse. And anyway, the tone of her voice suggested that if he didn't come down there, she would come and find him. She had sat him down in the chair by her desk.

"Do you know how sick your wife is?" she asked.

Marco had shrugged, and it was the wrong thing to do, because Dr. Montrose went right ahead and laid into him. "You have a responsibility," she had told him. "You impregnated her, she's bearing your child, she's alone, doesn't know anybody and her family's in Italy. How can you behave in such a disgraceful way, as if she doesn't exist?"

The wee doc was really furious, although it was none of her business, and ought just to be between him and Francesca. He felt a bit scared of Dr. Montrose's anger, although she was smaller than him and only a woman, and he finally promised to visit Francesca the next day. The thought of her, of that great bloated belly, nauseated him. What a terrible mistake he'd made with her. He must have been absolutely crazy to even think of marrying the woman; she didn't know any English, didn't care about the restaurant, didn't even like sex, not after the first few times. But that might have been at least partly his fault, he had to acknowledge, because he did get a bit rough sometimes, and one time he'd shouted Caroline's name by accident, and she had taken a very dim view of that. Marco didn't want to remember the exact happenings around that time, before he married, when Caroline had taken up with that jerk. It had seemed really serious then, and the thought of anyone touching her, let alone making love with her, made him almost physically sick. So Marco had gone off to Ibiza on a package tour, met this tiny Eytie girl who smiled so nicely at everything he said, and seemed so sweet and nice although they could only communicate with signs; it didn't take too long for those signs to get bolder and more intimate. They made love for the first time two days after they met, and although she tried to teach him a few key words in Italian, he couldn't remember them and soon lost interest.

By the time they'd been married a few months, Caroline had already got rid of the fellow he'd been so upset about, and taken up with Brian, that yellow-bellied imbecile who worked at the garage.

And Francesca didn't care much for Marco's parents, and even less for Caroline, although Caroline had really tried to be nice to her, but she eventually gave up when Francesca kept on pretending not to understand a single word she said.

Marco put the bottle back in the rack and took out another one. After Francesca had the kid, he thought, he'd divorce her and send her back to Turin to her parents if her parents wanted to pay the fare. Divorces didn't even cost that much these days, and if she wanted to, she could get the marriage annulled by her local church. That would cost her parents a bit, he thought. He'd heard that annulments cost about three hundred pounds minimum in the UK, but he had no idea how much it would be in Italy. Nor did he care. If he got a divorce, he reflected with a gleam of hope, it might even help his chances with Caroline, because now, every time he touched her, she threw Francesca back in his face.

Chapter 11

Next morning, Jean went early to the hospital to see Francesca.

She was lying in bed, the great bulge under the sheet looking like a strange, foreign mass that couldn't possibly be part of her tiny body. She seemed asleep; her head was over to one side, her mouth was open, sagging under the force of gravity, and her breathing was regular, half sigh, half snore. But it was her face that concerned Jean. Her eyelids and cheeks were so puffy it made her almost unrecognizable, and a red patch on each cheek added an unhealthy, febrile glow to her appearance.

Francesca made a grunting noise, stirred, and tried to open her eyes. They were so swollen that Jean could see only a thin crack of dark between the lids. Jean took her hand and sat down in the chair beside her.

"Did you sleep well?" she asked gently. Francesca's hand was dry, listless, and hot. Somehow it felt detached, as though it didn't belong to a living person. Francesca shook her head once, as if it didn't matter, one way or the other. She started to talk to Jean in her halting English, as if she was continuing a conversation she'd been having in her head. "He was so beautiful, so nice... He picked me out of all the girls. Me! Can you imagine? Me, the little nothing girl from Turin... I was working in a place that made shoes and I saved money for three years to go to Ibiza. My friend Lorita who worked with me, we had planned it for a year, but she got pregnant and didn't come...." Francesca's voice was low, almost rambling, and Jean wondered whether she really knew where she was. "So I went by myself. The first night, they had a, what you call, a get-together at the hotel. There was a man with a white jacket who stood up and told everybody to dance with someone they didn't know. . . ."

Two nurses came in with a tray with medications on it and Jean stood out of the way while they gave her an injection. Her thigh was swollen and waxy looking, and oozed bloody fluid from the needle hole after it had been pulled out. The older nurse kept dabbing at it impatiently with a piece of gauze until Jean said she'd put some pressure on it until it stopped.

When the nurse had gone, and Jean had taken her hand, Francesca started talking again, but it was as if her life had been re-running through her head like a film, and hadn't stopped for the injection. "It was at the wedding that I first knew . . . realized . . . that Marco didn't love me. I didn't understand it at first, because I was so happy at the time. . . ." Francesca tried to sit up but the effort was too much and she lay back panting, her nostrils flaring with the effort. She said nothing for a while, getting her breath back, but she started again before she was really ready, so her sentences were broken up by her breathing. "He . . . Marco was in love with his sister, and married me because . . . because . . . I don't know." A tear escaped from between Francesca's swollen eyelids and made an irregular track down her cheek. "He used to say her name when he was asleep, Caroline, Caroline, until I thought I was going mad. Once he even called me by her name." The red spots on Francesca's cheeks became momentarily brighter. "I thought that having a baby would make him see *me*, see that I was a real person, who loved him, not just a . . . thing, a substitute."

"Maybe it will, Francesca," said Jean comfortingly. "I spoke to him yesterday, and he's coming to see you."

"If he comes, it's because *you* made him," replied Francesca. She tried to smile. "I don't want to see him. He hit me too often. I want to die, that's all. If it wasn't for the baby . . ."

When Jean left Francesca's room about twenty minutes later, she had trouble keeping back the tears.

Before leaving the hospital, she tracked Peter Macintosh down in the doctor's lounge, where he was having a cup of coffee.

"We're all very worried about her, Jean," he said, getting to his feet, "and about the baby, too. We have her on the fetal monitor, I suppose you noticed, and the baby's heart rate went up again since yesterday, and had a couple of bouts of irregularity."

"What are you going to do?"

"I'm trying to decide. I think probably the best thing would be a Caesarean, but the baby's so small." Peter shook his head. "But it looks as if we may have to, to save the mother's life."

"I'm afraid you're right, Peter." Jean's heart felt like a piece of lead.

"Talk about being between Scylla and Charybdis. . . ." Peter hesitated, then said suddenly, "I'm almost as worried about her attitude as her medical condition," he said. "She just lies there, completely unresponsive. She doesn't make any attempt to help herself, to get herself in a positive frame of mind. I hate to operate under these circumstances."

Jean didn't know what to say. Luckily she had confidence in Peter, and knew that he would do whatever was best for Francesca.

"God bless, Peter," was all she managed to get out, then almost ran out of the hospital. She nearly collided with Marco who was coming through the main door, and Jean pulled herself together quickly. She put a hand on his arm. "She's not feeling at all well this morning," she told him. "I don't think you should stay very long, Marco, but it's very important that you make an appearance.

Back at the surgery, everybody was busy. The usual Spring epidemic of colds had struck, the waiting room was full, and when she came in Jean could hear the muffled sneezes and coughs through the door.

"If there's anybody in there who doesn't already have

a cold," said Eleanor, nodding at the waiting room door, "they soon will."

"Any messages?" asked Jean, but Eleanor was telling her that she'd read that a mixture of lemon juice, honey and tea, when drunk out of a pure copper mug, made colds disappear like snow in the sun.

Jean went into the little lab where the electric kettle was, and made herself a cup of tea. "Are there any biscuits, Eleanor?" she asked. Eleanor went over to the filing cabinets and took a box out of the bottom drawer.

"Why do you keep them in there?" asked Jean, who had often enough looked around for biscuits without being able to find them.

"Because if I put them with the tea things, there never would be any," she replied, adding, "and I lock them up at night."

Eleanor took two digestives out of the tin and gave them to Jean, who by now was feeling slightly irritated at her school-teachery attitude. It wasn't as if Eleanor were *paying* for those biscuits.

Jean went into her office, balancing her cup and the biscuits on the saucer, and was closing the door behind her when Helen Inkster appeared and came in behind her, waving a folder of papers.

"We have some new official guidelines on prenatal care," she said in her booming voice. She sat down in the patient's chair. "Listen to this. 'The months before birth is a particularly important period for both mother and child,'" she read, "'and special care and attention has to be taken if the pregnancy is to be completed free of complications.'"

"Wonderful," said Jean, taking a bite out of her biscuit. "I wonder who told them."

"That's just the beginning," said Helen, reaching for the second biscuit on Jean's saucer. "It gets better." Helen flipped a page. "Here we are. 'Unfortunately, statistical analysis of figures derived from earlier studies suggests that the cohort composition of pregnant females was not accurately predicted, based on a chi-squared test applied using the predeterminant criteria as outlined in our earlier publication number 045/842. . . .'"

"Maybe if they'd used pregnant *males* it would have come out right," said Jean. "Anyway, what's a cohort? I thought it was a Roman legion, or something like that."

"Who knows? Just take a look at the signature, if you please."

Jean took the paper. "Mary Crandell . . . Not *our* Mary Crandell, the one who . . .?"

"The same," said Helen. "The one who was thrown out of nursing school because she didn't have the right attitude. It just shows you. She's probably got a luxurious office with a secretary, over in Dundee, and I bet she earns a lot more than we do."

"I wonder how they learn to write like that," said Jean, amazed. "It must take years of practice."

"Not at all," replied Helen. "They give them a list of key terms, like predeterminant, cohort, series regression, and all those other words, then they spend their day making up a kind of soup with them. I'm sure you or I could do it, no trouble, after a quick, intensive course."

Eleanor poked her head in the door. "Your patients are waiting, Dr. Inkster," she said. "And by the way, Jean, that Inspector Niven called, a while back. He wants you to call him as soon as you come in, please."

"What's this *Jean* bit?" asked Helen sternly. "It's Dr. Montrose, if you don't mind."

Eleanor withdrew rapidly and closed the door.

"How's that little Francesca doing?" Helen asked, turning back to Jean. "She's such a tiny thing, you wonder how she could carry a baby at all."

Jean told her how sick Francesca was, and how concerned Peter Macintosh was about her.

After Helen had gone off to see her patients, Jean remembered that Douglas Niven had called. A sudden fear took hold of her. There seemed to be something wrong with all the pregnancies she was involved in, and she wondered if maybe something had happened to the recently pregnant Cathie.

Doug wasn't in his office, and they put her through to the dispatcher. "We'll raise him for you, ma'am," he said cheerfully. "I'll have him call you right back."

Sure enough, Doug called back within a minute.

"Jean?" His voice sounded so grave that Jean gave an involuntary shiver. "I'm over on Christie Street, number 73, flat 3B, on the third floor. There's been a murder here, and it's someone you know. I think you should come over right away." He paused a moment. "Jamieson's on guard outside the building," he went on. "He has instructions to take you straight up."

PART TWO

PART TWO

Chapter 12

Christie Street was only a few minutes away from her surgery, and Jean decided to go on foot, because she felt too flustered to drive, and finding a parking place at this time would almost certainly be difficult. Her heart was pounding as she walked quickly along William Street. Suddenly she stopped; she'd forgotten her black medical bag. She only hesitated for a moment. Douglas had said *murdered*, so there was no possibility that she could do anything, so her bag would just be an extra, unnecessary burden. My God, she thought, who could it possibly be? Why hadn't Doug wanted to tell her on the phone? Somebody you *know*, he'd said. Did that mean a patient, or a friend, or somebody everybody knew, like the postman? She couldn't think of anyone she knew who lived in Christie Street, in the middle of town. Jean found herself running, but soon had to slow to a walk again. And Douglas had sounded really upset himself, although murders, if not quite his daily bread, were certainly common enough in his line of work.

By the time she came close to Christie Street, Jean was panting and felt lightheaded. She paused before the corner to get herself together. She certainly didn't want Constable Jamieson to see her until she was in full control again.

There were three police cars outside number 73, all with their lights flashing. Douglas's plain blue Ford was parked behind them. A line of pink police tape fluttered in the wind, enclosing the space around the entrance. Number 73 was just a doorway between a travel agent and a small grocery store, with three steps leading up to it. Constable Jamieson was talking to Mr. Fox, who owned the grocery store. He saw Jean cross the road, murmured something to Mr. Fox, and came over to lift the tape for Jean to pass under.

"He's waiting upstairs for you, Dr. Montrose," he said. His voice was quite impassive, but Jean knew that he would never forgive or forget the time she'd almost killed him in that deserted house when Douglas Niven and he were investigating the death of the little Lumsden baby. "Second floor," he called up after her. When she reached the first floor, Jean rested for a few moments against the banisters on the landing. One of the doors on the corridor opened just a crack, and a woman's face appeared for a second before disappearing again. Jean heard the thud of the closing door, then the sound of heavy bolts being drawn.

On the second floor, there was more pink tape across the corridor, with POLICE BARRIER DO NOT CROSS written in continuous black capitals along it. A detective holding a notebook was talking to an old man in the doorway of the flat next to the one that had been closed off. Nobody paid any attention to Jean, and she ducked under the tape and rang the doorbell. The door opened almost immediately. Douglas said, "Come in," and stood aside to let her pass into the flat.

"Who is it?" Jean's anxiety overflowed, but Douglas still didn't say anything. She tried to observe her surroundings as she followed him through the hallway. It was an old building, and the rooms were dark, with high, yellowed ceilings and silver-painted central heating radiators that growled and banged. There was a woman's umbrella leaning up against the wall, and just inside the front door, a gray raincoat hung on a hook under an oval mirror.

Jean could feel the tension building up inside her; she didn't know what to expect and cringed internally as she walked into the front room behind Douglas. There was a sofa with pink and silver stripes, a matted gray carpet, two armchairs of different types, a television on a stand to the side of the fireplace. It was on, but the sound had been turned off. A game show appeared to be in progress, and lights were flashing, indicating that someone had won. Two people were in the living room, a man and a woman, both in uniform, dusting the various surfaces with whitish powder. Jean recognized the fingerprint team; she'd seen them often enough, but never spoken to them. Intent on their work, they didn't even look up. The window faced the street below, and as she passed, Jean got a quick glimpse of a small crowd gathered on the opposite side of the street; she could see several upturned faces as they looked up in her direction.

Doug stood at the door of the bedroom. Inside, Jean got a glimpse of the police photographer, a pretty girl with long straight blond hair. The flashes from her camera came every few seconds as she moved around, taking pictures from every angle.

"Go on in, please, Jean."

The body was on the bed, naked, legs apart, but the first thing Jean noticed was the blood. It was all over the sheets and blankets, on the body itself, and dark streams had congealed into jellylike blobs all the way down to the floor. From the shape of the legs, Jean could tell it was a female. She forced herself to look at her belly, the lower part of which had been ripped open in the middle, and a loop of gray intestine stuck out and hung over the edge of the cut. The body was on its back, with both arms stretched out and projecting beyond the edge of the bed. Jean reached out tentatively and touched the hand. It was cold and stiff. There was blood on the fingers, and the arm resisted her attempts at movement. She looked quickly under the woman's fingernails and saw some tiny shreds of whitish tissue under a couple of them. Reluctantly, Jean's eyes moved up to the chest, the breasts, the face with bloody matted curly blond hair over it. The eyes were wide open, glazed, the corneas dulled.

"Oh, no!" Suddenly Jean recognized the face and turned away, nauseated and horrified.

"Could you give us a guess at the time of death, Jean?" Doug's voice was close, insistent.

With a quick fury, Jean turned on him. "Why did you get me to come here? I'm not your police surgeon! How dare you impose on me like this!"

Douglas stepped back, shocked. "I'm sorry, Jean. I thought . . . She was your patient, so I called you first, obviously."

At that moment, they heard the noise of someone being let into the flat and a few seconds later, Dr. Malcolm Anderson, the pathologist, bustled into the bedroom.

He grinned at Jean. "Well, quine, you always seem to get to the scene before me." Then he saw Jean's pale, strained face and came forward quickly, thinking she was about to faint. He took her arm, and with Douglas on the other side, they helped her unresistingly into the living room and sat her down in one of the armchairs.

"Can I get you anything?" Dr. Anderson asked. "A glass of water?" He sounded so concerned, so different from his usual blustery, jovial self that Jean smiled, although rather faintly.

"No," she said. "I'm fine. It was the rush of getting over here, and going up those stairs, I think." She got to her feet. "Now," she said, looking at Douglas straight in the eye, "to come back to your question. Judging from the coagulated state of the blood, the loss of tension in the eyeballs, and the amount of rigor mortis, I would think Caroline died about twelve hours ago, but I'm sure after Dr. Anderson's had a chance to examine her, he'll be able to give you a more exact time."

Chapter 13

"The next thing we have to do is to go and tell her parents," Douglas said to Jamieson. He had done all he could do at the scene, and was about to leave the flat in the hands of the forensic team. At this moment, they could hear the high whine of a powerful vacuum cleaner going over every inch of the room, searching for fibers from clothing, hairs and other minute debris that could, when magnified, identify the killer.

"They live over the restaurant," replied Jamieson. "It's only two streets away."

This was one part of his job Douglas hated. Coming up to some innocent, smiling person and telling him or her that a brother or husband or lover had been killed. So many times he had seen that smile freeze then start to disintegrate at his words.

"How did you get the tip-off, sir?" asked Jamieson.

"Somebody called from her office. She hadn't showed up, and wasn't answering the phone at home. The dispatcher sent a car. . . . " He stopped talking when they got to the street level and encountered the reporters and a portable TV camera.

"Sorry," he said in his official monotone, not breaking his stride when they shoved microphones into his face. "We have no further comment at this time. An official bulletin will be released to the press later today."

They crossed the street and after two minutes of brisk walking they reached the Kinross restaurant. The door was locked, and a sign indicated that opening time for lunch was still two hours away.

"There should be someone in the kitchen," said Doug, and they walked around the corner and tried to look in the window. Finally they rang the bell of the Frasers' flat, and after a moment the buzzer went; Jamieson pushed the door open and they went up the carpeted stairs. A door opened on the first floor and Mrs. Fraser appeared. Both Jamieson and Doug knew her, and had been in the restaurant, which had become something of a landmark in Perth.

She put both hands up to her cheeks. "What's happened?" she asked, while they were still on the stairs. Her voice was sharp with fear. "Who . . . Something happened to Marco! He did something! Oh my God, what did he do now?"

"Mrs. Fraser, do you mind if we come inside?" Doug's calm voice was set at just the right pitch, and Mrs. Fraser, trembling visibly, opened the door for them. Below them, the street door opened and Marco came bounding upstairs, taking the steps two at a time. He stopped abruptly on the top step when he saw Doug and Jamieson.

"Thank God!" said Mrs. Fraser. "Oh, Marco love, I thought . . . They . . . " Her voice failed her, and she rushed out on to the landing and hugged Marco in a tight grip.

Marco looked over her shoulder at Doug. "What do you want?" he asked, sounding slightly truculent. His relationship with the Perth Police had been strained by several warnings and one arrest within the last year, but the charges had been dropped.

"Let's go inside," said Doug. He felt pretty sure Mrs. Fraser would react very badly to his news, and he didn't want her to run out into the street screaming in her grief. Marco watched them, then went as pale as death. "It's Caroline," he said. "I know it's Caroline."

As soon as the door was closed, Douglas told them briefly what had happened, leaving out the more gruesome details.

Marco started to scream. At first it was a low moaning noise, and his mother tried to comfort him, but he pushed her away with a force that almost knocked her down. Jamieson made a move toward him, but Doug put a restraining hand on his arm and they watched, fascinated, as Marco put his head back and the moan became the howl of an animal in pain; the veins in his neck stood out and he banged his fists against his head before collapsing in a heap on the floor, letting out screams and shouting obscenities, apparently not to anyone in particular. After Doug felt it was safe to leave them, and a neighbor had come in to help Mrs. Fraser, they clumped down the stairs.

"I never heard a man scream like that before." Jamieson sounded awed. "Especially a strong young chap like him."

Outside, the sun was bright, and as Caroline's office was also a short distance away, Doug decided they would walk there.

The pavement was crowded and people had the cheerful look that comes when Spring begins to settle in. The incongruity shocked Doug; even though he was experienced in these matters, the first sight of Caroline's body and all that blood had made a deep impression on him, and walking and jostling among these cheerful, chattering pedestrians made him feel he was living in a separate, weird and menacing world.

"Have you, sir?" Jamieson's voice at his side brought him back.

"Have I what?" His voice was sharper than he wanted it to be.

"Ever heard a man scream like that, sir?"

"Yes, Jamieson, but only on the stage."

The moment they stepped inside the Macandon offices, there was a flurry of activity around them. Donald came out of his office, looking shaken and concerned, and Aileen was clutching and twisting a spotted blue handkerchief in her hand like worry-beads.

"Is Caroline all right?" asked Donald. "She hasn't shown up yet." He swallowed. "This is the first time . . ."

"I'd like everybody who works in the office to come here," said Doug, interrupting. "And I'll want to talk to each one of you individually."

The outside door opened and Peter Duggan came in, triangular-faced, studious-looking, a short pony-tail tied with an elastic band. "Good morning all," he said, then looked curiously at Doug and Jamieson, who were both in plain clothes.

"I'm Detective Inspector Niven," said Doug heavily, using his ponderous official voice. "And who might you be?"

"I'm Pete Duggan," he replied. "Now if you'll excuse me, I have . . ."

"Is everybody here?" asked Douglas, paying no attention to him, and addressing Donald.

"Except for . . ." Donald swallowed again, "Except for Mac MacFadyen, and . . ."

"And who?" asked Doug.

"Miss Fraser," replied Donald, looking at her desk as if he expected her to materialize there.

"I'm sorry to have to tell you that she's dead," said Doug after a pause. "She died in her flat, probably last evening." He looked around them again grimly. "And I can tell you now that foul play is suspected."

A choking sob escaped Aileen, and an expression of shock appeared on Donald's face. Only Peter's face didn't change.

"Do you know who did it?" asked Donald.

Doug ignored him, and a quick flush spread over Donald's face.

"I want to talk to each one of you," Doug said, then turned to Donald. "Can I use one of your offices?"

"Certainly," said Donald, sounding flustered. "Use mine, by all means. I can use Mac's. I'm sure he won't mind."

"Where is he? MacFadyen?" asked Doug.

"I don't know. I phoned him when . . .when Caroline didn't arrive and didn't answer her phone, but there was no answer there either."

"Do you have his address, please, and his telephone number?"

Donald motioned to Aileen, who hurriedly wrote them out on a piece of paper and handed it to Doug, who passed it to Jamieson. Doug noted that she didn't have to look it up.

Jamieson stared at the piece of paper, then at Douglas.

"Find him," said Douglas in a low voice, hiding his irritation at Jamieson's slow-wittedness.

After the door closed behind Jamieson, Doug went into Donald's office. Donald came behind him and hurriedly cleared some papers off the top of his desk. Before sitting down, Doug surveyed them again, then said to Donald, "I think we'll start with you, sir, if you don't mind."

Jean left Caroline's flat a few minutes after Malcolm Anderson's arrival, and walked slowly back to the surgery, oblivious of the fine weather, the traffic, everything except the memory of that still, lifeless, mutilated body. It bore so little relation to the vibrant, attractive Caroline Fraser whom Jean could still see so clearly walking toward her in the park only two days before. A dreadful thought struck Jean, and she stopped in her tracks, right in the middle of the pavement. What had Caroline wanted to tell her, when she'd met her walking around the North Inch? Jean hadn't even asked Helen what she had said; the entire episode slipped her mind.

Eleanor had a small list of messages for her, and looked at her curiously when she came in. Jean didn't have the will even to try to look normal, and she knew that the shock of what she had just seen must be written all across her face.

"Is Dr. Inkster busy?" she asked.

"She's seeing a patient right now, but I can get her to come out if you like." Eleanor was overflowing with obvious curiosity, and got up, ready to go and fetch Helen.

"Just ask her to come through when she's done," said Jean. "There's no hurry. Meanwhile, I could use a cuppa, please, if the tea's on."

Eleanor got up and went to get the tea, and Jean went gratefully into her office, and closed the door. She put her elbows on the desk and her head between her hands. She was still feeling dizzy and sick, and felt very annoyed at herself for almost fainting in Caroline's flat. As if she'd never seen a dead body before! Jean remembered the first day in the anatomy department when she was an almost-new medical student, unwrapping the corpses for dissection. Jean hadn't blinked an eyelid, although two of the other students at her table had fainted. But then, she hadn't known who those bodies had belonged to.

There was a knock on the door, and Jean sat upright. Eleanor came in with the tea, and Helen Inkster came in right behind her, looking curious and concerned. Eleanor must have said something to her, Jean thought, or she wouldn't have come so fast.

Jean waited while the door closed behind Eleanor, although she hung around for a minute, hoping to be included in the discussion.

"Helen, do you remember Caroline Fraser. . . ." The name almost stuck in Jean's throat. "When she came and talked to you, a couple of days ago, that very pretty girl?"

"Yes, of course. She didn't say much, though. She'd

been having urinary symptoms. I took a culture, gave her some ampicillin, told her to come back next week if it wasn't better. No big deal, I didn't think."

A slow, apprehensive heaviness settled over Jean's soul. Whatever it was, whatever fear she might have had, it didn't sound as if Caroline had confided in Helen.

"Was there anything else?" she asked. "Did she mention that anything was bothering her, anything like that?"

There must have been something in Jean's tone that alerted Helen, because she looked hard at her. "No, she didn't," she replied. "Now, what's this all about? You're not suddenly asking me about her for no reason."

"Caroline Fraser was murdered last evening," said Jean steadily. "I was wondering if she might have said anything to you that might throw some light on the matter."

Helen's face changed, and her mouth opened slowly. "Oh, my God! Is that where you were, just now?"

Jean nodded, not trusting herself to speak. There was a long silence while Helen stared at her, appalled.

"Was there any . . . any indication of who did it?"

Jean shook her head. "I don't really know. Doug Niven didn't seem to think so, but I can tell you it was a violent, horrible scene. Whoever it was must have either been insane or really hated her."

"She must have had a few enemies around town," said Helen quietly. "Caroline always had men hovering around her like flies around a honeypot, and she had quite a reputation for leading them along, although how far she went with them I don't know."

"Fiona always said she was irresistible." Jean tried to smile. "She said Caroline could get any man she ever wanted."

"I can't imagine why she'd bother," said Helen, a trifle tartly. "Personally, I've never met one worth the effort."

"Well, I suppose I'd better get some work done," said

Jean, dully. "I have five visits to do before lunch, then I'm going to see my mother."

"How is she doing?" asked Helen.

"Not bad, I suppose. She's a worry, though. One day, they're going to stop putting up with her tantrums, and I'll have to find another place for her."

Helen was surprised, but said nothing. She knew how caring Jean was about her mother, and she rarely sounded so negative about her.

Eleanor had made a list of the patients Jean had to visit, so she checked the contents of her black bag and went off. She saw all her patients, listened attentively to their problems and treated them with her usual kindness and consideration, and they never imagined that anything was wrong. But by the time she got to the nursing home in Barossa Place, Jean didn't remember a thing about the patients she'd seen or what she'd prescribed for them.

The matron, Mrs. Kimball, seemed to have been waiting for her, because no sooner had Jean come in, and the old honey-colored spaniel had wiffed mildly at her, than Mrs. Kimball appeared from her room. Jean's heart sank when she saw her expression.

"Well, she did it," she said. "I told you last time she was about to do something."

Jean sighed and waited.

"They didn't find out until the morning shift came on and was serving breakfast," went on Mrs. Kimball. "The first thing that happened was when the fire alarm went off. . . ."

"The fire alarm!" Jean put her hands up to her head, then looked along the corridor to see if there was any obvious fire damage.

"Oh, it's all right, Dr. Montrose," said Mrs. Kimball. "We got it in time. Luckily we have a smoke detector on the ceiling in each room. I think she'd forgotten about that."

Everything was getting too much for Jean; what with Caroline Fraser and now this, it was more than she could take, and to her embarrassment she felt the tears coming into her eyes. She took a tissue from her bag and blew her nose. "Tell me what happened, Mrs. Kimball."

"Well, you know how she likes a cigarette from time to time, and we don't allow the patients to smoke in bed, and we prefer them not to smoke in the rooms either, for that matter. They can go in the lounge, or outside."

Jean felt relieved; if it was only an illicit cigarette that had set off the smoke alarm, it wasn't so bad. But her relief didn't last long.

"The night nurse always looks in before she goes off," explained Mrs. Kimball. "When she came into Mrs. Findlay's room, your mother was sitting up in bed smoking. So quite correctly, she took the cigarette and her matches away, and apparently told her off." Mrs. Kimball shook her head. "Maybe that wasn't too clever, because we knew she was all ready to get up to some mischief.'

There was a clatter of trays and cutlery from the direction of the kitchen, and an aide came out, pushing a stainless steel trolley into the corridor, followed by another. "They're late," said Mrs. Kimball, looking at the clock. "The fire upset everybody."

"What happened?"

"Well, about half an hour later, when the smoke alarm went off, the nurses came running in to see what was going on, and she'd scrunched up yesterday's paper, put it in the middle of the room and set fire to it."

"Oh, my God."

"They put it out easy enough with a couple of jugs of water," said Mrs. Kimball, "But there's a hole in the carpet that'll have to be fixed, and her chair got singed."

"We'll pay for that, of course," said Jean quickly, hoping that Mrs. Kimball wasn't going to tell her to take her mother to another nursing home.

Mrs. Kimball looked at her, hesitated for a long moment, then said, "Dr. Montrose, if it was anybody else's mother . . ."

Mrs. Findlay was in bed, and her eyes were firmly closed when Jean came into her room, but Jean knew she was wide awake. There was still a strong smell of burned carpet and newspaper, although the window had been opened and the curtains were billowing gently in the breeze. Jean had brought some oranges and a bottle of Dry Sack; she put them on the bedside table, sat down in the chair, and waited.

"So when am I leaving? Where shall I be moved to?" Mrs. Findlay opened her eyes wide. Her voice and expression were unrepentant and truculent.

"You're not going anywhere," replied Jean. "Where did you get the matches?"

"I have my sources," said Mrs. Findlay. "Anyway, they found them and took them away."

"Mother . . . Why ever did you do such a thing? Don't you realize you could have set the whole place on fire, and burned yourself and all those other people to death?" Jean tried to keep her voice calm, but she felt ready to crack.

"In the first place, it would be the best thing for most of them," replied Mrs. Findlay. Her eyes were firmly closed again. "They're just using up air other people could use."

"Air?"

"Yes. And food, and care, and medicines."

"And so you appointed yourself the judge? And the executioner?"

"Yes. Nobody else would have the guts. Anyway that's not why I lit the fire."

Jean shook her head and said nothing.

"They were infringing on my rights."

"You mean smoking in bed?"

"I pay for this room," said Mrs. Findlay in a strong

voice. "And it isn't cheap. If I was in a hotel, I could smoke when and how I liked. Nobody would dream of coming in uninvited, and telling me to put my cigarette out. Can you imagine?"

"So that's why you tried to set the whole place on fire?"

"I had to make my point, get their attention, somehow," Mrs. Findlay grinned. "And I think I did."

Jean looked at her watch and got up. "Mother," she said, coming over to kiss her on the forehead, "I don't know what to say to you, except please, try not to cause any more problems."

In spite of herself, Jean's voice cracked. There was just too much going on, too much for her to cope with all at once. "Mother, I'm sorry but I have to go now."

Chapter 14

"Could I have your full name, please, and your home address, Mr. Tarland?"

Doug automatically fell into his interrogation routine; everything slow, everything methodical. Over the years he had found that the way he set about his questions had a strong influence on the results he got. Guilty persons got a sense of inevitability, a knowledge that sooner or later he would come to the truth, then he'd put a heavy hand on their shoulder and take them away. The clever ones would get irritated with Doug's slow, laborious style, and could be annoyed into saying things they later regretted. Even better, some assumed that he was stupid, and were thus predisposed to fall straight into one of his carefully prepared traps.

Donald Tarland didn't seem to fit into any group. He just sat there passively, looking numb and shocked, and answered the questions in a monotone.

"What was your relationship with the deceased, Mr. Tarland?"

That seemed to get his attention, thought Doug with some satisfaction. Getting under their skin was sometimes a useful technique.

"My relationship?" Donald was momentarily flustered. "She worked for me, and for Mac, of course."

"Is that all?"

Donald flushed. "I'm a married man. . . ."

"I know that, Mr. Tarland. That's not what I asked you."

"That was all."

"Did you ever visit her at home?"

"Certainly not. I don't even know where she lives."

"Did you notice anything unusual about her recently? Nervousness, tears, anything like that?"

Donald shook his head.

"Mr. Tarland, I have to write your answers down. I'd appreciate it if you'd say 'yes' or 'no'."

"No."

"Any private phone calls at the office? Do you know of any emotional attachments she might have had?"

"I don't know. Aileen could probably tell you, as they work in the same office. I only see them when they bring stuff in, or if I go out there."

"Do you know if anybody ever threatened her in any way?"

"No, not that I know of." Donald was hesitating, and Douglas waited.

"Can I come back to your question about emotional involvement?" he asked.

Douglas still didn't say anything. Sometimes it was better to give no encouragement, no approval, because the mere sight of him sitting there, attentive and silent, was often enough to fluster a witness, if that was what he wanted to happen.

"I've been wondering . . . for the last few weeks, my partner, Mac Macfadyen . . . Well, he's been sort of taking more of an interest in Caroline. I'm sure it's nothing, but I didn't want you to think I was suppressing information." Donald essayed a smile, and his round lenses glinted doubtfully. "I'm sure he'll tell you himself."

"What do you mean by *taking an interest,* Mr. Tarland?" Doug looked up from the lined pad, and his pen hovered in the air above it.

"Well, you know . . . " Donald was wriggling with a

prudish discomfort. "I think he may have gone out with her a couple of times, just for dinner, I'm sure, but again you should ask him, not me."

Doug looked at his watch. "Where do you think he is? Does he usually come in this late?"

Again Donald looked flustered. "No, I can't imagine . . . I don't think he had any trips scheduled. Let me check with Aileen." He went to the door, opened it and had a brief conversation with her. Doug got a momentary glimpse of Aileen's face, pale in spite of her excessive makeup.

"No. He should be here. I hope . . ." Donald blinked several times, then took off his glasses. Without them he had a naked, defenseless look. "I hope *he's* all right."

"Let's just take one victim at a time, if you don't mind, Mr. Tarland," said Douglas, feeling a bit of a bully, and enjoying it. "Now, is there anything else you can think of about Miss Fraser that might shed some light on this crime? Anything at all?"

Donald shook his head.

"Well, if you think of anything, you know where to reach me," said Doug. "Thanks for your help. Now if you'd send in Miss . . ." Doug looked at the name he'd written on the pad. "Miss Farquar, please."

Aileen stood in the doorway, still twisting the same handkerchief in knots. Her eyes were red, and some of the mascara had run down the side of her left cheek. She looked ready to collapse.

"Come in and sit down," he said. But Aileen stood there and started to sob loudly. Donald came toward her, awkwardly put a hand on her shoulder, then quickly took it off again, as if he'd taken an inexcusable liberty with her.

But Aileen couldn't or wouldn't stop crying, and finally Doug suggested that she get a taxi and go home. He told her that he'd talk to her later when she'd got a better hold of herself.

* * *

"Well, sir, what do you think?"

"Jamieson, I've told you before, this is the time to gather information and keep your eyes open. Thinking comes later, for some of us anyway, but you dinna need to worry about that." Douglas was feeling testy because nothing much had come from his preliminary interrogations, not that he'd expected much. Donald had been jittery and stingy with his information, nobody seemed to know where Mac was, Aileen had gone home and the bookkeeper had been no help at all. He lived at home with his parents and the evening before had gone with them to the cinema.

Thinking back over Donald's statement, Doug was left with a strong feeling that he *did* know a lot more than he was letting on, about both Mac and Caroline, and particularly about their relationship.

"When are they doing the post mortem, sir?" asked Jamieson as they drove into the yard behind the police headquarters building, an ugly, gray multistory built of prefabricated concrete panels.

"Jamieson, you're asking a lot of questions. Awa' and look for that MacFadyen chap again, and find out where he was last night. And when you've done that, check if that Aileen Farquar got over her hysterics. I'd better talk to her, so bring her in if she's well enough, all right?"

On the stairs going up to his office on the second floor, Doug met Ian Garvie, his colleague in the narcotics section. "Got your man yet?" asked Garvie with a grin.

"It wasn't a man that did it, Ian," Doug replied solemnly. "It was an alien fae outer space."

"Aye, fairly," said Ian, proceeding down the stairwell. "That's a good description of most o' the druggies I have to deal with."

It had occurred to Doug that there was no proof that the perpetrator was a man, although judging from the brutality of the deed, it seemed most likely. The post mortem might give him some clues about that; Malcolm Anderson was pretty sharp and often came up with helpful ideas.

Meanwhile, Douglas knew only too well that the few murder cases that weren't solved in the first twenty-four hours were liable to drag on for ever, and the longer they lasted the more likely they were to finish up in the "incomplete" files. He sat down at his small metal desk, took out a pad of lined paper and a government-issue ball-point pen. What did he know so far?

"Victim," he wrote slowly at the top of the page.

"Twenty-three yrs. old," he continued. "Worked as secretary at Macandon, employed there just over a year. Known to be fast mover where men concerned." Doug tore the page out, crumpled it and threw it in the wastepaper basket before starting again. Sometimes the notes on a case were subpoenaed for a trial, and the defence lawyers would eat him alive on a written comment like that, however true it might be. Caroline Fraser had been a very attractive young woman, there was no doubt about that. Everybody in town knew something about Caroline, and quite a few embroidered on that, not so much out of malice, but rather to add spice to their lunchtime gossip. Although Douglas knew that most of the rumors that had blown around town about her were false, his experience told him that her death probably had something to do with sex; jealousy, rejection, betrayal. There were plenty of possibilities.

Caroline didn't have many real friends, as far as he knew, although she was attractive and popular enough, even with the girls. Doug suddenly remembered that Caroline's best friend was Fiona Montrose. Well, that was certainly a help, although Fiona was not too happy with him right now. He shook his head. It was flattering to have a pretty girl like Fiona so obviously fond of him, but sometimes it got a bit embarrassing. Anyway, he'd have to talk with Fiona, and of course Jean as well. Douglas sighed, realizing that right now he wasn't too popular with her either. Jean had been really angry with him for getting her to come to Caroline's flat, but surely she knew that he hadn't done it to upset her. Caroline had been her patient, and he was still surprised at the way Jean had turned on him. A medical doctor, surely she was immune to seeing dead people by now. He made a mental note to ask Cathie about it. Maybe she'd have an explanation for Jean's sudden and astonishing hostility.

Doug turned his attention back to his lined pad. What else did he actually know about Caroline? He chewed on the rubber end of his pencil. There had been so much gossip about the girl; Doug didn't usually pay much attention to that kind of thing, but rumors and gossip seemed to swirl around Caroline Fraser like moths around a street lamp. There was that young chap Brian something; even Douglas had heard about him. He wrote his name down. Brian X. They'd pull him in and give him the once-over. Cathie, who always had a pretty good idea who was doing what with whom around town, would remember his surname.

Cathie. He felt a warm feeling coming over him, just thinking about her. Her whole body was changing now she was pregnant; there was a kind of smoothness about her, a roundness, although her tummy hadn't changed shape yet. It was quite extraordinary; she did the same things around the house, but there was a direction, a new quickness and confidence about what she did, as if her life had been refocused. Doug couldn't quite explain what he noticed, but he liked it and it excited him. And her breasts were full, and he loved the feel of them in his back when she turned toward him before going to sleep.

Caroline, Caroline, Caroline Fraser. Doug thought about her waxy-looking corpse lying splayed out on the bed, with those terrible mutilating injuries. At the time, Doug had wondered whether she was naked when she was killed, or had the murderer undressed her after she was dead? Malcolm Anderson had pointed out that the blood had dried on her skin, and there had been no blood or knife holes in the clothes on the chair by the bed. Did that mean that she'd been surprised while sleeping naked, or did it mean that the killer knew her intimately? One way or another it appeared that the killer had been in some kind of frenzy.

And that raised its own problems. Was that frenzy caused by love, by jealousy, a desire for revenge, or by fear? Or could she have been stalked and then attacked by some psychopathic killer?

Listen to your own advice, Doug told himself after ten minutes of fruitless speculation. Don't think until you've got your facts.

He thought for a moment, wondering who would be the best person to ask for more information, then reached for the phone. It rang just as he grasped the receiver. Jamieson was reporting that MacFadyen was not at his flat, or at least not answering the door or the telephone. None of his neighbors had seen him since yesterday.

"His car, man, what about his car?"

"It's gone too, sir. He has a reserved parking place behind the building, and it's empty."

Doug thought for a moment. At this time, there wasn't very much linking Mac with Caroline Fraser, except for Donald Tarland's comments, and an all-out search might simply prove embarrassing to one and all.

"All right, Jamieson. I'll pass the word out to keep an eye out for his car. Do you have his vehicle description and registration?"

"It's a Rover, sir, forest green, 1988 model. . . ."

"Good, Jamieson," said Doug when he had all the details written down on his pad. "Now awa' you go and see if Miss Aileen Farquar has got over her attack o' the vapors."

"Sir?"

"Yes, what?"

"About Mr. MacFadyen, he's on Inspector Garvie's active drug user list."

"Oh, he is, is he?" Doug thought fast. That might throw a different light on the case, and again it might not. "All right, I'll take care o' that side of things. Anything else?"

"Aye. Her brother Marco tried to commit suicide after we left. They just took him to the hospital."

"Jesus, Jamieson . . .!"

"Yes, sir?"

Doug gripped the phone tight. "Nothing. Report back as soon as you've seen Aileen Farquar." He paused for a second, recalling that Jamieson tended to be literal-minded. "Let me rephrase that, Jamieson. Report back *after you've talked to her and found out her whereabouts last night.* Also see if she knows anything about where MacFadyen might be, all right?"

"Right you are, sir."

Doug found Marco coming out of the hospital emergency department with his mother. He looked pale, and there was a big bandage wrapped around his left wrist.

"What happened?" asked Doug, stopping them.

"It was an accident," said Louise Fraser quickly. "He was upset, and, well, he was holding a knife and it slipped. He's not hurt bad." She turned to her son. "You don't want to catch cold out here."

"How's your wife doing?" Doug called after him.

Marco looked around. He didn't answer back, but his expression sent a quick chill down Doug's back.

Chapter 15

Constable Jamieson was elated; Doug had entrusted him with the delicate task of interviewing Aileen Farquar; he knew that Douglas would normally have done that himself, which obviously indicated that Jamieson had achieved a new level of trust and responsibility in his eyes.

He parked his car outside Aileen's home and climbed the three steps up to the front door, trying to remember the way his boss conducted his interviews. Douglas's words came back to him; "Always start off by getting them to agree with you about something, even if it's only the weather. Be understanding, try to get their confidence. Watch them all the time, but especially right at the beginning, before the interview starts. Look at their expression, their hands, note whether they're comfortable. You can learn more at that time than during the rest of the session. Keep your most telling questions for the end, after they think the interview is over, then you get them by surprise."

With all these thoughts running through his head, Jamieson rang the doorbell, a good long ring, to show it wasn't just the milkman calling.

Aileen came to the door, still tearful, yellow strands of hair trailing over her face.

"Come in," she said, looking over his broad shoulder to see if any neighbors were watching.

"Yes, well," he said, filling up the entire hall with his

bulk. He took the notebook out of his pocket and watched Aileen closely for signs of guilt. "I'm here about the Fraser case," he said in his most ponderous and official tone. "I have to warn you that anything you say may be taken down and used in evidence against you."

"Don't be ridiculous," said Aileen sharply. She seemed to have recovered her poise since he'd last seen her in the office. "And don't just stand there," she said, "come into the living room."

Jamieson, quite taken aback, obediently stepped into the large living room and sat down in the chair Aileen pointed out to him. She remained standing and went over to the window where she stood with her back to it, facing him.

Jamieson squinted up at her, his chair was positioned right in the middle of a square of bright sunlight from the window.

"Well, what do you want to know?" Aileen's voice was dull, lifeless-sounding.

Remembering his instructions, Jamieson smiled in his friendliest way, and scrunched up his eyes to see Aileen's expression, but all he could see was her dark outline against the window. "It's lovely weather we've been having, isn't it?"

"Yes, it is. Did you come all this way to discuss the weather?"

"All right, then." Aggrieved, Jamieson opened his notebook. "Where were you on the evening of the seventeenth of the present month?"

"You mean last night?"

Jamieson nodded, annoyed. The sunlight was beginning to hurt his eyes, and the letters danced in front of him when he looked from the window down to his notebook.

"I was here."

"Alone?"

There was a pause, and Jamieson looked up again, every sense suddenly on the alert. He knew from his presence at many such interviews with Douglas Niven that this kind of hesitation usually meant the suspect had something to hide.

"Alone?" he repeated sternly, his voice a shade louder.

"No," said Aileen finally.

Jamieson was just able to suppress a loud "Aha!" Instead, he said, "May I ask who was here with you?"

"Mac MacFadyen."

"Do you know where he is now?"

Aileen's cat, a large, elderly-looking tabby with a hanging paunch, came through the doorway, paused, then came directly to Jamieson and jumped on his lap.

"No. He . . . I haven't seen him."

"Since when? Did you have breakfast together?"

"No, he left before I got up." Aileen looked embarrassed. "I think you should know that we're planning on getting married, sometime," she said, tilting her chin up and looking at Jamieson with a defiant but strangely vulnerable look.

Jamieson sneezed, and the cat jumped off his lap. Aileen came away from the window and sat on the sofa near him.

"He didn't go to the office this morning," said Jamieson.

"There are lots of places he could have gone," said Aileen with a forced brightness. "He visits suppliers, people like that . . ." Her voice faded.

"Can you think of anybody who might have wanted to kill Caroline?" Jamieson was getting back to his list of questions.

"No," replied Aileen, her eyes round. "Everybody liked her. It must have been a madman, some kind of insane killer. Maybe she was just the first of a string of murders . . ." Aileen shivered, then got up. "I'm going to make some tea," she said. "Would you like a cup?"

A little while later, Jamieson got ready to leave.

"I'm afraid," said Aileen, looking up at him. "What if I'm next on the list?"

Jamieson, feeling large and protective, told her to keep her doors and windows locked, and to be sure she knew who she was letting into her home. Furthermore, he told her, if she ever felt she had any cause for alarm she was to call him immediately.

As he left, he remembered Douglas Niven's Parthian Shot. "By the way, Aileen," he asked her, "do you happen to know if Mr. MacFadyen has been . . . seeing Miss Fraser?"

She shook her head indignantly; Jamieson didn't see the momentary flash of panic in her eyes. "No, certainly not," she replied. "I'm the one he's been seeing, and if he has me, why would he want somebody else?"

Driving back to the station, Jamieson went over in his mind what he would put down in his report. He hated writing reports; nowadays they seemed more important than real police work, at any rate in the eyes of his superiors. One of Douglas Niven's most over-used expressions, one that always made him grit his teeth, was "If it's not written down, Jamieson, it didn't happen." Jamieson was quite sure that those of his colleagues who had made it up to sergeant had done so because of their slick and facile use of the written word, not because their basic police skills had been any better than his.

As he turned into the garage area behind the main building, Jamieson realized that he didn't really have very much to put down in his report, considering the time he'd spent there. He could hardly write down his main impression, which was that the interviewee's home-made shortbread was delicious, or that he hadn't been able to evaluate her reactions to most of his questions because she had been just a silhouette against the sunny window. A dim suspicion blinked faintly somewhere in his mind, but he dismissed it instantly because Aileen Farquar had been such a nice lady. Jamieson prided himself on being an astute judge of character, and he was sure that she was incapable of misleading him, let alone doing anything as horrible as what had been done to Caroline Fraser.

No, he thought, not her. And not Mac either, obviously, if he'd been with her all evening and had spent the night there, although he'd have to check that out. He didn't think much of Aileen's idea about a crazed killer roaming the streets of Perth; the most likely perpetrator was probably someone Caroline had been having a fling with, who had got angry at her for some reason and killed her. Jamieson had learned that violent crimes are most often committed by family members or lovers, and that was where his efforts should be concentrated.

But still, as he came up the concrete stairs at the back of the building, Jamieson worried about the continued non-appearance of MacFadyen, and wondered if they should put out an all stations for him, his alibi notwithstanding. Of course, he might have turned up while he was interviewing Aileen.

He knocked on Douglas's door and was about to walk in when the door opened abruptly and Douglas came out and cannoned into him.

"I have to go," he said. Jamieson looked at him in surprise; Doug's face was pale, and he was obviously in a hurry. Jamieson turned and walked back along the corridor with him. "Did you talk to Miss Farquar?" asked Doug.

"Yes, and I'm pretty sure she didn't . . ."

"Good. Did you find MacFadyen?"

"No, I was about to check a few places he might . . ."

"Well, get on with it, then. I'll be at home if anything happens, or else I'll phone in."

Doug disappeared down the stairs, indicating that he didn't want Jamieson to accompany him. At the bottom of the stairs, he pushed hard against the bar of the emergency exit and let himself out, hoping the alarm wouldn't go off. It didn't. His car was just around the corner and he climbed in, searching for his keys. His hand fumbled when he put the key in the ignition, and he let the clutch out so suddenly he almost stalled the engine. Four minutes later, he pulled up outside his house, jumped out and ran in, his heart pounding.

The front door was unlocked. "Cathie?" Even to him, his voice sounded unnaturally loud.

"I'm in the bedroom." Her voice sounded faint, but the mere sound of it reassured Doug. He took a deep breath and walked through.

"What happened?" He took Cathie's hand. It felt cold.

"I don't know. I started to bleed down there but it's stopped now. Oh, Douggie, it really scared me."

Doug got down on his knees by the bed and hugged her very gently.

"Did you phone Jean?"

"I was about to, but then it stopped. I thought I'd wait until you got home." Cathie's arms were clasped tightly around his neck. "It's not me, it's the baby I'm worried about."

"How do you feel now?" Douglas was taking charge again, and stood up. "I'll phone her right now. I don't know if she'll be at the surgery, but they'll know where to reach her."

When he phoned, Eleanor answered. She recognized his voice but was very helpful when he said that Cathie was having a problem.

"Dr. Jean's out," she said. "She's up at the hospital, and I'll try to reach her there."

Half an hour later, Doug and Cathie heard a car pull up outside. "That's her," they said simultaneously.

Douglas let her in, and Jean bustled in looking more cheerful than she felt. She didn't waste any time on civilities, but sat on the end of the bed, her eyes scanning Cathie's face.

"What happened?"

"Douglas, would you like to make us some tea?" Cathie asked, to get him out of the bedroom.

"It started about two hours ago," said Cathie, rearranging the top sheet into a straight line. "I'd just gathered the laundry and I got this funny pain." She put her hand over her lower abdomen. "It was a bit like a period pain, so I was surprised, like, because I'm nae due another period for about a year." She grinned at Jean, hiding her fear. "Then I felt it at the top of my leg, a wee trickle, and I was real scared then and I went into the bathroom to look. There was blood, no' a lot, but enough to be right feared. So I lay down on the bed and phoned Douggie."

While she was talking, Jean took out her sphygmomanometer, wrapped the cuff around Cathie's arm and checked her blood pressure. "That's fine," she said, rolling up the cuff and replacing it. "Now, let's take a look down there."

There was a drop of blood on her underwear and on the sheet under Cathie's legs.

"Are you still having the pains?"

"No, that stopped after a few minutes."

"Let's see, now, you're what, about seven weeks gone now?"

"Almost eight," replied Cathie.

Jean pulled the sheet back over her at the same moment Douglas came in with a tray.

"Oh Douglas, nae the mugs, for ony's sake!" Cathie was half amused, half mortified; she had a nice set of china, and liked to use it when an occasion presented itself. Douglas sighed, put the tray down and went back to the kitchen.

"I think you're going to be all right," said Jean. "But there is a wee chance that you may lose it." She was careful not to use the word "baby," but even so, Cathie's eyes filled with tears.

"What do I have to do? I'll do anything you say, Jean. I've waited five years for this baby."

"Well, for a start, I think you should just stay in bed for the rest of the day, and tomorrow too. I'll come in to see you in the morning. Otherwise, just take it very easy. No heavy washing, obviously, and don't carry anything heavier than a cup and saucer until we see which way things are going, all right?"

Douglas came in and poured the tea.

"Lovely cups," said Jean, holding her one out and examining it. She took a sip and put the cup down. "Now, Douglas," she said firmly, "for a few days you're going to have to do just about everything around the house. Cathie has to have complete rest."

After Jean had gone, Cathie gently pulled Douglas down on the bed beside her. He lay there, feeling very tender and protective, and put an arm rather tentatively around her.

Cathie stared thoughtfully up at the ceiling. "Douggie, if this had to happen, I must say it came at just the right time. The machine's broken and they can't fix it until next week. I was just going to start the week's wash by hand, so if you do this today, you won't need to do the vacuuming until tomorrow. The shopping list is on the kitchen table, and there's a couple of my skirts and your gray jacket you'll need to pick up at MacKay's dry-cleaners before they close."

Chapter 16

Jean had got the call about Cathie just as she came into the hospital to see Francesca, so she had simply turned about and driven straight to Doug and Cathie's house. Now she had to decide whether to go home for lunch or see Francesca. She decided she could live on her reserves for a few hours, and went back to the hospital.

Francesca didn't look any worse, but she didn't look any better either. Her black hair straggled across her brow and tiny beads of sweat stood out on her forehead, and there was a general air of pallor and limp weariness about her. Even the tiny action of turning her head to see who was coming in seemed to be too much for her, and she closed her eyes as soon as she'd smiled at Jean.

Jean had picked up some grapes on the way and put the bag on the bedside table before sitting down in the chair by the bed. *"Buon giorno, Francesca. Come sta?"*

Francesca smiled again, but didn't open her eyes. *"Bene, grazie, e lei?"*

Jean had shot her bolt as far as her Italian was concerned. "Have you seen Dr. Macintosh today?"

"Yes, he came early in the morning. He said maybe he operate soon for the baby, he was not sure."

Jean looked over at the fetal monitor. The baby's heart was going nicely at about 120 beats per minute, but every so often the beat seemed to falter, then it picked up and went back to normal. Jean thought about when she was having her own babies. If she'd had a monitor there and seen every little irregularity of her baby's heartbeat, it would have driven her crazy.

Francesca turned her head and looked at Jean. The puffiness had gone with the diuretic treatment, and now those deep brown eyes that had always seemed big, were huge in her pale, drawn face.

"Dottore Jean, I do not want this baby, I do not want to be alive."

Jean put her arms around Francesca. "You're going through a bad time right now," she said quietly, "but when this is all over, and you're holding a beautiful baby in your arms, you'll feel differently."

Jean felt an overwhelming sympathy for the young woman, and tried to imagine how she'd have felt under the same circumstances, far from home, without a family, and married to a husband who couldn't stand her and of whom she was afraid.

Francesca was saying something, but so softly that Jean had to lean forward again to hear her. "Do they know who killed Caroline?"

Jean shook her head, and wondered how she had heard the news. "Bob, he came and told me yesterday. He is a nice man, very sad."

Jean knew that both Bob and Louise Fraser had been kind to her, although they were both too afraid of Marco to interfere much. Caroline also had done her best to help, but she had always been too busy with her own very active life to pay much attention to Francesca.

Something about the way Francesca spoke alerted Jean; she seemed to want to say something else, but was either unsure about whether she should, or couldn't find the words. Jean held her hand, and waited for Francesca to go on.

"Could I have some water?" asked Francesca.

"Are you allowed to drink?" Jean glanced up at the IV. Francesca didn't say anything, and Jean figured that a sip wouldn't do her any harm.

She went to the sink, ran the water until it was cold, and half filled a glass.

Francesca took a sip, then another, as if she were dying of thirst. "That's probably enough," said Jean, anxiously. "Here, let me take the glass."

Francesca smiled, and wiped a drop of water from her lower lip with a finger, and put it into her mouth.

"I think Bob knows who killed Caroline," said Francesca, her voice barely audible. There was a long pause, and then she said, "And I think I do too."

Brian Wooley lay on his bed, unwilling to open his eyes. His alarm clock had gone off about two hours before, and he had fallen out of bed in a panic, still so drunk he could hardly find his way back into his bed. He'd knocked the alarm clock off the bedside table, and the noise drilled into his head as if vibrating nails were being hammered in. Eventually it stopped, and he went back to sleep, but his sleep was full of strange, nightmarish dreams, with a naked Marco chasing him through the streets with a knife, then he turned around and vaporized him with a ray gun, while Caroline, somewhere in the distance was beckoning to him, and laughing, laughing.

Brian propped himself up on his elbows, suddenly remembering that the alarm had gone off. The movement caused a sledgehammer to rise from somewhere about his knees and slam into the top of his skull with a ferocious crash, exploding into a thousand shards of light. His breath came fast and shallow, and he slid slowly down the bed again. He didn't think he could survive another pain like that. The bile flowed up from his stomach and into his mouth with a bitter, coppery taste, and he gagged, starting the pain in his head again. He gasped and choked, not knowing exactly where he was, or what was happening to him. He knew that he was scared, full of vague and frightening memories that he could only hope were dreams.

After lying still for about ten minutes, Brian tried again, very slowly, as carefully as if he were balancing a pan brimming with boiling oil on his head. This time he was able to roll out of his bed, and make his unsteady way into the tiny bathroom.

A dim memory of the events of the evening before came back to him, and he started to tremble so hard he couldn't shave without risking cutting himself. He'd decided to get drunk, he remembered that, and had gone to the Bridge Bar to do it. Little islands of recollection floated around him, just out of reach. After he'd had a few drinks that awful aching feeling had come over him, and he knew he had to see Caroline, come what may. He'd finished his drink and gone out into the cold air, heading for where Caroline lived. He remembered that it had been cold but he didn't feel it, although all he was wearing was a light jacket. And then he knew he had to be totally insane, to be climbing around there in the dark when he could barely stand up. Then lights, and Caroline . . .

The memory floated away, and Brian shook his head with frustration, and the resulting pain made him stand motionless for several minutes while the pain ebbed and flowed inside his head.

Finally he got dressed and went out to get a paper, and the bright sunlight outside struck him like a blow. If there were no mechanics' jobs to be had in Perth, he'd go to Edinburgh or Glasgow. And he knew a man who worked in Cordiner's garage in Aberdeen, who could put in a good word for him.

When he saw the blaring headline of the *Courier*, Brian's knees started to shake, and he leaned up against the wall of the newsagent's shop, feeling deathly faint. A few moments later, almost without warning, he vomited.

"Closed until April 18 due to death in family." Jamieson read the sign stuck to the outer glass door of the Kinross restaurant, and wondered if it contained anything besides its obvious significance. The letters were handwritten in strong block capitals, and he peered at the sign for obvious traces of sorrow, such as shakiness of the hand or tear stains, but there were none.

Jamieson seemed almost to have acquired a new life, a new, super-alert personality since Doug had retired temporarily from the fray. Doug had asked Bob McLeod, his Chief Inspector, if it was all right for Jamieson to follow up a few leads on his own, just for a day or two, and Bob had reluctantly agreed. They were short-handed, and anyway there wasn't that much Jamieson could do to get into trouble.

"I want a personal report from you every day at four-thirty," Bob had told Jamieson. He was already having second thoughts about allowing Jamieson out by himself, and had no difficulty recalling occasions when Jamieson had got the entire department into trouble. "And if you have any problems, tell me." Another painful memory struck Bob. "Not a single word from you to the press or the TV, OK?" he said sternly. "If they want any info, refer them back to me."

So Jamieson had made a list, just the way Douglas always did, putting what he considered the most likely suspects at the top. Aileen Farquar was on the list, simply because he knew he couldn't leave her off entirely, but he left a space between the second-last name and hers, and wrote her name in smaller letters than the others.

And now he was going back to talk to the Frasers. He'd done some research on the boy, Marco. His colleagues told him he was an undisciplined, violent and thoroughly unsavory character.

Ignoring the sign, Jamieson knocked firmly on the door of the restaurant, a good loud rat-a-tat-tat, to show he meant business. After trying two more times, attracting only the attention of a few curious passers-by, he finally gave up and went around the corner to the entrance to the Frasers' flat where he was admitted immediately.

Bob Fraser was there, gray-faced, pacing the floor, and Louise was in a chair by the fireplace, doing the restaurant's accounts. Marco was in his room and wouldn't unlock the door until Jamieson banged on it and ordered him to come out.

Jamieson sat down in the middle of the sofa facing the fireplace, and asked Bob to sit down too. Marco came out of his room with thunder in his face, barefoot and in a dressing gown, the bandage still around his wrist.

"I'm here making inquiries about the death of your daughter Caroline," he said heavily, looking from Bob to Louise. Bob watched him, his gray eyes full of pain, but Louise kept her eyes down.

"I have some questions I need to ask all of you." His gaze moved piercingly from one to another. To his annoyance, Louise didn't even look up from her ledger. "I'd like to start with you, Mrs. Fraser," he said loudly. She sighed, and folded her hands. She isn't going to be a cooperative witness, thought Jamieson, and mentally prepared to treat her accordingly.

"Where were you on the night of the crime?" he asked, then quickly licked the end of his pencil.

"I was here, of course," she replied. "Ask Bob."

"Can you corroborate that statement?" Jamieson turned to Bob.

Bob looked puzzled for a moment, then said, "Yes, she was here, most of the time."

"Ah!" said Jamieson. "What about the rest of the time?"

"Didn't you go to see Francesca?" Bob asked Louise, who scowled at him.

"Yes, I did, but that was earlier," she replied brusquely. "After that I was home."

"What time were you at the hospital?" asked Jamieson, feeling that he might be on the scent of something.

"Visiting hours," said Louise. She closed the ledger with a smack and suddenly became voluble. "It's really terrible, they don't let you go when it's convenient for you, only when it's convenient for them. Mrs. Farrow, next door, when she had her boy in there with an abscess in his neck, and she was on the evening shift at her work, she could never get in at the right time, until finally . . ."

"Visiting hours," said Jamieson, writing it down. All this extraneous chatter was confusing him. "And when was the last time you saw your daughter?"

"She helped in the restaurant last night. She was here until about ten-thirty. She didn't stay to help with the clearing up."

Jamieson was busy writing, and didn't look up when Bob let out a strange, sad noise, a combination of a cough and sob.

"Did you have any conversation with her that might lead to an arrest of the guilty party?"

"Do you mean, did she tell me who was going to kill her?" Louise's voice was sharp, sarcastic, and Jamieson looked up from his notebook, astonished.

"I don't suppose she did that, Mrs. Fraser," he said heavily. This did not seem to be an appropriate time for her to be indulging in levity. "What *did* she tell you at that time?"

"There was some trouble at her office, but she didn't say what it was. She was upset by it, though."

"Was she frightened?" asked Jamieson quickly. "Afraid?"

"No, I don't think so." There was something strange in Louise's tone, and this time Jamieson looked up. He paused for a moment before writing down her answer, and glanced up at her suspiciously a couple of times as he wrote.

"Was she close to you? I mean, did she tell you about her problems and stuff?"

Before Louise could answer, Marco said in a loud, aggressive voice, "No, she didn't. My mother hated her, and it was because of her she left home and got her own flat, and . . ."

"Marco! Please! That's enough!" Bob spoke for the first time, and Jamieson turned his eyes over toward him. Jamieson knew the man fairly well; Bob was a big, lumbering, gentle sort, who always seemed pained and confused by the warring that seemed to go on all the time in his family, for reasons that totally escaped him.

Jamieson expected Louise to come back with a vicious reply, but to his astonishment, her eyes filled with tears. "You know that's not true, Marco," she said. "It was for *your* sake, for your own good that we got her into that flat."

Marco glowered at her but said no more, and Jamieson made a note to come back to that topic when he got around to interrogating Marco.

"What about her friends?" Jamieson asked Louise, doggedly sticking to the list of questions he'd made out before coming. "Who were they? Did any of them have a grudge against her?"

Marco cut in again. "She doesn't know. She never wanted to know her friends, she didn't care." He stood up, still glaring angrily at his mother.

"Sit down, Marco," said Jamieson, with the patience of a large man who knows his strength. "You'll get your turn to talk in a minute. Meanwhile, sit down and shut up."

Once again Marco subsided, but he continued to throw angry glances at his mother. To Jamieson, Mrs. Fraser seemed more distressed by her son's anger than by the loss of her daughter.

"Caroline's friends," said Jamieson, going back to his list.

"Well, her best *girl* friend was Fiona Montrose," replied Louise, her glance flickering uncertainly over to Marco. "Caroline temped over at the place where Fiona's a management trainee. I think Fiona was a good influence on her."

Marco snorted.

"What about her men friends?" asked Jamieson.

There was a long silence.

"How about that boy Brian Wooley? Wasn't she seeing him?" prompted Jamieson.

"Not any more," said Louise, deliberately not looking at Marco. "They broke up quite a while ago."

"But he's still sniffing around her," exploded Marco, then let out a loud, unexpected sob. "He *was*, anyway. He couldn't stay away from her, even after . . ."

"He took it very badly," interrupted Louise hurriedly. "I mean Brian. He got far too serious about her. Caroline wasn't ready to settle down yet, and told him it was all over."

There was a silence while Jamieson wrote. It was broken finally by Marco, who said in a choking voice, "When I find out who did it, I'm going to kill him."

As it wasn't an answer to one of his questions, Jamieson didn't write that down.

Chapter 17

"Cathie, can you manage by yersel' for a wee whilie?" asked Doug, his Glasgow accent heavy on him. He put down the phone. "I have to go in."

"Aye, of course," said Cathie, watching Douglas. He was excited, and his eyes were shining. "What's up?"

"Did you ever hear of Brian Wooley?"

"He went for a while with that Caroline," replied Cathie. "He works over at the Station Garage with Mike Chivas."

"Aye, that's the one. Well . . ." Douglas looked at the phone as if for confirmation. "He's waiting to see me at the office. Jamieson says he was there when he came back from the Frasers, just a minute ago."

Doug took a big breath, as if he couldn't quite believe what he was going to tell Cathie. "He told Jamieson he wants to confess to Caroline's murder, but he'll only talk to me."

Ten minutes later, Douglas opened the door to his office. Jamieson had already installed Brian in the visitor's chair. He looked dreadful; he was unkempt, hadn't shaved for several days, and a miasma of stale alcohol hung around him like marsh gas. He looked haggard and undernourished, and barely looked up when Douglas came in.

"Would you like a cup of coffee?" asked Douglas. "Or a cigarette?" Brian shook his head.

The door opened and Jamieson came quietly in. "Did you read him his rights?" Doug asked him.

"Yes, sir," replied Jamieson.

"Good. Now, Brian. I believe you have something to tell me?"

"I think I killed Caroline," said Brian, speaking in a dull lifeless voice. His head was lowered and his words were barely audible.

"Oh yes?" said Douglas, glancing at Jamieson. "And what makes you think that?"

"I got drunk last night," started Brian.

"And the night before, and the night before that," Jamieson interrupted in a quiet voice.

"Shut up, Jamieson," said Douglas. "Go on, Brian."

"Then I went to see Caroline. I had to . . ." Brian lifted his head and stared glassily at Douglas.

"About what time would that have been, Brian?" asked Douglas silkily.

"It was dark, that's all I can tell you. And there wasn't much traffic. I don't know . . ."

"Did you go to her flat? Did she let you in?"

Brian put his head in his hands. "I don't know, I can't remember. But I had this dream, later, that I'd killed her, and Marco . . ."

"A dream, Brian?" Douglas's voice was beginning to take on an edge. "How did you kill her, in your dream?"

"With a knife," replied Brian, and Douglas sat up suddenly. "I didn't want to," went on Brian, "because I loved her, but somebody was telling me I had to do it."

"Was that somebody a person you know?"

"I think so, but I don't know. I've been trying to remember . . ."

"Where was she, Brian, in this dream? In the kitchen? In the bathroom? What was she wearing?"

"She opened the door," replied Brian, staring somewhere above Douglas's head. "She was wearing white, a white, shimmering gown. She was so beautiful . . .Then she went over to the window, and I followed her. It was open, and the curtains were billowing . . . When I stabbed her she rose up and floated out through the window, slowly, like a great ship. Oh God!" A great sob escaped from Brian. "I called after her, I shouted and tried to get her to come back, but she didn't even look around . . ."

Douglas sighed.

"Brian, when did you last eat anything?" His voice was kindly enough, so he was surprised when Brian started to weep softly. Soon he was racked by sobs, and couldn't speak at all.

"Jamieson, go and get him something to eat and drink from the cafeteria," said Douglas. "He can eat here, then take him home."

"In a police car?" asked Jamieson, unsure about using official transportation for such a purpose.

"Yes, Jamieson. In a police car. And if you need me, I'll be at home."

Jamieson hesitated, and looked at Douglas as if he were waiting for something. Douglas sighed, took a five pound note from his wallet and gave it to Jamieson for the food. "Leave the change in my desk," he said.

Mac was picked up at about eleven that morning. An alert sergeant in a patrol car was stopping at the last set of lights on the Glasgow Road, almost at the limit of his patrol area when he saw a forest green Rover coming in the opposite direction, slowing for the red light. He checked the number on his dashboard pad. Sure enough. He switched on his lights and signalled to the driver to pull over.

"He seemed fine, sir," he reported back to Douglas on the phone. "Cheerful, very good spirits, no sign of alcohol abuse. I just told him to go straight to the police headquarters because there had been an accident." He paused. "I didn't realize you weren't coming in today."

"No problem," said Douglas, a trifle brusquely. "I'll get Jamieson to see him."

"Just wanted to let you know, sir."

"Thanks. That was a good piece of work, Sergeant."

Jamieson used Doug's office for the interview, although the aroma of Brian Wooley was still heavy in the air, and rejoiced for a moment in the unfamiliar feel of his boss's swivel chair. The power of the office seemed to pass from the seat right into him. He leaned back, and a small piece of plaster detached itself from the wall behind him and fell to the floor. Jamieson surveyed Mac MacFadyen just as Doug would have done.

"Your full name and address please, sir."

Mac was looking very cheerful, well dressed, and his movements were quick and decisive.

"Would you tell me what this is about, please?" he asked. "All I was told was that there had been an accident."

"That's right. Now if you'll give me your full name and address . . ."

Mac shrugged and complied. An old Army man, he was used to going along with military procedure, which wasn't much different from this, except they'd be asking for his name, rank and number, in that order.

" . . . if you could tell me your movements last night." Jamieson's voice was so neutral that Mac missed the first half of what he was saying.

"Yes, of course." He hesitated. "Actually that's rather a delicate matter, and unless there's a really important reason, I'd rather keep it to myself."

"There's been a murder, sir," said Jamieson, sounding as portentous as he could. "Of a person who works in your office."

"In my office!" Mac jumped out of his chair, and it occurred to Jamieson that he was acting a bit hyper. "Who?"

"Miss Caroline Fraser," said Jamieson, watching Mac carefully.

Mac sank back into his chair. "Caroline! My God! When? Who did it?"

"That is the question we are presently investigating," replied Jamieson. "Now, you were about to tell me what your movements were yesterday evening."

"Well, I left work, did some shopping . . ."

"And what shops might you have visited, sir?" Jamieson was getting more and more portentous by the minute, and he watched Mac's every move like a hawk. The suspect seemed nervous, jumpy, and there was an indefinable something that told Jamieson that Mac knew what had happened to Caroline Fraser.

"Marks and Sparks, for a start," replied Mac.

"Do you have a charge card there, sir?"

"No, cash on the button." Mac laughed. "Then I went to the wine shop on South Street."

"And what did you purchase there, sir?"

"A bottle of Glen Grant, a couple of bottles of Chablis."

"And then, sir?"

"Then? Then I went home."

"And about what time would that have been, sir?"

"Oh . . ." Mac looked at his watch. "About five-thirty, maybe six o'clock, I suppose.

"You are an ex-Army man, sir, are you not?"

"Yes indeed. Captain, Royal Artillery."

"And used to making accurate statements concerning time?"

Mac grinned good-naturedly at Jamieson. "I left the Army over two years ago."

Jamieson's interrogation went on for another half hour, during which time he established that Mac had had dinner at the Towers restaurant with Aileen Farquar, taken her home, gone in for a cup of coffee and a small whisky, then gone home.

"About what time would that have been, sir?"

"Oh, around ten, maybe ten-thirty. I didn't look at the time."

"Did you go out again, sir?"

Mac hesitated for a fraction of a second. "No," he said. And actually that was perfectly true. He simply hadn't gone straight home, but Jamieson hadn't asked him that.

"Let me get this exactly correct, Mr. MacFadyen." Jamieson spoke in a loud voice, as if a third party were listening next door and he wanted to be sure nothing was missed. "You took Miss Farquar to dinner, drove her home, spent a short time in her house, then went home and stayed there? Is that right, sir?"

"You got it in one, Constable," replied Mac. He seemed very relaxed now, and Jamieson's antipathy to him grew. He was obviously not taking Miss Farquar seriously, a nice lady who seemed to really love him. But these officer types were like that, he thought. All glamour and nice clothes, but when something bad happens to one of your people, well, that's just tough. No real sense of loyalty, the kind of loyalty you find among the men in the trenches.

"Do you have any witnesses as to your movements last night, sir?"

"After I left Miss Farquar? No."

"Mr. MacFadyen," he said, "your account of your movements last evening does not agree with that of other persons."

"Like who?" asked Mac.

"Like Miss Farquar," replied Jamieson. "She says . . ." He could feel his indignation rising. "She says you spent the entire night at her house, with her."

Mac's nose wrinkled. He was feeling very edgy and euphoric, and wondered if his last hit had not been stronger than usual. Maybe that accounted for his next comment, which he would certainly not have made under normal circumstances. "No way," he said, laughing. "I'd rather spend the night with one of Macbeth's witches."

Jamieson's jaw dropped, then his whole expression hardened into one of strong dislike. "Off the record, sir," he said, "and between you and me. No gentleman would ever say a thing like that."

"You're probably right, *Constable*," replied Mac, still laughing, though he didn't want to. He could feel the heroin buzzing in his veins and he didn't care what he said or who heard him. "And now can I go about my business?"

"Yes. But I'll be needing to talk to you again, Mr. MacFadyen."

As Mac opened the door, Jamieson said, with a smirk, "And by the way, sir, I believe you'll also be hearing from the Drug Enforcement people in the near future, so please do not leave the confines of the City of Perth without our permission."

Donald Tarland had an appointment for his six-monthly medical checkup that day, and decided it would be silly to cancel it. When he showed up at Jean's surgery promptly at four, Jean noticed that he seemed pale and distraught, and quite understandably so, she thought.

"You must all have been so upset about Caroline," she said sympathetically. "A lovely girl. That was such a tragedy."

"Yes, it was terrible," replied Donald. "We're all . . ." he hesitated. "Everybody in the office is in shock, and of course so is Teresa."

Jean shook her head. "In Perth, of all places. It's scary; you'd think we were in Chicago or somewhere like that. Now, let's get down to business . . ." Jean checked his chart. "How have you been? Any problems?"

Donald, always very concerned about his health, mentioned that he'd had a few headaches and blurring of vision. "I hope it isn't a brain tumor," he said, joking, but there was anxiety in his voice. He had a number of other complaints; Jean went through the list of routine questions, taking each system in turn. Indigestion had been a problem since early adulthood, but was controlled with antacids. He'd developed some bladder inflammation, he thought, and Jean told him that the urine test would reveal if he had anything to worry about. Jean tried to concentrate as he went on with his list of symptoms, but her mind kept wandering elsewhere. She didn't have time to deal with hypochondria, even mild cases such as his. He was occasionally constipated, he said, and was developing some stiffness in the knees, but that bothered him only in the mornings. Donald's overanxious concern about his body went along with the rest of his personality, she thought. According to Teresa, he was rather boringly meticulous about everything, an anxious individual who insisted on correctness, propriety and order in every aspect of his life. Donald was an elder of the church and the president-elect at the local Rotary club. Altogether an admirable man, Jean admitted, but not somebody she could really like, although Steven was enthusiastic about both him and Mac.

"Your blood pressure was a wee bit high the last time," said Jean. "Why don't we start with that."

She did a complete physical examination and found very little to report.

"You're in pretty good shape, Donald, as far as I can tell," she told him. "We'll check your blood to make sure you're not diabetic or anemic, and if that's all right, you have a clean bill of health."

Jean said goodbye, and was glad to get back to her other patients, the ones who really had something the matter with them.

The post mortem was done in the pathology department of the Perth hospital. At first, Jean had emphatically not wanted to attend, but certain aspects of the case were already troubling her, so as soon as she finished her morning surgery, she went through to Helen's room and told her where she was going.

"Well, Jean, it's up to you." Helen, at her desk, sounded unusually harassed. "Honestly, I don't know what good it's going to do, you being there." She looked up at Jean, who was staring at her, looking guilty and crestfallen. The last thing Jean ever wanted was to have Helen think she was shirking her duties in the practice. "But, knowing you," Helen went on, "there's a very good reason for your wanting to be there. I'll expect a thoroughly detailed report when you get back."

Jean realized that Helen had been gently teasing her, and shrugged nonchalantly. "Right, I'll try to explain it to you in language you'll understand," she said, heading quickly for the door before Helen had a chance to put in any further repartee.

The pathology department was in the basement area of the hospital, next to the laundry, and Jean left her car near the service entrance. Two shiny hearses were standing outside, waiting; the black-capped drivers were standing together smoking and grinning over a joke.

With a leaden feeling in the pit of her stomach, Jean walked past a row of empty gray canvas laundry hampers with the hospital's name stencilled in large letters on them, and along the white plastered corridor past the double doors that led to the kitchens. Above the door at the end of the corridor was a large new red-on-white sign, "*Pathology Department. Authorized personnel ONLY.*" The door was locked, but there was a bell push at the side, installed since her last visit there, and Jean rang it.

After a few moments she recognized the technician's voice on the intercom. "OK, Dr. Montrose," he said. "Push the door when you hear the buzzer."

Both autopsy tables were occupied. Malcolm Anderson, in his red-stained rubber apron and long red rubber gloves, was standing at the first table. His face behind the wraparound plastic goggles was less jovial than usual. He saw Jean glance momentarily at the other table, where the remains of a thin woman with gray, straggly hair were lying. Her mouth was wide open, and she could see something pink inside it.

"That al' wifie?" said Malcolm, watching Jean. "She's from one o' the nursing homes. Choked to death on her dentures, poor cratur."

Jean felt her insides quivering as she approached the table that bore Caroline. In death, her spirited beauty was gone; the first incision down the middle of her breastbone had already been made, and the skin, muscles and those fine breasts of hers had been peeled back to each side, to expose the front ends of the whitish ribs, which projected slightly between the red of the muscles between them. The small loop of intestine that she had seen projecting from the cut in her belly was still there, only now it was wrinkled, dry and brownish in color.

Jean took a deep breath, and the smell of formalin assailed her. Come on, girl, she said to herself sternly. You'd think this was the first post mortem you'd ever attended. Shape up.

"Well, quine," said Malcolm, "this is a tragic business, for sure."

"I knew her quite well," replied Jean, remembering how she had almost fainted in Caroline's flat. "My Fiona was her best friend."

"Will you need to do the head?" asked the technician.

"Aye, because you can never tell," said Malcolm. He turned back to Jean. "About a year ago, there was this bairn that the police thought had died from abuse. He had bruising around the eyes, and they arrested the parents because he was dead on arrival at the hospital. When we opened up his head we found that he'd had a brain hemorrhage from an aneurysm, nothing to do with

the parents at all." Malcolm grinned happily at the recollection; it wasn't often that he felt he'd done somebody
any good.

Carefully, holding the heavy scalpel between his
thumb and forefinger like a surgeon, Malcolm opened
the belly from the lower end of the breastbone to the
pubic hairline. He went around the cut in the belly so
that he could examine it from the inside. Jean tensed,
and couldn't help herself from flinching, as if she could
feel the knife cutting into her own skin.

Malcolm picked up the pair of heavy black scissors,
attached to the side of the table by a metal chain, and
completed the incision, cutting through the membranous
peritoneum to expose the glistening abdominal cavity, in
which the intestines floated like islands in a sea of dark,
half-clotted blood.

"They must have got her aorta," said Malcolm, delv-
ing in and pulling the intestines out of the cavity. They
slithered out with a slurping noise, and for a heart-
stopping second it sounded as if Caroline had come back
to life.

"Aye, they did," he confirmed, peering into the yawn-
ing cavity. "Look there, quine, see the cut, just to the left
of the spine?" He pointed with a pair of big forceps, and
Jean looked but all she could see was blood, and she
quickly took a step back from the table.

While Malcolm dictated his findings on the voice-
activated microphone, the technician came over and with
the scissors cut the stout membrane that kept the liver in
position, and brought it out, a nice, clean, young-looking
liver, as Malcolm pointed out. He put it on a tray with
the spleen, then went back for the intestines.

"Do you do routine cultures?" asked Jean. "Checking
for infections, things like that?"

"Oh aye, that's part o' the protocol," replied Malcolm,
picking up the spleen. It was about the size of Jean's fist,
a dark bluish red. "We do them on the lungs, blood and

urine, and of course in this case, we do vaginal ones too, with smears, looking for infections and spermatozoa. That's already been done, right?" He looked over at the technician.

"Done at the scene, repeated here," he replied. The tech was a rather saturnine individual who never spoke an unnecessary word.

A few minutes later, Malcolm came back to the table, put his gloved hand inside the gaping, empty abdomen and felt around the back of it, then down into the cavity of the pelvis. Suddenly his hand stopped moving.

"Put on a pair of gloves, quine," he said to Jean. "Then come and feel this."

Overcoming her reluctance, Jean went to the rack and selected the smallest pair of red rubber gloves, which were still too large for her.

"Feel that, down there, in the middle, going over to the left a wee bit, about the size of a pear? Aye, that's her uterus, and I believe she'd be about a couple of months pregnant, but we'll know better when we open it up on the dissecting table."

Always enthusiastic about an unexpected finding, Malcolm pulled the abdominal wall back with one hand and with the other pointed his forceps at something deep in the pelvis. "See that, quine? Those adhesions?" Jean forced herself to look, but couldn't see what he was talking about. It all looked dark and it was difficult for her to distinguish one organ from another. "She had an infection of some kind . . ." Malcolm raised his head and beckoned to the technician. "We'll need some more cultures here," he said. The tech took a long cotton swab-on-a-stick from a sealed test tube and poked down where Malcolm showed him, then went to the bench and smeared it on a series of Petri dishes with different culture media, before breaking the end off into another tube and sealing it.

There wasn't much else to see, Malcolm Anderson

told Jean, sounding regretful. He'd let her know if anything showed up in the head, but he felt pretty sure it would be normal.

"Can you make any guesses about who might have done this?" asked Jean.

"Aye," replied Malcolm. "Probably a right-handed male, judging from the force used, but it could certainly be a female. That was a savage blow," he said, pointing back at Caroline's abdomen. "And made with a long knife. Maybe some knowledge of anatomy, maybe not. Hard to tell. No trace of sperm in the vagina, from the preliminary smears at any rate. . . ."

Jean left the pathology department feeling overwhelmed with sadness, but at the back of her mind there was a germ of intuition that told her there was already some disturbing correlations in the case, but they floated elusively around in her head, and by the time she got back to the surgery, they had not been resolved.

Chapter 18

Washing the load of clothes was harder work and took Douglas longer than he expected, but he wrung them all out as directed and went into the garden carrying the heavy green plastic basket to hang the clothes up on the line. To his left he caught a quick glimpse of Mrs. McIver, their irascible neighbor, peering at him over the fence. At the sight of him coming out through the kitchen door wearing one of Cathie's frilly aprons and carrying the laundry basket, her jaw dropped and she scuttled back inside her house.

Douglas was wondering about Mac MacFadyen and whether he'd showed up at the station. If he turned out to be anything but an innocent bystander, he, Douglas, would be in deep trouble for not making serious efforts to find him from the beginning. The clothes line kept getting away from him; he carefully folded the top of one of Cathie's pink knickers over it, then reached down into the basket for the wooden clothes pegs. The knickers promptly slid off and landed in the grass. Douglas considered the problem for a few moments. He couldn't hold the damp knickers in position with one hand and at the same time reach for the pegs. When the telephone went and Cathie called for him through the open door, he had just about worked it out, and he had four clothes pegs gripped between his teeth when he ran into the house. Again he caught a glimpse of Mrs. McIver's astounded expression, this time from the safety of her first floor window.

Jamieson told him about his interview of Mac Mac-Fadyen and the discrepancy between what he and what Aileen Farquar had said.

"Good work, Jamieson." If Jamieson caught the tone of surprise in Doug's voice, it didn't bother him. "Do you think she was just covering up for him? Or was she trying to get herself an alibi?"

"I believe you're right, sir," replied Jamieson, and at the other end Douglas shook his head in momentary confusion. Sometimes he wondered how the thoughts in Jamieson's head were processed, and he got an immediate vision of a traffic jam on a narrow road. But Jamieson was still talking.

"Inspector Garvie says McFadyen's a heavy heroin user and our theory, sir, is that he came up to Miss Fraser's apartment to get money for drugs, she refused and he killed her."

"Quite possible," replied Doug. "But of course that's just conjecture. By that I mean guesswork, Jamieson."

There was a tone of ineffable self-satisfaction in Jamieson's voice when he told Doug that he was on his way out to arrest Mac.

"You're going to *what*? Jamieson, don't even consider it." Doug took a deep breath. "You can't just take him in on the basis of a guess; you'd need something that ties MacFadyen much more directly to the murder. I'm talking about something like a knife in his hands with her blood on it, stuff like that, direct evidence."

"Oh yes, sir, we have the knife. Didn't I mention it? It was handed in by a couple of children this morning. They saw the handle sticking out from the grating over a drain at the corner of her street. There weren't any useful prints, but it had blood on it, it's human and the lab says it's her group."

"Jesus, Jamieson! It's time I got back over there," said

Doug speaking mostly to himself. "What I'm trying to tell you is that you don't have anything that directly links MacFadyen to the crime. If you arrested him, his lawyer could get a habeas corpus and have him out quicker than you could read the 'situations vacant' column in the paper."

"Sir!" Jamieson's voice was just as confident as ever. "That knife, sir, is part of a set of four. The other three are in a box in Mr. MacFadyen's kitchen according to Inspector Garvie's men, who raided his flat earlier this morning with a search warrant, looking for drugs, sir."

There was a long silence, almost palpably filled with Jamieson's huge satisfaction.

"OK," said Doug finally. "Go up right now to Bob McLeod and tell him the whole story. Don't do anything else until you've talked to him. He'll tell you what to do."

When Jean came back to visit Cathie, the first thing she heard when she came to the door was the high whine of a vacuum cleaner, which died down after she rang the bell for the second time. She was all ready to tell Doug off for letting Cathie out of bed, and Cathie for doing housework, but when Doug came to the door, grinning broadly in his short, frilly apron and holding a long attachment for vacuuming under furniture, she relaxed and grinned at him. "I was getting ready to give you a piece of my mind," she said. "How's our patient?"

"Fine," replied Douglas. "She says she hasn't had such a good time since we went to Blackpool, and that was four years ago."

In fact, Cathie looked like a queen, dressed in a cream negligée, propped up in her bed with big pillows. She was reading a mail-order catalogue, and had an open half-pound box of Black Magic chocolates beside her. On the other side was a small tray with tea things.

"Look at this, Jean," she said, pointing to the catalogue. "If I buy this genuine hand-hammered wok, made in the ancient Republic of China, at their new low price, they throw in a' the bits wi' it, a scraper, a wee brush to clean it, a hook to hang it on, a'thing you need. What do you think?"

Jean took the catalogue and looked at the brightly colored picture. "It looks wonderful," she said carefully. "I didn't know Douglas liked Chinese cooking."

"He can learn to," said Cathie. "He already won't drink anything but China tea, these days."

"That's because I dinna get anything else," said Douglas.

"Awa' ye go back to your vacuuming, Douggie lad," said Cathie. "The doctor has tae examine me."

Jean smiled at them. Douglas and Cathie were inseparable, and had a very happy marriage. For some reason, Douglas, with his responsible job and good powers of leadership, actually seemed to enjoy the fact that, at home, Cathie led him around by the nose.

Cathie had no further bleeding or pains since the day before, and Jean decided to let her get out of bed a little, as long as she promised not to do anything in the least strenuous.

"Good," said Douglas when he heard the news. He sounded very relieved as he took off the apron and headed for the door. "And if it's all right with you, Jean," he said, "I'm now going back to work."

Jean stayed to chat with Cathie for a few minutes, then drove back to the surgery. On the car radio, she heard that a local businessman and Falklands War Hero, Mac MacFadyen, was helping the police with their inquiries in connection with the recent murder of Caroline Fraser, and Jean was shocked. Mac was not the one she would have put at the top of the list of suspects, but she realized that of course the police knew a great deal more about the case than she did. But already there had been indicators that had pointed her in other directions.

Back at the surgery, there was a message for Jean to call Dr. Peter Macintosh, and with a sinking feeling in the pit of her stomach, she phoned him back.

"It's about Francesca Fraser," he said, "She's not doing well, and I'm getting more concerned about her baby. I've decided to do a Caesarean, first thing tomorrow morning, and I wondered if you'd like to come and assist me."

"I'll be there," promised Jean. "But I hope you'll have somebody with more experience there too."

"I'll meet you in the operating theater, then, a few minutes before eight o'clock."

Jean put the phone down. Luckily it wasn't her turn to do the new home visits the next day, and she knew that a Caesarean section shouldn't take too long. That was, she reminded herself, if things went according to plan. She thought about Francesca, facing this operation alone, and decided to look in on her later that day. Poor little thing, she would be feeling so lonely and frightened, and Jean's kind heart went out to her.

When Doug got back to his office, he found Jamieson sitting in his office chair.

"Out!" he said, and Jamieson jumped up as if he had been shot. "I was just using the phone, sir," he said, abashed. Actually he had been sitting there, enjoying the luxury of privacy, wondering how much his success with the Fraser case would help his chances of promotion. The lamp of ambition had been well and truly lit in his heart, and in his euphoria Jamieson had been promoting himself upward through the ranks, first regarding Doug as his equal, then, as he ascended on the basis of sheer merit to the dizzying heights of chief inspector and then superintendent, as his obsequious inferior. All that fantasy was wiped out in an instant when Douglas came into the office.

"Where's MacFadyen?"

"In the cells, sir. He's called a lawyer, Mr. Edward Imrie. He's going to be here shortly to apply for bail."

"He'll get it, you can be sure of that. A war hero, is Mr. MacFadyen, with a Military Cross to his credit, no less. Any way, I'll go down and have a chat with him. You'd better come with me."

They walked in silence down the back stairs to the lowest level of the building. Jamieson evidently couldn't understand why Doug wasn't falling over with admiration for his astute handling of the case, and felt annoyed and aggrieved.

Mac MacFadyen was in the third of eight cells, next to a drunk who was singing quietly to himself in a rusty-sounding baritone. Mac stood up when the guard unlocked the door and Douglas and Jamieson came in. He looked grey and ill, and Jamieson was shocked at the sudden change in his appearance. His brow was beaded with sweat, and he spoke quickly to Doug. "Look, Inspector, I'm taking medicine, and I need to have it now, otherwise I could get into serious trouble. I have it at home and I'll be perfectly happy to have somebody come back with me, but I need it . . . I need it now."

"What sort of medicine is it?" asked Doug. "If you have a prescription, we can send someone out to get it for you."

Mac's knuckles were white with strain. "It's not a prescription medicine," he said, his voice rising in spite of himself. Doug felt momentarily sorry for this man, who had become an addict through no fault of his own. However, he realized that if ever there was a time to get information out of him, this was it.

He motioned to the guard, who brought in a chair. Doug sat down in it, and stared impassively at Mac.

"Maybe we can arrange for you to get your medicine," he said, ignoring the hiss of Jamieson's indrawn breath, "but first there's a couple of things I'd like to discuss with you."

"Sure," said Mac. "Go ahead." Douglas, watching him closely, hoped he wouldn't go into a withdrawal convulsion before he'd finished with his questions.

"You cautioned him?" he asked Jamieson, without taking his eyes off Mac.

"Yes, sir. When he came in." Jamieson's voice was clipped, aggrieved.

Douglas could see he didn't have long to get anything out of Mac.

"Did you visit Caroline Fraser in her flat, the night she was killed?" he asked Mac.

"Look, Inspector," said Mac. His voice was low, almost croaking, and his whole skin seemed to be tightening around him like a shrink-wrap. "First let me go home, then I'll tell you anything you want the moment I come back. Right now, I'm sick. . . . " He held up his hand and looked at it. It was shaking, and didn't look as if he had much control over it.

"We were talking about Caroline," said Douglas, forcing himself to sound relaxed, but not taking his eyes off Mac for a moment. "Did you go to see her?"

"Yes, I did." Mac's voice rose, almost to a yell. "Now let me go. I'm warning you, I'm . . . going to. . . ."

"She was killed with your knife," said Douglas, trying to calculate exactly when Mac was going to break.

"No. No!" Mac's face was now a waxy white and drenched with sweat. "She's not dead. She was angry, but not dead. There wasn't any. . . ." He started to mumble, and the sweat was pouring off him.

Douglas thought there was maybe one more answer left in him before he disintegrated. "Why did you go there, Mac? Why did you go to see her?"

"I needed money. To buy my medicine. She didn't have any and she was angry. . . ." Mac's whole body started to shake, and the left side of his face started to twitch spasmodically.

"Did you kill her, Mac? She wouldn't give you any money so you killed her, right?"

"No!" Mac got up, swayed to one side and fell back. Jamieson, watching him, thought he might be faking, but obviously Douglas took it seriously.

"OK, Jamieson," he said quickly, hoping he hadn't left things too late, "call Dr. Montrose and ask her to come up here right away."

Chapter 19

Teresa was out in the garden planting onions when she heard the sound of Marco's old Vauxhall turning the corner into the drive.

"You came just at the right time, Marco," she called out with a smile of genuine pleasure. As he came up to her, Teresa could see that he was angry, but that wasn't too unusual. The bandage on his wrist stuck out from under his shirt sleeve.

"Here, Marco. Pass me an onion when I've made a hole for it." She stuck the T-shaped wooden hole-maker in the soft ground. "What's on your mind?"

"Did you hear the news?" he asked in a low voice.

"You mean about Mac being arrested?"

"Yeah, about Mac being arrested."

Teresa busied herself for a moment making a series of onion-holes. She could feel the suppressed violence emanating from Marco.

"I'm really sorry, Marco. It's a really tragic business," she said.

"I don't think it was him," said Marco. He passed her a small, golden onion.

"Who do you think it was?" asked Teresa, looking up.

"Brian Wooley," replied Marco. "He's been hanging around Caroline like a leech. He watches her in her apartment from a roof opposite. And he's nuts. I've warned him once already. And I can't find him."

"It's probably just as well you *didn't* find him," said

Teresa, thinking of Marco's explosive temper, and the violence that permeated his life. She moved along to make the next series of holes, and Marco pushed the box of onions with his foot so that it was within her reach. He watched her, thinking that Teresa was about the nicest and most sensible person he'd ever met.

"Marco, I'd leave poor Brian well alone, if I were you," said Teresa. "It seems pretty clear that he didn't do it."

Marco opened and closed the fingers on the side he'd sliced his wrist. They were stiff and a bit swollen. The doctor said he was lucky not to have cut any tendons.

"Is your hand hurting?" asked Teresa. She stood up and took off her gardening gloves. "Let me see." She massaged his hand gently and bent the fingers one by one, then straightened them out again. "Does that feel better? " she asked after doing it a few times.

"Yes, thanks, Teresa." Marco gazed at her with pure adoration.

"OK. Now let's get back to work," said Teresa briskly. She smiled briefly at Marco, put her gloves on again and got back down on her knees.

"You can see how they go in, Marco? Point up, about four inches deep." Teresa pressed the onion firmly in position, then covered it with soil.

"Let me do some," said Marco.

"No. You'd just get yourself all dirty. And your bandage. You can pass me the onions when I'm ready to put them in."

"You really think Mac killed my sister."

Teresa put down her hole-maker. "Marco, I have to tell you something, even if it's only to protect Brian Wooley." She paused, considering how she should present the information she wanted him to have. "Mac is a drug addict, Marco. We didn't find that out until recently. He's even been stealing from the business to get cash to buy his drugs. . . . "

"What's that got to do with Caroline?" asked Marco, his voice rough.

Teresa paused. "Donald says Mac's been having an affair with Caroline for a while."

Marco stared at Teresa, and a flush spread slowly across his face. The very thought of Mac even touching Caroline made his entire being bulge with violent intentions.

"That doesn't mean that Mac killed her, Marco, I'm sure you understand that. But honestly, we think the police are probably right. He probably did go to her flat, wanting money, and when . . ."

Abruptly, Teresa stopped talking, picked up her hole-maker and started to stab holes in the ground so fast that Marco had trouble keeping up the supply of onions.

After about ten minutes of frantic work, Teresa stopped, stood up and stretched. "I'm going to take a break. Would you like a cup of coffee?"

In silence they went back to the house, past the big, white-painted French doors to the side door that let straight into the kitchen. Teresa scraped the mud off her boots, then stepped out of them. She had small, dainty feet that suited her petite, elegant and meticulous person.

Marco followed her into the kitchen. As always, everything was exactly in its place, the counters were spotless, and everything shone as if it were a display in a home furnishings exhibition.

"You keep this place beautiful," said Marco, his anger momentarily sidetracked. "You should see my mother's kitchen. Stuff all over the place, pans, everything."

"Well, she has lots of other things to think about," replied Teresa. "Now, you'll find the coffee in the freezer, in a plastic bag. I like to grind it fresh every time." She washed her hands at the sink for what seemed like a long time to Marco.

He sat down on a stool and watched Teresa go her methodical, precise way about the kitchen.

"But him being a hero in the Falklands and all" Marco shook his head. "It's not the thing you'd expect a man like him, an officer, to do, is it?" The anger was creeping back into his voice.

"When people become addicted to drugs, particularly heroin," said Teresa rather primly, "they behave differently. They do things that normally they'd never do. They can stop being human, and turn into animals." Her fastidious nose wrinkled as she spooned an exact measure of ground coffee into the coffee maker.

"So you think he did it."

"That'll be up to the judge and jury to decide, Marco. But I know Douglas Niven, and I'm sure he wouldn't have arrested him unless he was *certain*. You remember all the other cases he's solved, like when the Lumsden baby was murdered, and that schoolteacher who was burned up."

Marco watched while Teresa took a large fruitcake out of its tin, put it on a wooden carving board and cut two big slices. She placed them in the exact center of two expensive-looking white china plates with a thin band of gold around the rim, then put a small dessert fork on each plate.

"What does Mr. Tarland think?"

"Donald knows Mac much better than I do." Teresa paused, wondering if she should go on with this discussion with Marco. "I'm sorry to say that at this point he's quite sure too. Now let's get away from this morbid talk. How's your mother bearing up?"

"She couldn't care less. In fact, sometimes I think she's glad."

"Marco! How can you say things like that? Of course she's not glad!" Teresa sounded mildly indignant. "Caroline was her *daughter*."

Marco kept silent. It would take too long to explain how he felt, and there were some things, some feelings that kept bursting out of him, feelings he couldn't even discuss with anyone, not even with Teresa, because he knew how wrong they would sound to people.

When Aileen Farquar came into work the next day, she checked to see that Donald was in his office, then made some tea. While she waited for the kettle to boil, she sat and tapped her pencil on the desktop, feeling sadder, angrier and more trapped than at any other time in her life.

Donald came out of his office and walked over to the window, and stood silently next to the table with the tea things. Even with Donald there, Aileen thought, the place had a funereal silence about it. Caroline's desk was eerily vacant, but Aileen could still see her there, working, watching everybody who came into the office, especially the men. And how they had come! People who had no real business there, men from other offices, men who had just stopped by on some pretext or another. One day, Aileen had come to work early, and by the time Caroline arrived, she had changed the desks around, so that she was now sitting nearest the door, and Caroline was by the window.

"Orders," Aileen had said, shrugging, and pointed to the inner offices, not indicating Donald's or Mac's in particular. Soon after that, Caroline had found that it hadn't been Mac's idea, and later that Donald had given no such order. Caroline had let her know that she knew, but by then, it wasn't worth fighting about, and anyway the traffic just went past Aileen and headed for the desk nearest the window.

"Well, it's just the two of us now." Donald broke the silence.

"Don't you think Mac'll be back?" asked Aileen.

"I don't know, to tell you the truth." Donald looked old and worried and his hair, usually so meticulously combed, was straggling and unkempt where he had run his hands through it.

"I hope we never see him again," burst out Aileen.

She then told Donald how she'd tried to protect Mac by telling the police that he'd spent the night with her, and tears of anger and embarrassment ran unchecked down her cheeks, and her long blonde hair came together in wet streaks on her face.

In her misery, Aileen remembered with painful clarity when she'd first met Mac. In fact she knew the day, the time, and exactly what she had been wearing. She'd been working for Donald for a few weeks while he was setting up his mail-order business, answering the phone, sending out letters and requests for information. At that time, of course, she was living with her mother, and taking care of her.

Twice she'd tried to leave home when she was younger, once to take up a better job in Edinburgh, and the other when she'd just had enough of Glasgow and her mother, but both times her mother had become so ill that it would have been impossibly cruel to leave her. So Aileen was blocked, although she was not without ability, had a quick mind and a decisive nature.

All this quickness of mind, all her decisiveness had turned to mush when Mac came on the scene. After Donald had interviewed Mac and brought him back to the office, Aileen had fallen in love. Just like that. It had never happened before, partly because of her mother's strictness with her, but also because her first experiences with boys had scared and disgusted her.

She'd heard Donald and this stranger laughing outside the door of the office, and Donald had fumbled with the key, as if he had had altogether too good a lunch.

"Aileen, I'd like you to meet Mac MacFadyen, or should I say *Captain* MacFadyen, who may be coming to join us."

"Everybody calls me Mac," he said, smiling.

Aileen had smiled back, shaken the firm hand, met the strong, friendly gaze, caught a faint trace of the discreet after-shave. She was also dimly aware of his powerful military presence and immaculate clothes, and a slight, well-disguised limp. But the *coup de foudre* had struck, she had fallen in love, though it was quite the last thing she was expecting.

After spending most of the afternoon with Mac, Donald had accompanied him to the door, and came back to Aileen's desk.

"Well, what do you think of him?"

"He seems very nice," replied Aileen, trying to make her voice non-committal, and hoping with all the force and strength of her being that he was indeed going to come back and work with them. Just in case she hadn't sounded enthused enough, she added, "He makes a very good impression, I must say." She knew that Donald needed someone to handle the sales side of the operation.

"That's just what I thought, too," said Donald. "He's got some money and would like to go into a partnership. He was in the Falklands War, got a Military Cross." Donald's usually serious face beamed happily in the reflected glory of Mac's medal. "Between the two of us we'd have the money we need to get things really rolling."

Aileen went home that evening and told her mother that not only had she met the man of her dreams, but that Donald was thinking of moving the business out of Glasgow. Her mother replied by telling her the doctor said she had a cancer of the stomach and wasn't going to live long. Then Aileen considered giving up her job, but the thought of spending every day watching her mother die was unbearable, and also if she did that, she wouldn't see Mac again, so she just soldiered on, coming home to cook and clean, just as she always had, only now she was only cooking for one, because the only food her mother could take was a whitish protein liquid that was injected through a tube into what was left of her stomach.

Mac came into the office several times in the ensuing weeks, sometimes with Donald's accountant, other times with Paul Solon, a corporate lawyer. Paul was just as meticulous as Donald, and insisted on covering every possible aspect of their business relationship, how much they would pay themselves, what the stock division should be, what would happen if they decided to split up.

"It's *essential* to decide that now, before you both sign the partnership agreement," said Paul. "Compared to a business partnership," he said, and he wasn't joking, "marriage is a trivial relationship."

"As we're each putting in a hundred thousand," said Donald, "couldn't we just buy the other one out at that price? I mean, if for some reason Mac wanted to get out, I'd buy his share back for the same hundred thousand he put in."

"Sounds reasonable," said Paul, putting his thumbs behind his wide red braces, "but of course that wouldn't work."

"Too easy," grinned Mac. "You wouldn't get a fee."

"It's not that," replied Paul. He had a fruity, well-educated accent that sounded intrinsically expensive, quite aside from the value of his professional advice. "The partnership will, I trust, be worth a lot more when and if you decide to separate, and to value it at one hundred thousand pounds would be unfair to the seller."

"Or crippling to the buyer, if things didn't go well and it was worth less." Mac shook his head. Going into business sounded a lot more complicated than he had thought.

"So what do we do?" asked Donald.

"And of course," went on Paul, "if one of you wanted to get out, the other might not have the money to buy him out."

"I'm putting in every penny I have," said Mac. "I certainly wouldn't be able to."

"Me neither." Donald was also finding himself a bit out of his depth.

The next day, Paul came accompanied by an insurance agent, who explained how, for a substantial premium, in the event of disabling injury, insanity or death of one of them, the other partner would be covered and the business could go on uninterrupted. It was at that meeting also that they decided to use Perth as their headquarters because the office rentals, and the fire and other insurance rates would be substantially lower than in Glasgow.

Finally, after everything was settled to Paul's satisfaction, they signed the papers, took a lease on an office and part of a warehouse in the center of Perth.

That evening, the three of them, Aileen, Donald and Mac went out for a small celebratory dinner, after which Donald took a taxi home, and Mac offered to drive Aileen back to her house.

"How do you like the idea of moving?" he asked as they drove out of the center of the city. It was raining, and the wipers slashed the windscreen clear from side to side, making the street lights flash and dart and trickle a little distance down the windows with each drop.

"I'm not sure," said Aileen. She told him about her mother, who had been taken to the hospital two days before and was not expected to last till the end of the week. Aileen cried, and Mac was very comforting and kind, and when they got to her house, he put his arm around her in the car and they just sat there for a while. Aileen was almost delirious with happiness; she'd never been really comfortable with a man before, and it was the most wonderful feeling she had ever experienced. Mac went to the funeral with her, and even helped her to find a good estate agent to sell her mother's house, and had kept an eye on the negotiations.

Aileen's anger flared again. Of course he'd kept an eye on things, because all the money would eventually go into his pocket, and from there into his veins. She clenched her fists, but it wasn't until some time later that Aileen realized that that was the moment when her love for Mac had turned into an equally overwhelming hatred.

PART THREE

Chapter 20

Doug and Jamieson were vastly relieved to hear Jean Montrose's quick footsteps coming down the corridor, accompanied by the more sedate steps of the guard.

There was a clink of keys, and the door swung open.

"In here, Doctor," said the guard.

Doug looked up. He was holding Mac's head; Mac had vomited, and the cell was full of the acid stench of it.

"I'm sorry," said Mac, making an effort to sit up. He was a pathetic sight; sweat matted his hair, his face was the color of putty, and a dribble of vomit ran down the side of his mouth.

Jean took one look at him, put her bag on the chair, and took out a slim prepackaged syringe. "Roll up his sleeve, please," she said rather curtly to Douglas, then addressed Mac. "I'm going to give you a shot of morphine, Mac. It'll make you feel better in a few minutes."

"Put it straight into my brain," he whispered, trying to smile.

Jean pinched the muscle just below the shoulder and stuck the needle in. Mac didn't flinch, although Jean noticed that Jamieson did. "It's in your deltoid," Jean told Mac. "It'll get up to your brain in just a few minutes."

She put the syringe back in her bag.

"I've made arrangements for you to be admitted to the Claremount Clinic, Mac," she told him in a calm voice.

"They have a detox program there, one of the better ones in Scotland."

The morphine worked quickly, and after a few minutes, Mac sat up, looking a bit more cheerful. He wiped his lip with his sleeve, and Jean took a couple of paper tissues from her pocket to give them to him.

"Douglas, could I have a word with you?" she said.

Her voice was calm, but to his dismay Douglas could see that Jean was furious. They stood by the door, and Jean's voice was low-pitched so that no one else could hear, but her words were precise and dipped in acid.

"Why did you let him get into that condition?" she asked. "Did you use his dependency to squeeze information out of him?" Doug had never seen Jean so angry, not even when he'd called her to Caroline's flat. But she wasn't finished with him. "And why call *me* out? Why not your police doctor? Do you think I have nothing else to do? I have to leave eight clinic patients to come here, and now I have to go to Claremount with him. Douglas, you're totally inconsiderate, and what's more, you're abusing not only your position but our friendship as well."

And with that, Jean turned on her heel and went back into the cell, leaving Douglas standing there with his mouth hanging slightly open and feeling very abashed.

Jean followed the police car to the Claremount Clinic in her white Renault. Douglas drove very carefully, making sure that Jean didn't get stuck at the traffic lights. He felt quite shaken by Jean's tongue-lashing, but had to admit that she was right on all counts, and he felt very apprehensive, not out of fear that she would turn him in but, because of all the people in the world, he didn't want to loose her friendship, and he knew that at this moment, there was a serious danger that it might happen.

Mac sat quietly in the back, looking straight in front of him. Jamieson sat stolidly next to him, and not a word was spoken until they turned in through the gates of the clinic.

"Stay here," ordered Doug as he pulled up directly outside the main entrance. He saw Jean's car come to a halt beside him.

A male nurse in a white coat came out, and Jean sent him back for a wheelchair. It wasn't only because Mac might not be able to walk up to the admission ward, but she knew that it was much easier to control a man sitting in a wheelchair than one walking along under his own steam.

Mac lost consciousness for a short time in the cell, and in spite of the injection of morphine sulphate that Jean had given him, he felt wound up as tight as a piano wire. He knew that his face was still and expressionless, but everything that happened around him, every noise, every light, screamed at him like a live, malignant being, intent on destroying him. Trying to cope with all this frightening sensory input coming in at him from all sides, Mac was only dimly aware of being placed in the wheelchair, and the rush of lights as he was pushed rapidly along the corridor made him dizzy and sick, and he closed his eyes. That didn't help; in fact it made it worse, because the sounds and sights of the war came back, the explosions, the flashes of his artillery, the face of Sergeant Jock Murphy who'd been standing next to him when he took a fist-sized piece of shrapnel in the chest Mac wanted to shout, to scream, anything to drown out the bubbling sound coming from Jack's chest, but he couldn't do anything, he couldn't even move or make a sound, because they were holding him down, smothering him, and the other animals were coming up right behind them

"We'll give him some methadone as soon as we get upstairs," said the nurse, looking apprehensively at Mac's chalk-white, twitching face. "Dr. Armstrong's up there, thank God."

Jean stayed long enough to make sure Mac was settled and being properly taken care of. She didn't have enormous confidence in psychiatric clinics; her past experience had shown them to be hives of incompetence, cruelty and carelessness behind a mask of sympathy and compassion, but there was nothing she could do about it. There was no alternative to using them, and well they knew it.

After leaving the Claremount Clinic, Doug went back to the offices of Macandon Industries. Aileen was in the outer office, instructing a temp sitting at Caroline's desk. She straightened up when Doug came in. She was wearing a plain but nice-looking blouse and skirt, and it occurred to Doug that Aileen was really quite attractive, with her blonde hair and quick blue eyes, when they weren't weeping.

"I'd like to talk to you for a minute," he said to her. "Is there somewhere private?"

"I'll just be a minute, Morag," Aileen said to the girl, smiling quite composedly, then led the way into Mac's office. "He's not here right now," she said. "Will this do?"

Doug glanced around briefly at the sparsely furnished office. It had only a desk with a telephone, two chairs and a pair of filing cabinets against the wall opposite the window.

"Please sit down," he said. Aileen was about to sit in Mac's chair behind the desk, when Doug said, "*That* chair, please," and pointed at the visitor's chair. Good try, he thought.

"We have a problem, Miss Farquar," he started. He took a copy of her statement to Jamieson out of his pocket. "According to this report, you spent last Thursday evening at home?" He watched her closely, but she seemed perfectly relaxed.

"Right," she said.

"Now, please think very carefully before you answer. Were you alone all that evening?"

Aileen hesitated, then looked him straight in the eye. "No, I wasn't," she said.

"Who was there?" asked Doug. His voice was mild.

"Mac," she replied.

"How long did he stay?"

"May I ask why you have to know?" said Aileen. "It's a personal matter, obviously, and . . ."

"It's like this, Miss Farquar," said Doug, deciding that there was no point in withholding information. "His statement conflicts with yours. He says he left your flat soon after taking you back from dinner. You told Constable Jamieson that he spent the night there, with you." Douglas paused. "Now, Miss Farquar, which version is correct?"

Aileen's hesitation was so brief that Doug might have imagined it. "That's right," she said. "He did leave. He brought me home from the dinner that I paid for, had a cup of coffee, then a small brandy, tried to get some money out of me, then left."

Doug's eyebrows went up at the obvious bitterness in her voice.

"He tried to get money from you?"

Aileen bit her lip. "Yes. He usually does. He was pretty desperate that night, because he was out of cash and needed his fix. I was angry, because so much of my money has gone into his arm, although of course I didn't know it at the time."

"Did you give him any? Money, I mean?"

"I only had five pounds. And that wasn't enough, not by any means."

"Did he tell you what he was going to do?"

"No. He . . . he just said that I wasn't his last resort." Aileen looked so hurt that Douglas felt sorry for her.

"You said you knew he was addicted to drugs, Miss

Farquar. How long have you known that, and how did you find out?"

"It doesn't take a genius," said Aileen. She seemed to be pulling herself together, and her voice was getting stronger. "After I realized it, and it wasn't any one particular thing, just everything came together. I couldn't believe it, and of course the money . . ." Aileen stopped talking, and Doug saw that she was having a hard time holding back her tears. "That was the only thing he wanted from me," she said, looking Doug squarely in the eye, "and once that was gone, he had no use for me at all."

"Did he ever threaten you, or strike you?"

"Not till that last evening, when he found I was broke," replied Aileen. She told him about how Mac had caught her by the hair and hurt her neck by jerking it backward.

"Did you think he was out of control, at that time?" asked Douglas.

"Close," said Aileen. "I certainly wouldn't have wanted to be around him an hour later, if he hadn't had his fix."

"Thank you, Miss Farquar," said Douglas, getting up from Mac's chair, "that will be all, unless you have any questions."

Aileen hesitated for a second. "I must say, I'm a bit afraid," she said. "What if he comes back? Should I answer the door."

"Well you won't have to worry about that," said Douglas, smiling. "I've just come back from taking him to the Claremount clinic. I suppose you've heard of the place?"

"Out on the Blairgowrie Road? I've heard of it. Will they keep him there?"

"Until they get him ready to stand trial, Miss Farquar."

"So you really think he did it, don't you?" Aileen had

a very strange gleam in her eye as she asked the question.

"That is the way all the evidence points at this time, yes, I'm afraid so," replied Douglas, and opened the door to let Aileen out.

Jean woke up early next morning, and right at the front of her mind was the prospect of assisting Peter Macintosh to do Francesca's Caesarean section. She lay quietly in bed for a few minutes, gearing herself to get up and face the day; Steven was still fast asleep. Long ago she'd noticed that when he was asleep, the rhythm of Steven's breathing would slowly get deeper for several breaths, then slow down and almost stop, then off he'd go again. Sometimes, if he fell asleep before her, she couldn't help listening, following the rhythm, and it could keep her awake for quite a while. Jean slowly eased over to the edge of the bed and put one foot out, then the other. There was just enough light for her to see her way to the bathroom. She held her pajama bottoms up with one hand, as wakefulness seeped slowly into her head like a sunrise.

Brushing her teeth, she thought about Francesca, and a cold premonitory feeling came over her. It was so tragic that the girl should be going through this all by herself. That Marco, he was bad news all around; he didn't seem capable of a normal relationship with women. He hated his doting mother, his feelings about Caroline had certainly not been brotherly, and poor little Francesca was treated as if she didn't exist. And that vicious streak of his. Jean had a thought that almost embarrassed her. Could Marco have seriously tried something with Caroline, then killed her? Or found out that she was pregnant? Or even . . . Jean put that last appalling thought out of her mind, and tried to think of other things. But the vision of Caroline's brutally damaged body kept on intruding while she was deciding what to wear. What about Mac? How well had he known her? Could he have had any reason to kill her? Jean pulled on her grey skirt; there was a button missing from the waistband, but she felt pretty sure the hook would keep it from falling down. She sighed, knowing that she should put it in the basket with the other clothes awaiting repair, but then she'd have to repeat some of the tiresome steps of getting dressed. I'll fix it tonight, she thought, giving her tummy a quick pat and taking a quick look in the mirror. Everything looked all right. Nobody was less vain than Jean, and she spent a minimal amount of time on her appearance, but she did like to look presentable. A little grey was reappearing around the temples—time to see her hairdresser again; there was no point waiting for an acid comment from Steven.

Downstairs, there was just enough light to maneuver around. Jean quietly unlocked the back door to let in Alley, their marmalade cat. He ran in as usual and made straight for his saucer, then looked back reproachfully at Jean.

"Just wait!" she said, "I'm coming." She opened the refrigerator for the milk and filled his saucer, then before he had time to complain again, Jean loaded his plate with Kitty Snaks.

Fiona appeared behind her, bleary eyed. "Oh my!" said Jean, starting. "I didn't hear you come up."

"I couldn't sleep," said Fiona, pushing the dark hair out of her eyes. "I keep thinking about Caroline."

A tear appeared on her cheek, and Jean sympathetically wiped it away with a finger. "I know, dear. We're all grieving . . . but we can't let it take us over, you know. There's too much to do out there." Jean waved vaguely in the direction of the outdoors. "Do you want some corn flakes?"

Fiona shook her head. "Just a cup of coffee—I'll make it," she said. "Does Doug know who did it?"

"Did what, dear?" Jean took a healthy serving of corn flakes and poured milk over them.

"Who killed Caroline," replied Fiona. "Doug hasn't been over for a while," she went on. "Did you have a fight with him?"

"Certainly not." Jean took her bowl, balancing it rather precariously, into the dining room because there wasn't room in the kitchen. "I expect he's just very busy."

Fiona persisted. "That never stopped him before," she said.

"He's having to spend a lot of time at home," said Jean. "You know Cathie almost lost her baby."

"She doesn't deserve to have it," said Fiona, her voice sharp. "*I'd* like to have his baby,"

"Don't be silly, dear," said Jean sensibly. "Remember Cathie's his wife, and he picked *her*."

"Well, I'll ask him anyway." Fiona's voice was barely audible and her mother didn't hear her.

Jean stood up, gave her skirt a little twist, then she was ready to go.

"Leave your plate," said Fiona. "I'll take care of the dishes."

The hospital car park was only half full when Jean got there, so she put her car as close to the entrance as possible. She felt lethargic, and even the thought of a walk across the parking lot made her feel tired. She had noticed a long time ago that any unpleasant or unwelcome task had that effect on her, but it never lasted very long.

She stopped for a moment to say hello to the woman at the desk, then took the lift to the third floor operating theaters.

"Good morning, Dr. Montrose." The head nurse took Jean to the nurses' changing room. "The doctors' one is men only, I'm afraid," she said, "but ours is actually nicer."

A few minutes later, Jean, feeling a little strange in a

green shirt and trousers, went into the theater. She hadn't been there for some time, and was very careful not to touch anything that might be sterile.

Peter Macintosh was already scrubbing up, and with an inner sigh of relief Jean saw that his registrar was with him. On the other side of the glass window Jean glimpsed the patient on the operating table, her belly making a grotesque dome under the drapes.

"Morning, Jean," said Peter, over the noise of the running water. "Have you met Dr. Ramasandra?" His registrar grinned and made a small bow to Jean.

"Our young lady in there . . ." Peter grinned through the window and shook his head. "This morning the foetal alarm went off twice, and the baby's heart rate slowed right down. I'm having Dr. Esslemont, the pediatrician, stand by. He's very good with neonates."

"Is Francesca asleep?" asked Jean. "If she isn't, I'd like to say hello."

"She's asleep," replied Peter. "I told her you were coming, and I think that cheered her up a bit."

Jean put on the blue paper hood and tied it behind her neck, then did the same with her mask. She stepped over to the third sink and started to scrub up. She remembered the technique, and lathered well above her elbows, scraped under her nails with an orange-stick, then, for the specified three minutes, used the stiff brush with enough vigor to make her hands and arms pink and tingly. Holding her hands in front of her and away from her shirt, she backed into the theater, where the scrub nurse gave her a sterile towel to dry her hands. Peter and his registrar were already gowned, gloved, and were putting sterile drapes on the patient. A little bassinet stood to one side, awaiting the baby.

"Jean, if you'd like to stand to my left," said Peter when she was fully garbed. Dr. Ramasandra stood opposite ready with the suction and electrocautery probe near his hands.

"Ready, Andrew?" Peter asked the anaesthetist, a portly, middle-aged doctor whose mask he had rather negligently allowed to drop below his nose.

"Ready as she'll ever be," he replied. "I'm keeping her as light as possible, so start slow, huh?"

The yellowish plastic adhesive film over Francesca's belly glowed in the light from the overhead bank of operating lamps. "No fancy Pfannenstiel incisions today," said Peter. "Just a standard down-the-middle. I want to get in and out as fast as we can." He held out his hand and the nurse put a wide-bladed scalpel into it. Very gently, Peter started the incision just below her umbilicus, but the abdomen moved beneath the knife. "She felt that," said Peter, looking over the ether screen at Andrew.

"OK, hold it just a minute," said Andrew. He took a syringe, stuck the needle into the port in the plastic intravenous tubing and pressed on the barrel.

"Try again," he instructed, after about a minute had elapsed.

This time Peter completed the incision without any visible resistance from the patient. Dr. Ramasandra was kept busy clamping the small bleeding vessels, and Peter and he tied off the larger ones and electrocoagulated the smaller ones. The smell from the little wisps of smoke made Jean feel nauseated, but she forgot about it when Andrew said to Peter, "You'd better get moving, the baby's heart is slowing right down." His voice had an unmistakable ring of urgency.

"I'll need the heavy scissors," said Peter, after making a swift opening in the fibrous layer between the abdominal muscles. He put two fingers inside, and with his other hand used the scissors to open the entire lower belly. The uterus was right up against the abdominal wall, red-brown and tense. "Pull on these retractors," he instructed Jean, who leaned back to give him as much

space as possible. "Where's Dr. Esslemont?" he asked
the circulating nurse.

"Right behind you," said a quiet male voice. Out of
the corner of her eye, Jean could see Dr. Esslemont staring at the monitor. "The baby's heart has stopped," he
said.

"Oh damn," said Peter under his breath, and his fingers flew. In a moment, he had grasped the uterus, made
a long cut in it, reached in and pulled out the baby. Jean
got a momentary glimpse of a blue-grey, waxy-looking
infant.

"Oh, my God," said Peter.

The umbilical cord was wound tightly around the
baby's neck. Quickly Peter unwound it, clamped and cut
the cord in seconds, and passed the baby over to Dr.
Esslemont. Nobody said anything, and Jean waited, ago-
nized, for the baby's first wail. It never came.

There was what seemed an interminable period, by
which time Peter, in total silence, had removed the pla-
centa and given an injection to tighten up the slack muscle of the uterus. After several interminable minutes, Dr.
Esslemont's voice was heard from the side of the room
where he had been giving oxygen and trying to make the
baby breathe. Jean looked around. His face was pale beneath the mask, sweat beaded his forehead, and his voice
was not steady.

"No go, I'm afraid," he said.

There was a long silence.

"Give me a heavy Dexon suture for the uterus," said
Peter to the scrub nurse. There was another long silence,
then Peter spoke again, very quietly. "Somebody'd better
go and tell the father."

Chapter 21

Two days after his unsatisfactory confession, Brian Wooley moved from the Kildrummy Arms back to the Bridge Bar, partly because it opened earlier, but also because the barman at the Kildrummy Arms had quietly come around the bar, told him to finish his drink, get out and not come back. Brian hadn't been making a disturbance, he was just making the other customers nervous. Since his visit to Douglas's office, Brian had been drinking almost continuously, moving around from one pub to the other, not even aware that Marco was looking for him. It was clear that whatever demons he'd tried to exorcise were still present and squirming inside his head. Now, Brian lived in a haze in which consternation, fear, and guilt were mixed in an inextricable tangle. Even at the Bridge, though, they were starting to regard him with suspicion, and he had no doubt that soon they too would politely ask him not to come back. Not that he caused any trouble; he just sat and drank, but there was something so solitary about him, about the way he sat alone, with his head down, and was never joined by friends, that the other, normally cheerful and boisterous regulars became uncomfortable. It wasn't a big bar, and they couldn't get very far from him. He looked thin, was unshaven and unkempt, and his long unwashed hair spread in matted clumps over his collar.

The day after Caroline's funeral, Mike Chivas, Brian's old foreman at the garage, came into the Bridge Bar with a couple of friends. He was shocked to see Brian; he couldn't believe that he could have changed so much in so short a space of time. Brian, head down, didn't see him.

"What's he drinking?" Mike leaned over the bar and spoke quietly to the barman, indicating Brian.

The barman shrugged. "Draught lager," he replied, "but I don't think he'd know if it was horse piss. Friend of yours?"

Mike told his friends he'd join them in a few minutes, took his drink and a pint of lager for Brian over to where he was sitting.

"Mind if I sit down?" he asked. Brian looked up for a second. His eyes were red-rimmed.

"It's a free country," he said. Mike sat down, not knowing quite what to say, but wanting to help somehow, and they sat in silence for a minute. Mike pushed the beer toward Brian and raised his own glass.

"Cheers," he said.

Brian sat, immobile, and for a moment Mike wondered if he was going to keel over.

"Brian, is there anything I can do? You were always a good worker until . . . well, until recently. I don't know what happened, and I'd like to help if I can."

Brian looked up again, his eyes unfocused. "Yes," he said, and Mike got the impression that he didn't really know who was talking to him. "Yes, you could do something."

Mike took a long drink, and hoped Brian wasn't going to ask him for money, "Good. What?"

"You could get the fuck away from me," Brian leaned forward and shouted at him, the rage flashing in his eyes. The barman looked up and was about to come round, but Mike shook his head, then got up.

"You know where to reach me," he said to Brian. "I was only trying to help."

He walked over to where his friends were sitting, and

wondered what terrible thing could have happened that had had such a disastrous effect on Brian. He knew that he'd started to get silent and withdrawn a few weeks ago, about the same time as he stopped talking about his girlfriend Caroline, the girl who . . .

"Oh, my God," he whispered to himself, and looked back at the still, bent figure of Brian, sitting all alone again. "Oh, my God!"

After the operation was over and Francesca had been taken to the recovery room, Jean came out of the operating suite hoping to find Marco in the waiting room, but instead she found Bob, Francesca's father-in-law, sitting there anxiously, trying to read a newspaper. He stood up as soon as Jean came in and came over to meet her. "How is she? Is she all right?" Seeing Jean's expression, he gripped her arm. "Please, don't tell me something went wrong."

"Where's Marco?" asked Jean, because really he was the first one she should give the bad news to.

Bob shrugged, but his anxious eyes didn't leave Jean's face for a moment. "Who knows? I've hardly seen him since Caroline died. Is Francesca all right?" He looked as if one more piece of bad news would do for him, so Jean made him sit down beside her.

"Francesca's all right," she said, although she knew that was not strictly true. "But the baby was born dead. I'm terribly sorry."

Jean put an arm around Bob's shoulders, expecting him to break down completely, but instead he said, "As long as Francesca's all right—the baby . . . To tell you the honest truth, Jean, maybe it's just as well that it happened this way."

"Where can I reach Marco? Is he at the restaurant?" Jean wanted to talk to him, to try to convince him to take better care of his wife. She would need help and comfort even more now she'd lost the baby.

"I don't know where he is," replied Bob. His eyes were full of tears, and he had the dazed look of a man being beaten over the head by an assailant he couldn't see. Jean held his big, wrinkly old hand tight.

He hesitated a moment, trying to find his voice. "I've seen him a couple of times in the street," he said, "just walking up and down, and he looks so wild. I honestly don't know, Jean. What did we do that made everything go so wrong?"

"You didn't do anything wrong," said Jean. "On the contrary, you brought them both up as best you could, just like we all do," Jean was thinking of Fiona and Lisbie, and thanking God they'd never caused her and Steven any real problems, though of course there had been times when they had both given them cause for worry.

Bob got up, and dabbed his eyes with his handkerchief. "I'll try to find Marco," he said, "and tell him to get in touch with you. Thanks, Jean, you're very kind, and I really appreciate it."

Jean watched Bob walk toward the door. He seemed to have aged ten years in as many minutes.

Jean went back to the recovery room to see how Francesca was faring.

"Her temp's down a bit," said Andrew Milne, the anaesthetist, who was looking very subdued, "and her blood pressure's swinging around, but that's what you get with pre-eclamptics. Otherwise she's doing all right. I'm holding off on giving her blood for a while. Maybe she won't even need it."

Francesca was looking as pale as a ghost, partly because of the lack of makeup. Jean remembered the first time she saw her; she'd just arrived from Italy with Marco, and she looked as pretty and bright and lively as anybody she'd ever seen.

Jean reached for her hand, lying limp, the same color as the sheet. The IV line ran into a vein on her thin little arm, and the veins were blue on the back of her hand. Francesca opened her eyes; they flickered rapidly, not seeing anything. She closed them again, and Jean pressed her hand then left quietly, feeling a guilty relief that Francesca hadn't been awake enough to ask questions.

"Did you remember you have a lunch date today?" asked Eleanor, looking up from the office diary. She had that superior tone of voice that always annoyed Jean.

"No, I didn't," she replied.

"Teresa Tarland," answered Eleanor. "At the Theater restaurant, at one."

"Oh dear," said Jean, almost to herself. She hesitated; the last thing she wanted to do after the events of the evening was have a social chitchat with anyone, even Teresa, but she had promised Steven, and also there were certain things she urgently wanted to discuss with Teresa Tarland. "Thanks, Eleanor. Now if you'd get me the list of home visits, I'd appreciate it. You know I like you to have it ready when I come in."

Eleanor reached for the appointment book, grumbling under her breath.

"Is that a problem?" asked Jean sharply.

"I can't do everything at once," mumbled Eleanor. Jean was about to make another comment when Helen came out of her office with a letter in her hand.

"Jean, this report came in from the Dundee bacteriology lab," she said. "It was addressed to you, but Eleanor put it in with my mail and I opened it. Sorry." She held it out to Jean.

It was a copy of the report to Malcolm Anderson on the bacteriological cultures taken from the body of Caroline Fraser, including the ones she'd specifically asked him to take, and Jean's heart sank as she read it. An additional problem was that it wouldn't mean anything to Dr. Anderson, so he couldn't do anything about it.

*   *   *

Just before one o'clock, Jean left the surgery and headed for the restaurant. It was on High Street, only a few minutes' brisk walk away. The morning was unusually fine for this time in Spring, and Jean wondered if they were going to have another hot summer like the last one. She shivered at the memory of the horrors that had accompanied that awful heat wave. She walked quickly up William Street, and waited for a break in traffic before crossing South Street. She saw a figure hurrying along the pavement toward her, and realized that it was Marco. She turned and caught him by the sleeve as he passed. He swung around like a snake, raising his arm at the same time, then dropped it when he saw who it was.

"Dr. Montrose, I'm sorry. I thought . . ."

Jean interrupted him, her voice urgent. "Have you been to the hospital, Marco?"

"My father told me," said Marco, lowering his eyes, but Jean could sense the rage in him.

"Marco, would you come and see me in the surgery this afternoon, after three? I really need to talk to you about several things."

"I don't know," muttered Marco. He shuffled his feet. "I'm rather busy this afternoon "

"Marco, please! It's really important. Important for you." It was the tone of Jean's voice rather than what she said that caught his attention, and he looked up at her with a question in his eyes.

"All right, then. Three o'clock," he said reluctantly, and hurried off. Jean crossed the road, wondering if he would actually come. He was such an erratic, unreliable person that she certainly couldn't count on his promise.

Teresa was already sitting at a table, and waved at her when Jean came in.

"My goodness, what a morning!" said Jean, flopping gratefully into the chair next to Teresa, who was looking her usual elegant and attractive self in a green and white striped silk shirt and summery white skirt. "You look wonderful. You'd think, the way I run around, I'd have a figure like yours."

"If you ate nothing but lettuce and carrots and felt hungry every minute like me,"said Teresa, smiling, "you would."

"Well, luckily Steven likes me the way I am," said Jean, picking up the menu. "At least that's what he tells me."

"Donald and I watch each other's weight," Teresa said in her firm way. "Just a couple of extra pounds, and we can make life hell for each other."

"What are you having?" asked Jean.

"Caesar salad," said Teresa. With a sudden recollection of the morning's operation, Jean wondered at the number of things Caesar had named after him.

"Well, I think I'll have the special lunch," said Jean, folding the menu hurriedly.

"Beef noodle soup, shepherd's pie, followed by caramel custard," read Teresa, grinning. "Do you want a calorie count on that? I taught Donald how to do it, and now he ruins everybody's meals with his calculations."

"I didn't have much breakfast," said Jean. "And stop flaunting your skinny bones at me."

"Did Donald remember to tell Steven about the brunch next Sunday? I think you'll enjoy it. We're having a couple of dozen people over, including Ken Oasaka, the new conductor of the Edinburgh Symphony, and Denis Price, or, I should say *Sir* Denis Price, who owns the Hillshire Hotels, is coming with Celia. I don't know about Ken, I understand he doesn't speak much English, but the Prices are such a lovely couple. Do you know them?"

"I know who they are, but I've never met them. Teresa, where do you find all those people? You've been here just over a year, and all the crème is already beating a path to your door!"

"Donald has a lot of contacts, you know," Teresa replied rather vaguely. "And we like to meet new people."

"Well, I'd hate to have to pay your food and drink bills," said Jean, smiling.

"Well, I say, when you've got it, share it," said Teresa.

"The business is doing well, so we don't see any sense in living like hermits."

"How's Donald faring?" asked Jean. "Caroline's death must have come as an awful shock to him."

"He's been terribly upset," said Teresa. "He really liked Caroline, and she did a very good job. It's a small office and everybody's very close, so it was like having a death in the family."

Teresa hesitated. "It's been especially tough on Donald," she went on, "because that's not all that's been happening at the office." Teresa's lips tightened. "Everything's falling apart there. Mac . . . Well, the police are pretty sure that he was the one who killed Caroline." Teresa glanced around. "They're just waiting for him to come out of the clinic, then they're going to charge him with the murder."

Teresa leaned forward, her voice pitched so that only Jean could hear her. "Do *you* think he could have killed her? Apparently he went up to her flat, and she let him in—somebody said she'd have let anybody in, as long as it was a man—but I don't believe that for a moment. Anyway, he wanted money for drugs, and she didn't give it to him, so . . . Did you know they found the knife? From his own kitchen set, apparently."

The waitress came to take their order, and the conversation was interrupted, but, watching Teresa, Jean could tell by the set of her facial muscles and the quick movements of her hands how upset she was in spite of the effort she made trying to look calm and collected.

"I'm sure it was all the result of his addiction," said Teresa. "That'll get him off, won't it? Like a plea of insanity, or something like that? I certainly hope so." As she talked, Teresa nibbled the crust of her roll, and watched Jean with her big eyes, looking, thought Jean, smiling to herself, like a junior schoolgirl having lunch with the head prefect.

After Jean's soup and Teresa's salad arrived, Jean mentioned that she'd seen Marco in the street. "You and Donald have sort of adopted him, haven't you?" she asked.

"He's really a very nice boy, under all that anger and resentment," answered Teresa. "When he's feeling rough, he comes and talks things over with Donald and me, and that seems to calm him down. And he likes to help me in the garden, so it's good for everybody."

"Does he mention Francesca to you?" asked Jean curiously.

"Hardly ever. Donald and I both tried to get him to act a bit more responsibly with her, but he feels he's in a trap he can't get out of, and can't bear to be in the same room with her."

"He should have thought of that before he married her," said Jean, rather tartly. It was amazing that the Tarlands, who were so meticulous about the correctness of their own behavior, should be so tolerant and kind with Marco. They didn't have any children of their own, so maybe they regarded him as a kind of son although they weren't that much older than him, maybe twelve or fifteen years. Of course Teresa, being a psychologist, would understand his motivations, but Jean wondered if Teresa and Donald fully realized how violent and disturbed Marco was. She decided to find out. "The thought had crossed my mind, Teresa," she said, pausing for a moment before attacking the shepherd's pie, "that Marco might have had something to do with Caroline's death."

Teresa's mouth opened in horror. "Jean! You can't possibly mean that! Caroline was his *sister*!"

Jean nodded apologetically. "Teresa, of course you're

right. Sometimes I get really weird ideas, and all those possibilities float around in my mind. Anyway he's coming to the surgery this afternoon—I hope."

Teresa changed the subject, but Jean could see that she had been deeply shocked by her suggestion. It crossed Jean's mind for a second that if Teresa and Donald did understand Marco's violent potential, they might be at risk by extending their friendship to him, and she decided to ask Doug later what his thoughts were about that.

Teresa was asking about Jean's roses.

"I need to do something to hide the wall at the side of my kitchen," she said. "I'd like to put in one of those old-fashioned climbing multifloras like you have on your end wall."

"That would look great," said Jean, glad of the change in topic. "But they're rather slow growing, and they'd take years to cover that wall. There are other variables   I got a catalogue in the post last week that had a whole lot of them. And maybe you could put some hollyhocks in front of them while they're growing   "

They chatted about their gardens for a while, then Jean looked at her watch.

"I have to run," she said. They divvied up the bill, and each left a tip under the saucer.

"See you next week?" asked Teresa.

"Next week's going to be difficult," replied Jean. "But I'll phone you."

Jean gave Teresa a hug as they parted at the street door, then she ran across the High Street. She really liked Teresa, who was interesting and when she stopped being prim and sanctimonious, could be slyly funny about the people she knew. Going to their house always made Jean feel domestically incompetent; everything was always in its proper place, their furniture looked as if it had just come out of the showroom, and it was obvious that no speck of dust would have the audacity to alight anywhere near their house.

Jean stopped at the French pastry shop and bought half a dozen croissants to take back to the surgery. At the back of her mind was a nagging worry about the Tarlands' relationship with Marco. Maybe they *could* calm him down, but on the other hand he could easily get angry with them for some reason, then they would become the target for one of his dangerous rages.

Jean turned the corner into William Street, thinking about the Tarlands and the brunch Teresa was having next Sunday. They were such a social pair . . . Jean loved to entertain too, but most of her friends tended to be rather easy-going like herself, and were more likely to drop in for pot-luck than expect the elaborate candlelit dinners with seating places that the Tarlands liked to put on.

But, of course, Jean and Steven had lived in Perth much longer than the Tarlands, and didn't feel the pressure to establish themselves in that kind of way.

Jean hurried along William Street, and thought of Teresa's attractive and slender figure with a touch of envy, but all that vanished as soon as she stepped back into the surgery.

Chapter 22

Douglas Niven came over to the Montroses' house that evening, after phoning to see if Fiona was going to be home. He wanted to talk to her about Caroline, if that was all right with her, but he also wanted to mend his bridges with Jean, who had not spoken to him when they left the clinic.

"He can talk to me about anything in the world," said Fiona, coming back to the table

"Except babies," taunted Lisbie from the other side of the table.

"Even about that, under certain circumstances," replied Fiona, and met Steven's and Jean's shocked gazes with a stubborn expression.

"That's not funny," said Steven. "And I suggest, young lady, that you take your attentions elsewhere. He's a married man, and that's that."

"I seem to remember something about you and a young lady by the name of Miss Blaikie. . . ." retorted Fiona.

"That's enough, Fiona!" snapped Jean angrily. She rarely got upset with either of her daughters, but she certainly was now. She glowered at Fiona. "That's a topic I will not have discussed here, and that's final!"

"Sorry, Mum." Fiona had spoken before thinking how her words would hurt her mother, and she was really contrite. Steven blushed a bright red and scowled fiercely at Fiona, but said nothing.

"Anyway, here he is," said Lisbie, who had heard Doug's car stop outside. Fiona got up hurriedly and went out to meet him. Steven, still furious, wouldn't meet Jean's eye. That whole miserable episode, which occurred when Jean was so busy with the Lumsden baby business, was long behind him, and although he and Jean had made up without apparent residual scars, he was finding out that his children had long and accurate memories, and had no inhibitions about voicing their opinions.

A few moments later, Fiona appeared at the dining room door hanging on to Doug's arm.

"I'm going to borrow your daughter for a little while," he said, smiling a bit sheepishly, and watching Jean's face to see if she was still angry with him.

"Why don't you keep her?" asked Lisbie. "She doesn't eat too much, and she's house trained."

"I wish I could say the same about you," Fiona flashed back.

"Use the morning room," said Jean, "nobody'll bother you there." Her voice was crisp, and there was a slight flush to her face. She did not look happy, and Douglas decided she was still thinking about Mac and still angry about being called out to see him.

"And scream if she attacks you," Lisbie called out. "We'll come in and rescue you."

In the morning room, Fiona became very quiet and sat demurely on the sofa. She wasn't looking forward to being grilled about her friend Caroline. Douglas sat down in Steven's big green easy chair.

"Well, Fiona, you know I widna bother you, especially when it's about your friend, but I need your help."

Fiona's big dark eyes studied Doug. He had a rather young, smooth-skinned, innocent-looking face, triangular in outline, and wore the old-fashioned round National Health glasses that gave him an air of mild astonishment, sometimes even alarm. His hair was short, bristly and of an indeterminate color, with the slightest touch of grey at the temples. It looked as if he'd touched them up to make himself look older.

Fiona had always had a crush on him, since he came to Perth from Glasgow as a newly fledged Detective Inspector a few years before. At that time, Jean, who knew everybody, had helped him find his way around, and they had been friends ever since. The only faintly discordant note was that Fiona professed not to like Cathie Niven, but everybody thought that was just funny, including Cathie and even Fiona herself, sometimes.

"We're trying to find who killed Caroline," Doug said, pulling out his notebook. "You were probably her best friend, so I think you may be able to help. And don't look at me like that. I have to be able to concentrate."

He grinned at her.

"What can I tell you?" asked Fiona. "I don't know anything everybody else doesn't know. Anyway, I thought you'd found out that it was Mr. MacFadyen who did it."

"Well, Fiona, there's a difference between knowing something and being able to prove it. We're pretty sure, aye, but we hae to convince a judge and a jury. And that's no as easy as you might think. "

"I'm still very upset," said Fiona, and her voice shook for a second.

"Do you know if Caroline was seeing anybody? I mean a man?"

"I don't know, Doug. She . . . well, you know that she'd gone around with a few men in her time. She never stayed very long with any of them."

"Let's see, now," said Douglas, prompting. "There was that young mechanic chap, Brian Wooley, for a start."

"No," said Fiona, "there were a few before him. But Brian was really nice," said Fiona. "We all went out a few times together. Was he in love! He couldn't take his eyes off her."

"What happened?"

"Well, Caroline was . . . she was very pretty, you know, and wanted something better. Brian was very nice and she really liked him, but he wasn't ever going to be able to buy her a Jaguar or a big house."

"So she dumped him?"

"Yes, I suppose so. I didn't hear exactly what happened."

"When was that, now?" Doug's pen was poised over his notebook.

"A couple of months ago, maybe a bit more. I'm not sure."

"Who replaced Brian? Was it Mac?"

"I don't know if anybody did. Caroline sort of acted a bit coy, and even hinted she might get married, but I've known her a long time, and she'd never want you to think she didn't have anybody."

"Did she get Marco to beat Brian up?"

"No. That was terrible. What happened was that Brian kept following her around and spying on her, and that really got her mad, because she'd told him in no uncertain terms to get lost."

Douglas listened carefully, and with an automatic gesture pulled out a cigarette packet from his breast pocket. It had been months since he'd smoked one, but he still carried the packet with a single dried out old cigarette, as a kind of talisman. He looked at the packet with an expression of surprise, then put it back.

"So she told Marco?"

"No, not till . . . Apparently one night Brian was caught peeping into her flat from a flat roof opposite. He'd gone up a drainpipe or a fire escape or something. Anyway somebody below heard the footsteps and called the police. He wasn't charged, but Marco got to hear about it, and that's when he came after him. That's what Caroline told me, anyway."

"Tell me a bit about Marco and her." Douglas sat back in the chair. Fiona shifted around, looking embarrassed.

"You know Marco had a thing about her?"

Douglas said nothing but his expression encouraged her to talk.

"He watched her all the time, too. Not like Brian; I don't mean he'd go up fire escapes and all that, but he was very jealous. He always wanted to know where she was, who she was with. That was the main reason she wanted a flat of her own, to get away from that."

"After Brian," asked Doug carefully, "do you think it could have been Mac MacFadyen?"

"He certainly doesn't seem like somebody who'd kill anybody, especially a woman. He's so . . . well, so cheerful and good-natured sounding. But you never know," said Fiona, sounding very wise. "I know Caroline went out two or three times with him, nothing serious I didn't think at the time, but for some reason . . . I don't know, but I wondered about that, because a couple of times she said something about being held up at the office, and she, well, you know, had that look." Fiona grinned at him. "It's something a woman would understand better."

"When was the last time you saw her?"

Fiona's eyes filled with tears, and she wiped them away with the back of her hand. "Two days before she was killed. We went to the Isle of Skye for a drink."

"Did you meet anyone you knew?"

"Not a soul. We didn't even stay that long." Fiona was remembering that Caroline had been anxious to go home. Was she planning on meeting somebody, or was she going somewhere else?

"Did she say that she was seeing anybody?"

"You already asked me that. No, she didn't."

Douglas tried a different tack. "Do you know Aileen Farquar, who works at Macandon?"

"Slightly. I'd know her if I saw her. Quite nice-looking, dresses well, but a bit spinstery, right?"

Douglas wasn't about to touch that one. "Did they get on well? I mean, Caroline and Aileen?"

"Not too well, I don't think, just from what Caroline used to say about her. Aileen apparently had a terrible thing about Mac, and sometimes made life rough for Caroline, because she thought she was trying to steal him."

"Do you think she was?"

"Caroline? I doubt it. That wasn't her style. More likely she'd be making eyes at him just to get Aileen mad. But then, if they did go out . . . I mean Caroline and Mac . . . Doug, I honestly don't know what to say. Ask Mac."

Douglas checked the list of people he had intended to ask Fiona about. He covered Brian Wooley, Marco, Mac, and there still remained the Tarlands and Caroline's parents. He duly asked her about them, but Fiona didn't know much about any of them.

"Well, that's about all, then, Fiona," he said, flipping the elastic band over his notebook. "Shall we go back into the living room?"

"Yes. I'll make some tea. By the way, did you ever think that Caroline could have been killed by some lunatic who tried to come in and rape her? I mean somebody she didn't know and who didn't know her?"

"Yes, we considered that, Fiona," said Doug, getting up, "but I don't think it's likely. She let whoever it was into the flat, and there was no robbery. No . . ." Douglas took off his glasses and rubbed them on the front of his shirt. "It was somebody she knew well, and I would guess, intimately."

Back in the living room, the mood was lighter. Lisbie was telling Steven and Jean about the new partner who'd replaced Roderick Ferguson in the law office she worked in. "He's called Ivan. Ivan Aribal. His father's from Argentina, I think. So of course everybody calls him Ivan the Terrible, but he's really just a cuddly pussy-cat of a man, with a lovely smooth skin and a big moustache that looks as if it was stuck on." Lisbie put a down-curled finger under her nose, put her head back, and did a quick impersonation of her new boss. "Anyway, he's taken Mac on as a client, because Mr. Imrie doesn't like getting involved in criminal stuff. As if half of his nice clean business clients weren't doing criminal stuff. . . . Oh, Doug!" she said when he came into the room behind Fiona. "Did you know Mr. Aribal's thinking of suing the police for wrongful arrest on behalf of Mac MacFadyen?"

"That's a load o' rubbish," said Doug crossly. "And if that's something you heard in your office, doesn't that make it confidential?" He was not amused by the kind of shenanigans that some of the once-staid Perth lawyers got up to these days. They just made the police's job that much more difficult.

"How's Cathie today?" asked Jean hurriedly. "I didn't get a chance to stop by."

"Och, she's fine now. I hope you'll let her do a little bit around the house soon. Doing nothing doesn't suit her."

"It's just that you don't like vacuuming," said Lisbie. "Tell the truth," Everybody laughed, including Doug.

He left after a cup of tea, and as he drove homeward down Argyll Place, he went over what Fiona had told him about Caroline. Somewhere in all that talk, he felt instinctively, there was something that put a different light on the case.

He turned at the bottom of the hill, and switched on the radio, but he didn't hear the music. He was worried about Jean. As long as he'd known her, she'd had a calm, composed personality even in the face of the most stressful events. And now, in the space of a couple of days, she had lashed out at him twice in a really aggressive way. It wasn't that he didn't deserve it, that wasn't what was bothering him. It was just that it was so uncharacteristic of her.

Chapter 23

Aileen Farquar opened her clothes cupboard and pulled a chair up. She climbed up on to it, a little stiffly, and reached up to the back of the high shelf above her dresses and coats. The round hatbox with the thick blue stripe around it was at the back, and after sliding it forward and pushing the lid off, she rummaged inside. The gun was wrapped in a rag, and she climbed down, holding it tight. Inside the rag was another, oily, rag and she unwound that with a feeling of apprehension, as if she were slowly taking the wrappings off a mummy. The blue metal of the barrel had a brownish tinge in the recesses, where the oil had turned into a thick gum. With a strange feeling of dread, Aileen hefted the gun in her hand. It was heavy, but not as heavy as when she'd last held it. The gun, a .38 Smith and Wesson revolver, had belonged to Aileen's father, a captain during Word War Two. Gingerly holding the weapon, she remembered watching him sitting in a chair at the kitchen, holding it in both hands. He would push down a little lever near the root of the barrel, and the gun would break. Then he'd spin the cylinder, check each one of the chambers, peer along the inside of the barrel, aiming it at the light above the table so he could clearly see the rifling of the bore. Then he'd shown her, over her mother's objections, how to take the gun apart, clean it, then coat each part with a thin oil before reassembling it. Then he

wrapped it up and put it away in the same hatbox, on the
top shelf, out of her reach.

The bullets . . . Aileen went back up on the chair.
There they were, heavy in a grey-brown box of thick
cardboard, also wrapped carefully in a rag. She took one
out and examined it. The brass casing was dull, and the
rounded lead bullet would expand when it hit, and that
was just what she wanted. Her father had explained that
too, but all she remembered was that it had something to
do with the shape and it had some other kind of metal on
the inside. For the next hour, Aileen worked in a kind of
daze, cleaning the old gummy oil off, pulling a rag
soaked in her sewing machine oil through the barrel. She
even polished the brass cartridge casings with Brasso
until they gleamed. By the time she finished, her father
would surely have approved of her work.

Brian Wooley only dimly remembered the hand falling
on his shoulder as he sat in the Bridge Bar, and even
more dimly stumbling out, propelled by the pressure of a
strong arm. Then the stumbling run across the car park,
the lights dancing wildly inside his head. Brian was
pushed hard against the side of a car parked in the far
corner of the bar's car park. It was dark, but not too dark
for Brian to recognize Marco's slight but muscular figure. Marco was holding him by the collar, pushing
against his throat, and Brian was helpless. There was
something about Marco, something about the power of
his rage that paralyzed Brian, as it had in the past.

"You killed her, didn't you, you little fuck?" Marco's
voice was soft, but tight and sibilant as a snake's.

Brian couldn't breath, and tried to push the hands
away. He made a choking noise, and Marco loosened his
grip fractionally. Brian gulped and shook his head. His
eyes wouldn't focus, but he knew he was in deadly danger. Marco had tried to maim him before, and that was
before Caroline's death.

Before Brian could say anything, Marco pounced on him again, bending his head back over the bonnet of the car. His rage was so powerful it seemed to envelop him in an explosive cloud. Brian thought his neck was going to break, and his knees buckled and he slid down to the ground. Marco took a swift aim at his ribs and kicked him hard, but in the dark he missed, hitting him in the shoulder with a cracking thud.

"Before I kill you," he said, "I want to hear it from you. The truth!" He aimed another kick, which connected just where he wanted it to. Brian gasped with the pain, and couldn't breath. The lights on the bridge flickered and swam in front of him and he thought he was going to die right there and then.

Marco caught him by the jacket and pulled him up.

"No!" gasped Brian. His legs buckled again, but Marco held him up. Maybe it was the jolt of terror inspired by Marco, but for the first time Brian was able to remember what had happened the night Caroline died. "I saw the car," he said, forcing the words out. "It stopped outside her flat. . . ."

After Brian told him what he'd seen, Marco's fury seemed to redouble.

"Why didn't you tell the police?" he asked, his face right up against Brian's.

"I didn't remember until now," croaked Brian. "I thought maybe I did it . . . I just wanted to see her, that's all."

"You wanted to see her undress, didn't you?" Marco's fist struck Brian's nose and cheek with a crunch, but Brian hardly felt it. He was back up on the roof with his binoculars, watching Caroline open the door to her visitor.

"No," said Brian miserably. He could feel his face puffing up where Marco had struck him. "I just wanted to see her, I loved her. . . ."

The fist hit him again. "Don't say that word," shouted Marco. "You don't even know what it means!"

Brian felt his mouth filling with blood. He took a breath and spat a tooth in Marco's face with a desperate defiance, and that was the last thing he remembered.

Jean drove fast, and was at the hospital in just under fifteen minutes. She hurried up to the Intensive Care Unit; Bob and Louise Fraser were sitting anxiously on a bench outside and stood up when she approached.

"What happened?" asked Jean.

"We don't know. The first thing we heard was a doctor who phoned, but I couldn't understand all what he was saying," said Louise.

"Nor could I," said Bob. "She gave me the phone. I think he's Indian, maybe." He looked at Louise for confirmation.

Her anxiety made her features old and harsh. "Anyway, of course we came as soon as we could," she said.

There was a small group around the second bed on the left, and Jean headed straight for it. Francesca looked smaller than ever, and had a transparent greenish oxygen mask on her face; it was hissing with the volume of oxygen going through it. Jean came up and took her hand. Francesca's neck muscles tensed every time she took a breath and her nostrils dilated. She smiled at Jean, but it took a huge effort, and she couldn't sustain it. Peter Macintosh was there, at the end of the bed and looking very grim, with his registrar and the houseman, one on either side of him, and one of the ICU nurses.

"She's had a pulmonary embolus, Jean," said Peter. "A big one. I'm afraid there isn't a great deal we can do. We put her on heparin . . ." He shrugged his shoulders.

Jean's throat tightened, and she grasped Francesca's hand hard. A pulmonary embolus meant that a clot had formed probably in the veins of her pelvis, and detached and travelled up into her lungs. Without another word, Peter and his retinue left, followed by the nurse.

Jean pulled a chair up and sat down at the side of the bed. Francesca reached for her hand and held it tightly. She tried to say something, but didn't have the breath, and lay there panting for a while, trying to summon up her strength.

Jean talked quietly to her, and her presence obviously comforted Francesca, because the fear went out of her eyes, and her breathing became marginally easier.

"I'm going to die," she said.

"Francesca! Of course you're not. You have to think about getting better." Jean could feel her own heart beating fast, and she tried to smile encouragingly at Francesca.

"Jean, that's all I want, now." Francesca tried to sit up, but the effort was too much for her. A tear rolled down her cheek and she flopped back on the pillow, exhausted. After a minute she recovered enough to speak, but she had to pause for breath after every two or three words.

"Please understand . . . I'm glad, Jean . . . I'm happy to be dying because . . . my life is over anyway." She smiled at Jean again, and the fear had gone from her eyes. "I was . . . I was afraid that I might live and . . . just be ill," she went on. Jean could see that Francesca was getting rapidly weaker, and the heart monitor above the head of the bed was showing signs of irregular beats.

"Would you like Bob and Louise to come in?" Jean asked softly. "They're both outside."

"No," whispered Francesca, and her hand fluttered. It was china-white and so small and frail it brought tears to Jean's eyes. "Please stay for a while."

Jean stayed until Francesca fell asleep, then tiptoed out of the room. Bob and Louise had gone.

Jean remembered guiltily that she hadn't been to see her mother for two days, and although it was getting late, she drove back across the bridge, stopped off at Marks and Spencer's to pick up a fruit cake and a bottle of Beaujolais, then went on to Barossa Place. She parked outside the nursing home, looked at her watch, and hoped that back home one of the girls would be making dinner. They were used to her coming home late, sometimes very late, and both knew how to rustle up a quick meal. Years ago, Jean had taught them how a perfectly satisfactory dinner could be made in minutes from mince, tomato sauce and spaghetti, or their favorite, a casserole made by defrosting the frozen cod steaks she always had on hand, and popping them into the oven after emptying a tin of cream of mushroom soup over them. Steven always knew whether Jean was home from the smells emanating from the kitchen.

Mrs. Findlay was sitting up in bed reading the *Courier and Advertiser* when Jean came in.

"Well," she said, putting the paper down, "where have you been? I told the nurses you were probably busy finding out who killed that girl, and that's why you didn't have time to come here."

"No, Mother, I don't do that kind of thing any more." Jean smiled, and kissed her on the cheek. "There's a perfectly good police force to do that, thank you. I've just been busy."

"It says here that they're closing in on the killer," said Mrs. Findlay, nodding at the paper. "They always say that, and they always arrest the wrong person."

Jean put the fruit cake on the bedside table and the bottle in the cupboard by the window.

"Have you had supper?" she asked.

"If that's what you call that disgusting stuff they serve, yes, I have. It was spaghetti and some kind of tomato sauce all mixed up with mince . . . ugh!"

"That's what you would have had at home," said Jean cheerfully. "I hope the girls got home before Steven. He hates having to wait for dinner."

"It's really terrible," said Mrs. Findlay, fixing her daughter with a censorious eye. "The poor man works all day, comes home, and has to make his own supper. He should have married somebody who stayed at home and took care of him. Heaven knows what the poor man's socks and shirts look like."

Jean sighed. "Sit forward a bit, Mother, and I'll fluff up your pillows. Steven has the cleanest socks and the best-ironed shirts in town, I'll have you know."

"Thanks to Mrs. Cattanach," snapped her mother. "A good cleaning lady doesn't make up for not having a wife."

"Mother, I'm sure you're right." Jean looked at her watch. "Well, I have to run," she said, and headed for the door. "See you tomorrow. Lisbie said she'd stop in after work tomorrow too."

Mrs. Findlay said something, but Jean was already closing the door behind her. Driving home, she felt tense and guilty about her mother, but she had too many worries and so many other things to do, and really she couldn't stand her invariably critical comments for more than a few minutes at a time.

Chapter 24

Mac was feeling worse than he'd ever felt in his life. His stomach was cramping, and the medicine he'd been given made him not only woozy, but gave him a dry mouth that no amount of water could slake. They had taken away his clothes and his luggage, no doubt to search for illicit drugs. The worst was the dreams, that weren't really dreams, but events that blended with what he recognized as reality until the picture on the wall opposite his bed, a peaceful scene with several highland cattle knee deep in a stream, came to life, and the cattle climbed out of the picture and came menacingly toward him, changing their shapes into the most fearful of twisted monsters. He was drenched with sweat, and had a dreadful feeling that he was a violin, and somebody was tightening the strings, tightening them until he knew he would break . . . He screamed a co}ple of times, and the first time the white-jacketed nurse gave him an injection which made him sleepy but didn't help his other symptoms, and a feeling of sheer terror kept creeping up on him until he knew he was going to go mad. They always said that the first three days were the worst, but he had no idea how long he'd been there. It seemed as if his entire life had been spent in that room, between those walls that kept closing in on him. When he asked what day it was, the nurses told him, but he forgot instantly, and so he'd keep on asking until they stopped answering.

"For the last time, it's Sunday morning," said a thin

male nurse who flitted around the room, sometimes changing into a horse, when Mac would brace himself, waiting for him to rear up and fall back on him.

A little later, the door opened as he was groaning and moving around in his bed, and a nurse with a dark blue cloak over her uniform came in, closing the door behind her.

"Oh, God," said Mac, "give me something to make me feel better, please, nurse. I'm going mad. . . ."

Even in his pain, Mac noticed something familiar about the nurse, particularly her curly golden-blonde hair, but it wasn't until she turned toward him that he recognized the face. He tried to scream, but his terror was such that only soundless air came out. The last thing Mac ever heard was the sound of a gun exploding next to his head, muffled by the pillow that the nurse held over it with her other hand.

The morning was perfect for having the brunch outside, so about ten Teresa instructed the caterers to put the trestle tables up on the lawn outside the back of her house, where everyone could have a good view down to the river bank. Soon gaily colored parasols were in position over the tables, and a gentle breeze momentarily lifted the folded corners of the white linen tablecloths.

Donald was nervous as he always was before a party, and fussed and wandered around the kitchen. "Where's the band?" he asked, looking at his watch. "Shouldn't they be here? I'll go and phone "

"They're not due for another hour," said Teresa patiently. "There's no point having them standing around and eating the provisions."

"That reminds me," said Donald, easing his tie, "do you think we should have got two cases of red wine? We have two of white."

"People drink more white," replied Teresa, with a tone

of finality. "And now I suggest you leave everything to the people we're paying to take care of it."

Teresa, though she didn't show it as obviously as Donald, was also nervous. There were going to be a lot of important people coming, and she had the perfectionist's urge to check every little thing. And, of course, she did have other things on her mind.

When Jean and Steven arrived, Jean in a pretty flowered grey-blue and dark red dress, and Steven looking very natty in a lightweight grey suit and shiny black shoes, the party was already in full swing. The band was playing Scottish songs, and a kilted vocalist was singing, "Bonnie Dundee," but with a strong Glasgow accent, as Steven rather acidly pointed out to Jean.

Teresa came over to meet them, and introduced them to the famous Japanese conductor Ken Oasaka, who nodded and bowed but spoke no English whatsoever. Jean made a few valiant attempts, but only got a few more bows for her trouble.

Steven wandered off, found a glass of champagne and some people he knew, and was soon having a good time, and didn't see Jean being called away to the phone.

An accident. That's all that Doug had said, but if Mac had fallen or had a reaction to the medication, Doug wouldn't have been there, unless they'd been trying to question him when it happened.

Jean didn't usually drive fast, but on this particular Sunday the roads were clear and she went like the wind, slowing only when she could see the gates of the Claremo}nt Clinic. There were two police cars outside the main entrance, an ambulance with the lights still flashing, and Doug's unmarked blue Ford next to the dark blue van which belonged to the forensic team.

Constable Jamieson stood outside the top step, and watched Jean approach. "Inspector Niven's on the second floor," he said when she came up.

She hurried through the corridors, and passed a few attendants and nurses who were talking in low voices or clustered in small, nervous groups.

At the top of the main stairs, the corridor to the right was cordoned off. A policeman Jean didn't know, but who evidently knew her, raised the pink plastic tape and she slipped underneath.

"Fourth door on the left, Dr. Montrose," he said.

Doug came out of the room just as she came up to it.

"It's a mess in there," he said, remembering her reaction to seeing Caroline Fraser's body.

Having had more time to prepare herself, Jean went in without flinching.

As she had noticed on other similar occasions, there was a feeling of utter stillness in the room, even though there were several people inside, moving and talking in low tones. As usual, neither the photographer nor the fingerprint people looked up nor acknowledged her presence. For some reason, in the presence of death they stayed insulated and immersed in the exercise of their own particular expertise.

The bullet had been fired in a downward direction, so that most of the blood and bits of flesh and bone were on the bedclothes and the carpet on the side away from the door.

"He was found when the nurse on duty came around to do a routine check," said Douglas as Jean looked down at the mortal remains of Captain Mac MacFadyen. "The nurse is in shock, poor chap; I have a sergeant with him in the visitor's lounge, but I don't think he has much to tell us."

"It couldn't have been self-inflicted?" asked Jean. She knew of instances of suicide during drug detoxification, particularly in the most painful, early stages.

"No weapon," replied Doug briefly. "Malcolm Anderson just phoned. He can't be here for about an hour. Do you mind giving us a guesstimate on the time of death?"

Jean put her hand under the sheet and on to the chest. It was cool, but still well above room temperature, and when she bent his arm at the elbow it moved without any resistance. "Not long," she said. "A couple of hours at most, but surely you can tell better from checking the times of the nurses' visits?

"It's odd that he was still tucked up in bed," mused Jean. "You'd think that if somebody came in with a gun, he'd at least have got a foot out, or made a move to defend himself."

"He was probably asleep, don't you think?" said Douglas. "The nurse said they'd given him drugs to counteract his withdrawal symptoms, and that could have made him sleepy, right?"

"Can I lift the pillow?" asked Jean. "I mean the top one."

"Of course, You can't get prints off a pillow. Lift it from this end, because the other one's stuck to his head."

The pillow showed the fan-shaped black powder burns radiating out from the center. A small, brown-rimmed hole had been burned where the muzzle of the gun had been, and a ragged track of torn cotton showed where the bullet had sped on its destructive way.

"That was probably a .38," said Douglas, looking over her shoulder, "but when Dr. Anderson finds the bullet inside his skull somewhere, we'll know for sure."

Jean carefully laid the pillow down. "Any idea who . . . ?" she asked very quietly.

"None. Being a drug user, he probably had some enemies, just like that Graeme Ferguson, if you remember him."

"Oh, yes," said Jean. "I remember him all right." After that case, she and Douglas hadn't spoken to each other for several weeks.

The door opened and Sergeant Flynn poked his head in. "Can you come through for a minute?" he asked Doug. Without being invited, Jean accompanied Douglas to the lounge where the young bearded male nurse was sitting, his hands twisting in his lap, his face pale as a snowdrift.

"He saw somebody, he thinks," said Sergeant Flynn, standing with his back to the door. "Now tell the Detective Inspector, Victor."

Victor looked up. His eyes were of the palest, watery blue. "I was going to give Mr. MacFadyen the hundred milligrams of seconal he'd been ordered. I had the capsule in a wee paper cup on a tray, just the way we're supposed to." Victor looked from Doug to Jean, as if he had been accused of some dereliction of duty.

"Go on," said Douglas, sitting down and sprawling comfortably back in one of the easy chairs.

"Well, it's always busy up here," continued Victor. "On the admission ward, there's people coming and going, nurses, aides, attendants, therapists, sometimes even a doctor. . . ."

Douglas's friendly grin acknowledged Victor's attempt at humor, and he added a nod of encouragement.

"Well, this nurse brushed past me, going the other way. Normally I wouldn't have noticed, but she was wearing a cape, and none of the nurses who work here wear capes." Victor paused and shook his head. "I didn't even think about it at the time. We have nurses coming in and out with patients from hospitals or other clinics."

"Aside from the cape, what did she look like?"

"Honestly, I don't know. I was in a hurry. I have fifteen patients to take care of." Victor looked anxiously at his watch. "The meds are all overdue, and they're all going to be so angry with me."

"You must remember something about her, Victor, if you noticed her cape," said Douglas reasonably. "You're a trained nurse, and part of that training is observation, right, Victor?" Jean noticed that Doug was forcing Victor to agree with him, and also that there was just the suspicion of a hard edge to Doug's voice. He'd quickly taken Victor's measure, and was pretty sure he knew how to deal with him.

Victor put his hand up to his head. "Honestly. She was just going along normally. I didn't notice. . . ."

Doug stood up and walked over toward him.

"Long legs? Nice shape?"

Victor shook his head.

"Come on, Victor." Doug could be quite intimidating when he wanted to. "You can do better than that. What was she wearing on her feet? Ballet pumps? Green wellies? Was she taking little steps? Skipping? Running?"

"She wasn't running . . . I don't know. She wasn't wearing green wellies, though."

Doug bore down on him. "You did notice that, eh? Did she look at you, Victor? Did she wink? Did she have dark eyes? Was she somebody you'd like to go out with?" Doug's voice was getting louder, and Victor put his hands defensively over the top of his head.

"She didn't look at me. She just went along the wall, and I didn't see her face. Really."

"Why not, Victor? Normally, when you're walking along the corridor, and you meet me, you see my face, right? Even if you're not looking directly at me you see something, a nose, eyebrows, a mouth, right, Victor?"

"I didn't see her face, sir . . . She turned her head a bit, and her hair sort of came around so I couldn't see her face at all. I'm sorry, I didn't think I'd ever be asked. . . ."

"What color of hair?" asked Douglas quickly. "Do you remember that?"

"It was blonde," replied Victor.

"Long? Short?" The urgency in Doug's voice was unmistakable.

"I really couldn't tell you," said Victor, looking astonished. "I don't believe I really remembered that she was even blonde. I just passed her in the corridor. . . ."

"Long, Victor? Was her hair long?"

Victor put his hand up to his shoulder. "About here. It was actually rather nice-looking hair, a kind of golden blonde."

Doug and Jean exchanged a quick glance. They were both thinking of the same person.

"Thanks, Victor. You'd better get back to your patients now and start passing out the tranquilizers," said Doug, putting a kindly hand on his shoulder. "Otherwise they may tear you apart and eat the pieces when you come in."

Chapter 25

As soon as Victor left the room, Doug called headquarters on his portable radio, and told them he was on his way to see Miss Aileen Farquar at 15 Ainslie Place in Perth, and that he was leaving the crime scene in the hands of Sergeant Flynn.

"You want to come?" he asked Jean.

She hesitated, then her curiosity got the better of her and she followed Doug and Constable Jamieson down the stairs and out to their car. Doug told Jamieson to sit in the back, which he did, barely able to suppress a scowl.

"I have a feeling we're coming to the end of the line here, Jean," said Doug firmly as he drove |hrough the gates. The beautiful weather had gone, low clouds had drifted in, and it was starting to rain, a thin, dreary kind of Spring rain, and Jean wondered how things were going at the brunch. Poor Steven, she hoped someone would give him a lift home. The rain didn't slow Doug down one bit. His car slid and slithered as he passed and overtook other vehicles, and when they pulled up with a squeal of brakes outside Aileen's flat and the car had come to rest, Jean felt she was drawing the first breath of the whole trip.

"Do you always drive like that?" she asked, unfastening her seat belt.

"I took the advanced Police driving course," said Doug, with some pride. He glanced up at the house.

"Now, I don't know what's going to happen, so I'd rather you stayed here in the car, if you don't mind. You know Aileen, don't you?"

"Yes. I've seen her several times in the surgery. Nothing serious, but I got to know her a bit."

"Good. If she's there, and we arrest her, I'll call for a woman officer to come out. Meanwhile I don't want you to get in harm's way."

"All right with me," said Jean, smiling at Doug's short memory. He hadn't had any such qualms about keeping her out of harm's way that night when she went into Strathalmond Castle by herself, and that wasn't so very long ago.

The car heaved as Jamieson ponderously extracted his bulk from the car, and Jean watched them go up the steps and ring the bell. It was now raining quite hard, and the two men stood on the top step with their backs to the door to avoid as much of it as possible, and Doug turned up the collar and lapels of his jacket. Nobody answered and, after a few minutes, Doug tried the big brass handle. The door opened and they went in.

Jean wondered if they hadn't all made a great big mistake by assuming that it had been Aileen Farquar up at the clinic, just because the person Victor had seen had golden blonde hair. There had to be lots of genuine nurses with that hair coloring, but Aileen's was certainly very noticeable and distinctive. Her mind went back to Mac MacFadyen, and she felt a deep sorrow for him. Of course everybody knew that Aileen had a big thing for him, but if she had taken the desperate step of shooting and killing him, he must have done something really terrible to her. Jean sat back in her seat and watched the rivulets of rain run down the windscreen. The radio suddenly crackled, and Jean jumped. It was a message for another car, and for awhile she listened to the chatter on the police frequency.

There was a knock on the window, and again Jean was

startled; it was Jamieson, who opened the car door for her.

"Is she there?" she asked.

"The Inspector would like you to come in," replied Jamieson. He spoke in his usual heavy, portentous way, as if everything he said deserved to be instantly transcribed into the National Archives.

It was still raining, and Jamieson had left the door ajar, so Jean ran straight into the house. There was no entrance hall, and the door opened directly into the front room, furnished with pleasant, chintz-covered easy chairs and a sofa. Long green satin curtains had been pulled to cover the tall windows. Jean looked around, but saw no one until she went into the bedroom, where Douglas was standing by the window, reading what appeared to be a letter of several pages. Aileen's fully dressed body was on the bed, legs hanging over the edge, and the smell of gunpowder was still in the air. The face was unrecognizable, but the golden blonde hair spread out over the pillow certainly was.

Jean gasped and felt the same kind of weakness that had come over her when she had been suddenly confronted with Caroline's body.

"She left this suicide note," said Douglas, looking up. "She says that Mac had betrayed her in the worst possible way, and this was the only way out."

He passed it to Jean, who turned her back to the bed and started to read. It was written in Aileen's concise, upright hand, and detailed the sad chronology of her affair with Mac MacFadyen. She listed all the clothes and jewelry and money she'd given him, including all that her mother had left her, and every penny she'd made from the sale of her mother's house. He was going to marry her, she'd been so sure of that, then he developed this relationship with Caroline Fraser. She didn't blame him for that, Caroline was very attractive and seductive, and he hadn't been able to resist her charms. But that last night, when Mac left her bed and went off to see Caroline, that was the last straw. Evidently he hadn't been able to get money from her and killed her in a fit of rage. He had been getting those recently when it had been too long since his last fix, Aileen wrote, and then he'd get so desperate he'd do anything.

Jean handed the letter back to Doug.

"There's nothing I can do here," she said dully.

Douglas hesitated for a second. "Right. I'll get Malcolm Anderson to do what's necessary. Jean, I'm sorry to be putting you through all this "

"That's all right, Douglas," she answered. "It was my decision to come here with you."

Jean calmly turned back to the bed and made a quick examination of Aileen's body. It was still warm, and the blood had not completely coagulated.

"Within an hour," she said to Douglas, her voice flat. "My car's still up at the clinic," she went on, "and I would appreciate a lift back."

"Of course," said Doug hurriedly. "I'll leave Jamieson here until the team arrives."

They left the room, Jean averting her eyes from the body, and went back outside.

"Stay here until the ambulance comes," Douglas told Jamieson as he opened the car door for Jean.

"How do I get back to the station?" asked Jamieson.

"Shanks's pony," replied Douglas. "You need the exercise."

In the car, Jean fastened her seat belt. "Please, Douglas," she said, "would you mind driving slowly this time? I'm upset enough without you terrifying me on top of everything."

Douglas drove very sedately. The rain had stopped, and the air was marvelously clear.

"Well, I suppose that wraps it up," he said, looking straight ahead. He was obviously preparing his report in his head. "It couldn't be clearer. Aileen was head over

heels in love with Mac, killed him because he'd taken all
her money and then betrayed her with Caroline, whom
he had killed in a fit of drug-deprived rage. She was at
the end of her tether, poor woman. The note is clear
enough on that point, don't you think?" Douglas paused
while he slowed behind a large Shore Porters' lorry. "I
can see that happening, all right," he went on. "I suppose
Mac would have been about her last chance to get a
man."

Jean shook her head at him and pursed her lips.

"Douglas, some days you're so sexist that I really de-
spair of you," she said.

Douglas looked at her with astonishment. "Me?" he
said, "Sexist? What did I say?"

Jean shrugged. There was no point in discussing it any
further, and anyway she much preferred that he concentrate on his driving.

Jean sat back in her seat feeling numb and sad. All
these unnecessary deaths, all the result of momentary de-
cisions made by each of them. If only they'd known . . . If
only Mac hadn't decided to try the street drugs to help the
pain in his fractured pelvis, and if Aileen had stayed on in
Glasgow instead of following him to Perth, and if poor
little Francesca hadn't been taken in by Marco's transparent glamour, at this moment they would presumably
still be leading peaceful and productive lives.

Douglas glanced over at her. "It's pretty clear, isn't it?
That that's how it happened?"

"I suppose so, Douglas," she replied, but clearly she
was not happy with his interpretation.

"Did I miss something out?" Douglas was so pleased
with the symmetry of the case that he resented any hint
that it might not have happened that way.

"It's Aileen," said Jean. "She didn't actually say anything in her note about killing Mac, and anyway I just
don't see her as a killer, except of herself."

"Probably she realized we could put two and two together, don't you think?" asked Doug, feeling slighted. "She didn't *have* to tell us, because she made it so obvious by her actions."

To his chagrin, Jean evidently wasn't convinced. "I don't know," she said. "Aileen was one of those unfortunate women whose mother used up all her youth, and I can see that she might kill herself, particularly after an unhappy affair, but dressing up and going to the clinic like that and shooting Mac like a dog . . . Well, I suppose I'm always learning a bit more about human nature. It's certainly possible."

"I suppose so." Douglas obviously didn't want to discuss the case further. There were always other possibilities, but Douglas was a policeman, trained to be pragmatic. It was all right with him if Jean wanted to mull it all over, but as far as he was concerned, when a case was solved, there was no point wasting time looking around for might-have-beens.

By the time they got back, a Grampian television truck had joined the police vehicles outside the Claremount Clinic, and the ambulance was still there, indicating that the forensic team was still at work and the body hadn't been removed. In addition, Malcolm Anderson's car was parked outside. Douglas dropped Jean off at her car before parking round the corner. While Jean drove off, he went straight upstairs. Malcolm Anderson was in the room, chatting with the police photographer, a pretty young woman with long, ash-blonde hair, who was packing her equipment.

"I was just telling her that she and I are like a couple of *calliphoridae*," he said as Douglas came in.

"Calli what?" asked Doug, puzzled.

"*Calliphoridae*," repeated Malcolm. "Bluebottles. Always there minutes after the death."

"You are a gruesome bugger," replied Douglas. He

glanced at the bed. "Did you find anything we didna know already?"

"Well, there was an eye hanging off the far edge of the bed," replied Malcolm. "Did you see that, huh?"

"Yes, we did," replied Douglas.

"Can you imagine," went on Malcolm, "after it was all over and they'd taken the body away, a nurse coming in to make up the bed, finding that thing looking at her?"

"I've just come from another one," said Douglas. "Self-inflicted. Suicide note and all. She did this one here, went home and shot her own self."

"Must have been love," said Malcolm. "Let me tell you, my boy, love is the most dangerous emotion of all. It kills a lot more people than hate."

"Aye. Well, I dinna think we need to waste any more time here. Do you want to see the woman?"

"No. Not if it's a clear suicide. The ballistics people will want to check the ordnance, but I've got enough other things to do, thank you all the same." Malcolm closed his large black bag and hurried off. Doug told Sergeant Flynn what had happened, the ambulance people wrapped Mac's body in his bed sheet and took him off under the harsh lights set up by the TV crew.

And now, thought Doug morosely as he drove back in to town, comes the exciting part, writing the report.

Going to pick up his car in the car park, a patron of the Bridge Bar found Brian Wooley unconscious, and went back in to phone the police. On arrival, they called an ambulance when they saw that he had been seriously injured, and he was taken to the hospital.

"He's got a fracture of the maxilla on the right," reported Dr. Angela Borthwick, the registrar on call, to her consultant. She had trouble hearing him, so she spoke louder into the phone. "Also his nose, three ribs on the right, and a probable skull. He's unconscious, breathing spontaneously, slightly hypothermic from exposure. His pupils don't react to light but are central and equal in size."

Angela put the phone down and shook her head.

"What did he say?" asked the nurse.

"He said, 'Go ahead, take care of it, call me in the morning.'"

The nurse snorted. "That's what he'd have said if you told him the patient had come in with his head under his arm. Anyway I'm glad he's not coming in. He *loves* to get people out of bed to do special tests and things."

"I'll put some strapping on his chest," said Angela nodding in the direction of the patient. "The ENT people can do whatever they want with his nose, and the maxillary fracture isn't displaced so we'll leave it alone right now. Then I'm going to put him in ICU," she said. "We have a free bed. Did you know that the girl died, the one who had a pulmonary embolus?"

"I heard," replied the nurse. "I also heard they couldn't find the husband to tell him."

"That's a shame, really. If my husband did that to me, I'd kill him." They both laughed. As they couldn't find anybody to move the patient, the two of them took him up to the intensive care unit themselves. The gurney had a wobbly wheel that made navigation difficult, and on a sharp turn the IV bottle fell off the pole on to Brian's chest, but he didn't feel it.

Douglas looked at his watch on the way back from the Claremount Clinic. It was almost one o'clock in the afternoon. He thought briefly about bringing the news of his partner's death to Donald Tarland in person, but on reflection decided that a phone call would be sufficient.

Teresa answered the phone, and Doug heard her sharp in-draw of breath when he told her about the two deaths.

"My God! I can't believe it! *Aileen Farquar*? She killed Mac? Are you sure?"

"Yes, of course I'm sure," replied Doug shortly. It seemed a really silly thing to be asking.

"You'd better talk to Donald," she said, and Douglas heard her call him to the phone.

There was a long pause after Doug outlined the events of the morning. "That's just terrible," said Donald in a stunned voice. "That's everybody . . . Everybody in the company. Except me. Oh, my God! Do you think I could be next?"

"No, I don't believe that you're in any danger, Mr. Tarland," said Douglas. "It seems to have been an entirely personal matter between the other people in your group."

"Thanks for letting me know," said Donald dully, and Douglas heard the click when Donald slowly put the phone down. He thought for a minute, then reached for the lined pad to write his report.

When he got home, Cathie was in bed, and when he crept in beside her, she half woke up and held him warm and close until they were both asleep.

Brian was unconscious for almost two days, and when he woke up, he had no idea where he was. They gave him a little warm broth, not the easiest thing with his broken jaw, but as he was missing several teeth, there were gaps through which they could insert a straw.

Later that day, Constable Jamieson came up to the hospital to get a statement from him, and with difficulty Brian told him what had happened in the car park of the Bridge Bar.

Marco was home when Jamieson and Ben Wright, a young policeman fresh from training school, knocked at the door of his parents' apartment. Marco didn't come quietly. In fact, as soon as he saw them, Marco made a bolt for the door, but ran right into Jamieson's large frame, knocking the wind out of him. Luckily Ben was quicker, and grabbed Marco by the arm. Marco swung

around, and in the scuffle Jamieson got a fist in the eye.
Ben was able to overpower Marco, and while Jamieson
sat on the floor moaning softly with one hand over his
eye, Ben slipped a pair of handcuffs over Marco's wrists.
Jamieson recovered enough to call on his radio for a
black Maria, and after Marco had been packed off to be
charged with attempted murder, resisting arrest, and as-
saulting a policeman in the course of his duties, they
started to search the apartment. Bob and Louise, who
had huddled together and watched the scuffle in terror
from behind the door, went back and sat in the living
room, shocked and silent, while Ben and Jamieson, nursing his empurpling eye, went through the contents of
Marco's bedroom. Brian had said that Marco had threatened and struck him with a gun, so they had taken the
precaution of coming with a search warrant.

"What's this, d'you think?" Ben pulled out a dark blue
garment, tightly rolled up, from the bottom drawer of the
chest next to the bed. He unrolled it, and out fell a curly
golden blonde female wig.

"Amateur theatricals, I suppose," said Jamieson, looking at the cape Ben was holding up. He shrugged.
"Don't waste time, and put that stuff back just the way it
was. It's a gun we're looking for, Ben."

Ben found it, wrapped in a waterproof case, in the
water tank of the toilet, and they bore it back in triumph
to headquarters.

"It's not registered," said Jamieson when he reported
to Douglas. "That gives us one more thing to charge him
with."

"You'd better get that eye seen to," said Douglas.
"Did you find anything else?"

"Well, no, sir. Were we supposed to be looking for
something?"

"Not specifically, Jamieson. But with people like him
you might expect to find a few joints, stolen goods, or a
cocaine stash, evidence of other illegal activities."

Jamieson remembered the wig, "He's maybe a trans-vestite, sir, but that isn't illegal, is it?"

Douglas was at the door before Jamieson's words pen-etrated, and he thought of Marco's game-cockiness and macho attitude. Hardly the kind to be parading around in female clothes.

"Transvestite, Jamieson? Are you sure that's the word you're looking for?"

Jamieson told him about the wig and the cape, and Douglas slowly went back to his chair, sat down and put his head between his hands.

"Go and get them," he said in a flat voice, "and bring them here. Now."

"What, sir?"

"The wig and the cape, you imbecile! Don't you see? MacFadyen was killed by a nurse with blonde hair wear-ing a cape. You find a blonde wig and a cape, and you come to the conclusion that Marco's a transvestite."

"Oh," said Jamieson.

"Get going! If that cape and wig have gone, Jamieson, so has your job."

Jean was in the surgery when the pathology technician phoned. Dr. Anderson would be starting the post mortem on Mr. MacFadyen in about fifteen minutes, if she wanted to be there.

When she arrived, Malcolm Anderson was doing the external examination and recording it using the voice-activated microphone.

"The body is that of a well-developed middle-aged male, apparently in good health previous to the fatal in-jury. Head and neck . . ." Anderson broke off when he saw Jean coming in.

"You're like the angel of death, quine," he said to her. "Every time somebody's murdered around here, you have something to do with it. One day somebody's going to put two and two together."

Jean nodded sadly. "That's exactly how I feel, sometimes," she said, trying not to look at the gory remnants of Mac's head.

"Head and neck," went on Malcolm as if there had been no interruption, "there is a single gunshot entry wound just above the right temple, with a black ring of gunpowder visible on the surrounding skin, indicating that the shot was made from within a few inches. Exit wound . . ." Malcolm paused and surveyed the damage. "Multiple bone fragments exited removing most of the left side of the face and orbit. Left eye was extruded, found separate from the body. Considerable amount of brain tissue extruded, not all recovered."

Malcolm grinned at Jean and turned away from the microphone for a moment. "A' that euphemisms," he said. "When there's brains all over the bed, the walls and the ceiling, you say it's extruded and not all recovered."

Jean smiled weakly back. Malcolm continued his meticulous examination. "Numerous intravenous injection sites noted in both arms . . ." He felt the arms as he talked. "Several thrombosed veins are noted in both antecubital fossae, several areas of recent and healed infection." Again he turned to Jean. "You see those surgical scars?" he asked, pointing at two intersecting white scars over the upper thigh. "Do you happen to know what these were from?"

"A horse fell on him," replied Jean. "He said he had several operations on his hip. That's why he had a limp . . ." Jean looked away sadly. "And that's why he was addicted to heroin. It was the pain from the injuries and operations."

"Bilateral scars are also noted in the groin from surgical interruption of the vas deferens," droned on Malcolm. "There is a large mole, probably of congenital origin, on the medial aspect of the left thigh . . ."

"Will you check all those operations when you open him up?" asked Jean.

"Aye, surely," promised Malcolm. "I'll send a copy of the final report."

Feeling sad and confused, Jean left the pathology department and went back to her surgery.

Douglas went down to the cells to talk to Marco, who was lying face down on the narrow cot. The day constable let Doug into his cell, and put a chair in for him. Doug stood silently gazing down at Marco, until, after several minutes, Marco turned around and snarled, "What do you want?"

Very deliberately, Douglas sat down facing the back of the chair.

"Marco," he said in his kindly older-brother voice, "it's going to be difficult to get you out of this one."

Silence.

"You see, Marco, we have two options here. Either we can handle this in an understanding kind of way, you know, making allowances, pointing out that you have an uncontrollable temper. The psychiatrists have a name for it, and with some help from us, you could get off very light."

"What's the other option?"

"Well, Marco, put yourself in our shoes for a minute. We like to help people who help us, but on the other hand, we can get really mean and nasty with the ones who don't."

Douglas moved in his chair, trying hard not to show his dislike of this young monster. "You know what the penalty is for murder. You could spend the rest of your entire life in prison, Marco."

"I didn't do anything. Those two cops came into my house and attacked me. My mum and dad can tell you."

"Now, Marco, don't be silly. And anyway, that's not why you're here, is it?" Doug paused for maximum effect. "You see, Marco, they found the cape and the blonde wig."

That got Marco's attention, and he sat up, but he looked as defiant as ever. "That's not a crime. I'm in a drama group."

"Good," said Douglas. He pulled out his notebook. "That'll help you a lot. Now tell me the name of the group; and the people in it, please."

Sullenly, Marco did so. "Now, Marco, do most of your group take their costumes home with them? Isn't there a wardrobe, or a place to put them?"

Marco shrugged, "I don't know."

"Of course you do. It was rather a brilliant idea, actually, to borrow a wig. How often do you meet?"

"Meet who?"

"Your drama group."

"Once a week. Thursdays."

"That explains it," said Douglas, sounding relieved. "You borrowed the wig and the cape last Thursday, when you heard that Mac was going to be admitted to the clinic, and of course you wouldn't need to return them till next Thursday."

"I don't know what you're talking about." Marco's voice had lost some of its confidence.

"All right," said Douglas, grinning broadly as if he were sharing a huge joke with him, "what's the name of the play? Where can I get tickets?"

"What play? What are you talking about?"

"The one where you play the part of a blonde nurse, with curly blonde hair that made you look just like your sister, Caroline." For the first time, Douglas's voice was tinged with acid, and Marco saw his eyes harden, but just for a second. "That really was poetic justice, wasn't it? Dressing up to look like his victim, and then killing him. I bet you scared him to death."

Marco didn't answer, and Douglas went on. "Marco, let's stop playing games, eh? We both know about what happened up at the clinic. There were witnesses, Marco. Do you remember a male nurse you passed in the corri-

dor. He *recognized* you, Marco. He's been to your
restaurant several times and will swear to it. Now, let's
get down to business while we still have time. You see,
if we handle this properly, you have a very good defence, because he'd killed your sister, right? Killed her
in the most brutal, disgusting way . . ." Douglas's voice
rose in indignation. "And like any normal brother would,
you wanted to avenge her, right, Marco? Between you
and me, I'd have felt exactly the same way."

Marco nodded dumbly. All the fire had gone out of
him. Sitting hunched up on the bunk, he looked now
more like a plucked chicken than a fighting gamecock.

Douglas stood up. "OK, Marco," he said in a firm but
kindly voice, "let's get this over with as quickly as possible. We'll go into the evidence room, get you a cup of
coffee and a cigarette if you want one, then I'll read you
your rights, all that routine stuff, then we'll get the detailed story all down on tape, so nobody can ever say to
you, 'Hey, Marco, that's not what you said.' OK?"

An hour later, Douglas went wearily back up to his office, feeling exhausted but pleased by the outcome of the
case. Even though the sequence of events had helped to
establish what had happened, he felt he could take a jus-
tifiable pride in having wrapped it all up, ready for the
press, Grampian Television, and the next staff confer-
ence.

Marco had been remanded in custody, his statement
was on tape, witnessed, and put away in the safe, and
overall, it was a satisfactory conclusion.

Jamieson came into the office. His eye was now a fine
plum color, and it gave him a kind of unlikely dignity.

"There's a Mr. Beckwith outside, sir. It's about the
MacFadyen death."

Douglas looked at the card he proffered. "Norman C.
Beckwith," he read, "Insurance Adjuster."

"Send him in, but tell him I've only got a min}te. It's late and I want to go home."

Mr. Beckwith was a tall, thin man with a long, lined face and a slight stoop. He reminded Douglas of a heron, with his crest of wispy, rather long blond hair and a loosely fitting grey suit.

"Afternoon, Inspector," he said breezily. "I won't keep you more than a minute." He sat down on the visitor's chair and put his briefcase on his knee. "This is just routine, but we have to check every case of this kind." He opened his case and took a buff file out of it. "Mr. MacFadyen, who died three days ago, partner in the firm of Macandon Industries, PLC. The two partners had what we call cross-insurance, for a very substantial amount."

"How can I help you?" asked Douglas.

"I just need to be sure there was nothing implicating the other partner, Inspector, or any beneficiary. As I said, this is routine, but we have to investigate every case."

"Was there any other beneficiary?" asked Douglas, fiddling with his pen.

Beckwith checked the papers. "No. There usually isn't in this type of insurance. But, of course, he could have had other policies we don't know about for his wife, children, etcetera."

"Well, you can set your mind at rest," replied Doug briskly. "MacFadyen was killed by a young fellow who is presently in custody, and who has just made a full confession."

"Well, congratulations, Inspector," said Beckwith, getting up slowly, as if he'd been hoping to spend a while there, chatting about this and that. "In any case, I'll be on my way to see Mr. Tarland. I only wish all my cases could be solved that quickly."

Douglas opened the door for him.

"Oh, and by the way, Inspector," said Beckwith, shaking Doug by the hand, "I do some personal insurance advisory work. If you'd like a careful review of your own insurance status, without any cost or obligation of course, I'll be happy to go over it with you. My home phone number's on the back of my business card."

When Douglas got home, dinner was ready. Cathie had recovered completely from her near-abortion, and to Douglas she seemed not only to be glowing with health, but with something else as well, a kind of radiance that had quite transformed her.

"That wee bairn's doing a lot for your figure," he said, coming up behind her and cupping his hands around her breasts. "You're getting to be a real handful, you are."

"Awa' ye go!" replied Cathie, lifting the shepherd's pie out of the oven, "I canna serve your dinner when you're clutching on to me like that."

"That's true," he said, "So just you put it down a wee minute, because I've got something to tell you."

Cathie put the hot casserole dish down on the counter and turned to face him, smiling. "Well, what is it, Douggie? Is this a confession I'm about to hear?"

"Aye, it is that, sort of," said Douglas, putting his arms around her. "I just wanted to tell you I love you, and that I'm very, very proud of you."

Chapter 26

That morning, Jean slept late, unheard of on a weekday, and Steven was up before her and made breakfast. She was awakened by the smell of frying bacon, and a few moments later she heard Steven coming slowly up the stairs. He came in with a tray loaded with cereal, eggs, and bacon, toast and marmalade, two cups, a pot of tea and the newspaper, and put them on the bed while he drew the curtains.

"Here," he said, "time to get up."

"Oh my," said Jean, sitting up. "What time is it?"

"About nine," he replied, sitting down on the bed. "Do you realize you went to bed about twelve hours ago? This must be a record."

Jean glanced at the tray. "Anything in the paper?" she asked.

"I haven't looked," he replied. "You missed the best part of the party," he went on. Jean started to get out of bed, but Steven said, "It's all right. I phoned the surgery and they don't need you until ten."

Jean eased back on the pillows and relaxed. "You know, Steven, with all the goings-on, you never told me about brunch at the Tarlands."

"Not much to tell, actually," replied Steven, "they all got into an argument about modern music. Celia Price said it was disgusting that the government paid grants and salaries for people to write music nobody could listen to, and the conductor chap, Oasaka, kept on clapping his hands and saying "Ah so, Ah so!"'" or something like that.

"And what did you say, dear?" Jean poured the tea, balancing the tray on her knees.

"Me? I talked to Donald. He's having a tough time, business-wise, although he tried to tell me Macandon's doing just fine. I wanted to tell him, if you're doing so well why don't you pay your bills?"

"I'm glad you didn't, Steven. After all it was a brunch, not a business meeting."

"What happened up at the clinic? Yesterday you wouldn't say a word about it."

Steven sat on the edge of the bed and picked up a rasher of bacon and nibbled on it.

Jean's face became very somber, and she told Steven what had happened.

"Aileen Farquar killed him?" said Steven. "That's hard to believe. Can you imagine her doing that?"

"I don't know. She was dead, left a suicide note. Douglas seemed pretty convinced she'd killed Mac first, so who am I to argue?"

Jean watched her husband take another rasher and idly start to nibble it. "Steven, if you're going to eat all my bacon, why did you put it on my plate?"

"Sorry. I'll make some more. Poor old Mac, though." Steven was silent for a minute, thinking about him. "It's amazing how a man, specially one like him, I mean a professional soldier, could get so addicted he couldn't control himself."

"They say heroin eventually wipes out all the difference between people," said Jean. "One long-term addict's the same as another, even if one was a president and the other a . . . well, I don't know, somebody who hasn't achieved as much."

"Well, it's still very sad. I wonder what Donald's going to do. Now he doesn't have anybody. His whole company's been wiped out. And that's not good news for the glass works, either."

Alley, their cat, came into the room and jumped up on the bed. Steven scooped him up on one hand.

"Did you remember to feed him?" asked Jean.

"Of course. Actually, Fiona did. He ate as if he hadn't been fed in a month."

"I wonder how Teresa's doing," said Jean. "I feel badly for her, poor thing. She must be terribly upset about all this."

"I'm sure she is," agreed Steven, "especially if it interferes with her social schedule."

"Steven! What an unkind thing to say! I thought you really like them."

"Well, I do, but it gripes me that they can afford to entertain like that when Macandon hasn't paid my bill for almost three months. And I know for a fact that I'm not the only one."

All day long, thoughts and conclusions about the deaths of Caroline Fraser, Mac and Aileen kept forcing themselves into Jean's mind, even when she was in the middle of talking to a patient, or writing up a chart. That afternoon, she phoned Dr. Anderson to make quite certain about a point in Mac's post mortem, and his answers fitted the appalling theory that was willy-nilly putting itself together in her head. Then, grasping a recent bacteriology report tightly in her hand, she talked at some length to the head of the Regional Public Health Office in Dundee, and what he said seemed to clinch the matter as far as she was concerned.

When she went home, her heart was so full of worry and sadness that she forgot to pick up anything for dinner, and Lisbie, seeing immediately how upset her mother was, took over and put together the emergency cod casserole. Her timing was perfect, and it was ready to come out of the oven when Steven came home.

They had almost finished dinner when the phone rang, and Fiona got up to answer it.

"It's for you, Mum," she called up. "It's my sweetheart. God, I wish he'd call *me* sometimes."

Slowly Jean went to the phone. She was feeling so tired her muscles ached.

"Jean? There's been some new action on the Mac-Fadyen case. Can I come over?"

Jean only hesitated a second. "Yes, of course. How's Cathie doing?"

"Fine. Nae problems at all. I'll be over in a few minutes, then."

Fiona was watching Jean with bright eyes. "Is he coming?"

"Yes, but to talk business. Please don't hang around, Fiona. I don't want him to be here all night."

"Oh, all right. Whatever you say. I have plenty of other things to do." Fiona flounced off and a moment later Jean heard her going down the steps to her room in the basement.

But by the time Doug arrived, Fiona was back upstairs, and ran out to meet him when she heard the car. She put her arm through his and escorted him in, and it took a very severe look from Jean to dislodge her.

Douglas sprawled back in Steven's green high-winged chair, feeling very good. He was looking forward to being a father, the Fraser–MacFadyen case was finally solved, and everything was going his way.

He told Jean about Marco, and how he'd got his confession out of him.

"You actually told him that Victor, that male nurse, had recognized him."

"Well, of course. No harm was done." Douglas smiled broadly. "That's partly what made Marco give up and tell me the truth about what happened. It's an interrogation technique we sometimes have to use, and it worked."

"I'm not sure that's entirely ethical," murmured Jean, but Douglas was not to be shaken from his position of strength.

"So what you're saying is that MacFadyen was having an affair with Caroline Fraser, got her pregnant, then one night came over to get money from her to buy heroin, and killed her because she wouldn't come across. Then, when Marco found out, he killed him out of revenge?"

"I couldn't have put it better myself," said Douglas. "Do you think Fiona's going to make us some tea?"

Jean looked at him with a curious expression. "Do you remember when I said I wouldn't get involved in any more of your cases, Douglas?"

"I certainly do," replied Doug. "That was when we finally found out what Ilona Strathalmond was up to."

"Right," said Jean. "Well, I'm afraid I can't stay totally out of this one. You see . . ." Jean got up from her chair. "You see, Douglas, this MacFadyen business, I'm afraid it's not quite all as easy and clearcut as you think."

When Douglas left about fifteen minutes later, his face looked as if it had been carved out of stone, and he barely acknowledged Fiona's smiling goodbye.

Chapter 27

The next morning, Jean felt thoroughly lethargic, and tasks that she normally would have done without a second thought became like huge unclimbable mountains. She really didn't want to go to work, and would have given anything just to have stayed in bed, but of course her conscience didn't allow her to do that. So off she went in her little Renault down Argyll Place, trying to read the list of house calls she had to make, without taking her eyes off the road. After the house calls, she stopped in at the main police station and, with Douglas's permission, spent about half an hour in the cells talking to Marco, so it wasn't until about ten that she finally got to the surgery.

Eleanor was at her desk, and glanced at the clock when she came in. "Twelve patients," she said in that slightly reproachable tone that made Jean grit her teeth. "Two new ones."

"Fine," said Jean. "And I'd really like a cup of tea, please."

Eleanor went in the little room behind her desk where the tea things were kept.

"And Mrs. Tarland's here," she said. "Actually she was here first, so she's been waiting since a little after nine."

"Oh, good," said Jean. "Send her in, and bring a cup of tea for her, and some extra biscuits."

"Well," said Jean, smiling, when Teresa was installed

in the patient's chair, "I haven't even had time to thank you for brunch. It was great, and I'm sorry I had to leave. Now, what brings you down to this part of town?"

It turned out that Teresa had a mild bladder infection, and after examining her, Jean took the usual urine sample and a blood test.

"I see from the paper that Aileen Farquar killed Mac and then committed suicide," said Teresa from behind the screen where she was dressing. "I'm sure that's not right. Aileen didn't kill Mac, I'm quite sure of it."

"That's old news, Teresa," said Jean, who was writing on the patient's record sheet. "Actually it was Marco who did it. Apparently he's made a full confession."

"That certainly makes more sense," said Teresa, appearing round the screen, dressed as carefully and elegantly as ever. "He's a very violent young man. It's a pity he chose that way to revenge his sister."

Jean put down her pen and looked squarely at Teresa.

"Whose idea was it, Teresa? Yours or Donald's?"

Teresa stared. "Idea for what?"

"The idea of killing Mac. You see, Teresa, I know Marco pretty well, as you do, and we both know that he not only has a violent temperament, but is very suggestible."

"Are you saying we got him to kill Mac? Donald's partner? Are you quite mad?"

"I wasn't sure, although it would have fitted the facts. So I went down to talk to Marco in his cell this morning. I've known him a long time, and I asked him what had convinced him that Mac had killed his sister, and sure enough, it was what the two of you had said to him."

Jean smiled, but it took an effort. "Before that, Marco was sure Brian Wooley had killed his sister, so maybe you save Brian's life. But, of course, Marco's too macho to ever admit it wasn't his idea, even though you told him that Mac had been put in the Claremount Clinic, and if you had the nerve and the courage, you'd have gone up there to kill him yourself."

"That was just idle talk," said Teresa, very relaxed. "Of course I'd no idea that he'd go ahead and actually do it."

"Well, it could never be proved in a court of law anyway, could it? As a psychologist, you seem to have known exactly which buttons to press, Teresa." Jean spoke in a tone of reluctant admiration.

Teresa sat there, looking thoughtfully at Jean, then made up her mind. As Jean had said, nothing could ever be proved, but she did want Jean to know how faultlessly she had arranged for the removal of Mac MacFadyen.

"It was Bob Fraser who started it," she said, "when he asked Donald and me to talk to Marco because he was being such a problem."

Eleanor poked her head in and asked if Jean was going to be long, because there were patients waiting.

"Ten minutes," said Jean sharply. "And make sure nobody interrupts us please."

As soon as the door closed, Teresa leaned forward, excited by the smooth way it had all worked out. "You see, Jean, from a psychologist's point of view, Marco is a fascinating individual. Did you know that when he was younger he used to dress up in his sister's clothes and go out in the street?"

"I'd heard that," murmered Jean, because an answer seemed to be required, but she didn't want to interrupt Teresa's account.

"Well, he was deeply in love with Caroline, in a weird kind of way. He wanted to be her, to live inside her skin . . . Do you see what I mean?"

Jean nodded.

"They always looked very much alike, and Marco felt he too should have been born female, like his adored Caroline. Hence the dressing up, the macho attitude, the aggression, the play-acting, the rages . . . Marco was so sexually ambivalent that he just oscillated between one behavioral extreme and another."

Jean had to agree. "It must have been very difficult for him," she said.

"But of course, anyone who understood this had a good chance of being able to manipulate him."

"As Caroline did," said Jean. "And then you."

"It was really fascinating," went on Teresa, her eyes sparkling. "There were certain key words and phrases that Marco responded to, like one of Pavlov's dogs. The idea of another man having sexual intercourse with his sister drove him wild, as did the idea of someone hurting her. The idea of revenge was close to the surface, too, so to reinforce his tendency to take the law into his own hands, I told him stories about the incompetence of the police, how nowadays even the worst criminals always get away with their crimes."

"Was that before Mac became a prime suspect?"

"Of course. Marco isn't stupid. And for a while he was pretty sure that Brian had killed her. Brian's lucky to be alive right now."

"Brian told him he'd seen Mac that night?"

"Yes. When Marco caught him in the car park of that bar. Brian had been on the roof again, but he couldn't bear to watch Caroline with Mac, so he came down."

"Before she was killed?"

"Yes."

"So you helped Marco put two and two together?"

"Yes, but the hard part was pointing him in the right direction. For instance, I told him that if it had been me, and I'd decided to kill him, I'd have dressed up to look like Caroline, so that Mac would have one last petrifying fright before he died. Marco really liked that."

"But why did you want Mac dead so badly, Teresa?"

"Do you mind if I smoke?" asked Teresa.

"No, go ahead," said Jean, for the first time breaking

the inflexible rule of the surgery, and trying not to look at the NO SMOKING sign hanging prominently on the wall. Teresa took out a pack of black Turkish cigarettes, and lit one.

"Mac was very bad news, Jean," she said, watching a coil of blue smoke rise from the tip of her cigarette. "You don't know what Donald's been through with him. Mac practically destroyed the company, although Donald didn't realize that until recently. He lost big orders, our suppliers stopped shipping goods, and now the bank won't lend the firm any more money. Mac lost us a great deal of money, and that's aside from what he embezzled."

"Oh my," murmured Jean. "I didn't know that."

"And, of course, being a heroin addict, his chances of his ever being cured were small. So Donald was faced with a huge loss as a result of his activities, and even if he was found guilty and put in prison, that didn't help us one bit."

"And he was insured?"

"Only if he died. And double indemnity if it was the result of an accident or violence."

"Ah . . . yes. Did Marco know that?"

"There was no reason for him to know. Anyway, he just wanted to be quite certain that Mac had killed Caroline, then he was going to make him pay the price."

Jean took a deep breath, and her hands tensed. She had no idea how Teresa would handle what was coming.

"Teresa, why are you so sure that Mac killed Caroline?"

"That's obvious. Mac was having this steamy affair with Caroline, hadn't been able to get any money out of Aileen, so he went to Caroline's flat that night to get money from her. Then he killed her when she wouldn't give it to him."

"How do you know that?"

"Well, from the best possible source, Aileen Farquar herself." Teresa drew in a long puff of smoke, and exhaled it in a long jet.

"Aileen told you that?"

"She told Donald. She was very upset, he said, and came and told him, although she'd said something different to the police to protect him."

"If I told you that Donald had embroidered on that story, what would you think, Teresa?"

Teresa's mouth opened slowly. "Embroidered? Why would . . ."

"Because, unfortunately, it was Donald who was having the affair with Caroline Fraser, not Mac."

Teresa jumped up, and the ash from her cigarette fell to the floor. "That's nonsense! How dare you say something like that?"

"Because it's true, Teresa. I'm really sorry, but there it is."

"I assume you have some kind of proof before making such an accusation?"

Jean sighed. "Yes, I'm afraid so. Now just sit down again, won't you, Teresa? For one thing, Caroline was about two months pregnant when she was killed. Mac couldn't have made Caroline pregnant, because he'd had a vasectomy. Dr. Anderson, the pathologist, confirmed that at the post mortem."

Teresa had gone very pale as Jean spoke. "Another thing," went on Jean. "Caroline had been on holiday in Bangkok a few weeks ago, and brought back an infection. It was a *chlamydia*, a transmissible vaginal and bladder infection, but of a type that's actually never been seen here, according to the public health people I consulted. Donald had it in his urine, and there's only one way he could have got it. No doubt it's now in yours too." Jean looked at the sample bottle on the table. "Of course, the final proof that he was responsible for her pregnancy will be in genetic fingerprinting of the foetus, but that's none of my business."

The cigarette in Teresa's hand started to shake. Jean felt truly sorry for her; she knew what it felt like to have her husband having an affair with another woman. But she had to go on.

"Oh, and by the way," she asked Teresa, "did you notice a scratch on Donald? On his arm, maybe?"

"No . . . Wait a minute, he did have one on his back. It's not even healed yet. He was cutting a branch and scratched himself, something like that."

"There was some skin under Caroline's nails, Teresa. But again, that's up to the police to match it up. I don't even know quite how they do it, but I know they can positively identify the individual."

Teresa looked at Jean with a kind of hypnotized fear, then suddenly she seemed to relax and her voice regained its confidence. "You forget that Mac killed her with his own kitchen knife," she said. "You can't get around that."

"I wondered about that," replied Jean. "According to Inspector Niven, Mac told him he missed it the day before Caroline was killed, the same day that Donald had visited him. I suppose. . . ." Jean hesitated. "I suppose Donald just stole it." Watching Teresa's drawn, frightened face, Jean felt weary to the bone, and disgusted with herself for causing so much misery in people's lives. Why couldn't she ever learn to mind her own business? "Anyway," she went on, the weariness showing in her voice, "it'll all come out sooner or later."

Jean glanced at the clock. Eleanor would be coming back in any minute. "They also found hair and clothing fibers on the floor that didn't belong to Caroline or Mac, and Donald said he'd never been in her flat. . . ."

Teresa's knuckles went white when she realized that an unbreakable noose was being gently slipped around Donald.

"You see, Teresa," went on Jean, "Caroline told Fiona that she was having a hot affair with somebody at the office, and she assumed it was Mac MacFadyen. But Caroline also said she was determined to marry this man, so she must have been really putting the pressure on Donald, as she already knew that she was pregnant. You know how Donald is about appearances, and how devastating such a scandal would have been to him."

Teresa stood up. "I don't believe it," she said. "Not any of it."

"By the way, Teresa," asked Jean, "do you remember the night Caroline was killed. Did Mac come to your house?"

Teresa hesitated. "Yes, he did. He was in a terrible state. He must have just come from Caroline . . ." She shuddered.

"Did Donald give him money?"

"Yes, a lot. Five hundred pounds. I don't know why, considering . . . Oh, my," Teresa put her head in her hands; things were beginning to clarify in her mind.

"So presumably he went off to get his fix."

"Mac said he was going to Glasgo , because there was nowhere he could get it in Perth at that hour. He knew where to get it at any time, down there."

"Then when Mac was safely out of the way, Donald went out, right?"

"He often goes out for a walk before going to bed. Sometimes he takes the car, if he wants to walk around the Inch."

There was a long silence, broken by Jean.

"Well, Teresa, I think you'd better go home now. Inspector Niven should be there; I know he was going up to see Donald about this time. I'm sure he'll want to talk to you too."

Teresa was shaking when she got up, and her features seemed to have become older and harsh.

"There's absolutely no proof," she said. Her voice was just above a whisper.

"Teresa, proof isn't my business," replied Jean. "You know what happened, and so do I. Whether it can be proved to the satisfaction of a court of law, I don't know. That's police work, and some time ago I promised to stay out of that."

Don't miss
Dr. Jean Montrose's
next mystery adventure in
A Torrid Piece of Murder
coming from Signet
in December 1994.

Perth Memorial Hospital stands on high ground overlooking the city, and on a clear day, looking out from the windows on the third floor, where the operating theaters and recovery rooms are, the rounded Sidlaw hills can be seen in the distance to the Northeast, hazy, blue, unthreatening.

Dr. Peter MacIntosh, head of gynecology and obstetrics, stood at the wide window with one hand on the sill, talking to the sister in charge of the operating theaters.

"Thank God it was just a benign cyst," he said, holding up the specimen bottle containing a floating red blob about the size of a plum. "I was really concerned."

"That *was* a relief," agreed Sister Jan Kelso, a small, pale, determined-looking young woman with a long nose and no makeup. She hesitated. "Lois is our church secretary, and to be quite honest, she's not exactly the most stable . . ."

They heard the quick sound of running feet along the corridor and Jan turned, annoyed. Nobody was permitted to run in her operating suite. Round the corner appeared a young woman in a student nurse's shapeless grey uniform, her thin blonde hair straggling from under her cap. Sister Kelso was about to greet her with a sharp rebuke when the nurse stopped, out of breath, her gaze fixed on Peter.

"Dr. MacIntosh, please . . . your patient, Miss Munday . . . in the recovery room, she's stopped breathing."

By the time she had the words out, Peter was racing down the corridor as fast as his long athletic legs would take him.

In the recovery room, several nurses and a technician were gathered around a bed, and he hurried over. He took one look at the dead-white face of his patient.

"She has a pulse, sir," said one of the nurses, but already Peter had put his hand behind Lois Munday's neck and put his face down to hers to start mouth-to-mouth resuscitation. He blew three hard, deep breaths and could feel her lungs expanding with his air.

"Get me a laryngoscope and an endotracheal tube," he said to the nurse. He held Lois's chin up, watching for signs of spontaneous breathing, but as these did not appear, he started blowing into her lungs again. After three more big breaths, he stood up, went behind the patient's head, put one hand behind her neck, took the laryngoscope in the other, opened her mouth and slid the curved blade of the instrument in until he could see the vocal cords.

"Tube." He held out his hand, not taking his eyes off the vocal cords. The nurse placed the transparent plastic tube in his hand, and he slipped it deftly between the cords and into the woman's trachea. He blew into the end of the tube, watching Lois's chest expand as he did so, then attached it to the corrugated respirator tubing. The respirator was next to the bed, and Peter secured the tubing and adjusted the controls. In a moment the machine was sighing air into the patient's lungs at 500 mls per breath, 12 breaths per minute, and within a minute, Lois Munday's face became pink again. Peter looked at the monitor above the bed. The heart rate was a little fast, but had not faltered during this life-threatening episode. A few minutes later, she was regaining consciousness and it was clear that the emergency was over.

Peter straightened up with a long sigh of relief and looked at the faces around him. "Where's Dr. Sutherland?" he asked. Dr. Sutherland was the anesthetist who had been on the case.

A quick glance passed between the nurses.

"We called for him first," said one, plucking up her courage, but her voice was hesitant.

"Well?"

"He didn't answer his pager," she said. "I called the operator and she said he'd already left the hospital." The nurse, knowing the implication of her words, looked at her feet.

Peter's mouth opened in surprise, then his face hardened. "Thank you," was all he said, but they could see how angry he was. Anna McKenzie, one of the other anesthetists, came into the recovery room, and Peter explained what had happened. Anna looked shocked and hurriedly offered to take care of Lois from this point. Having handed the case over to her, Peter strode to the door and ran down the back stairs to the ground floor, heading for the administrative offices. He marched past the secretary and barged straight into the hospital director's room.

Roderick Michie was seated behind his desk, and when Peter started to tell him what had happened in the recovery room, Roderick nervously shook a cigarette out of a packet of Marlboros, lit it and took great, deep puffs, frequently tapping the end of the cigarette on the ashtray. He watched Peter's face and didn't say a word until he finished.

"I'll talk to him," he said finally, putting out his cigarette in the ashtray, which already held a dozen fag-ends. Roderick was a pudgy man in his middle fifties, with suspiciously black, thinning hair combed across the top of his head. He rubbed the side of his nose distractedly. "You know this isn't the first time, Peter . . ."

"I know," said Peter. "Apparently he had some major problems in Aberdeen before he came here. Did you know that?"

"It's all in his file," replied Roderick, avoiding Peter's angry stare. "There's nothing I can do about it. You know the system. We had a vacancy, and he was the only applicant. Sometimes we have to take who we can get, and that's not always who we want."

Peter took a deep breath, started to say something, then changed his mind. It wasn't going to help if he lost his temper.

"I hope you can do something, Mr. Michie," he said in a carefully controlled voice. "Otherwise, sooner or later, there's going to be a serious accident, and someone's going to die as a result of Sutherland's negligence."

A few moments later, Peter was on his way back to the recovery room to check on his patient. He was still tense with indignation and anger.

Less than fifteen minutes before, Derek Sutherland had just brought Lois Munday back from the theater when he was called to the phone in the recovery room. Within minutes of hanging up he was dressed and out of the hospital, forgetting in his haste to tell the nurses that he was leaving. He drove out of the car park and headed down the hill, his mind full of what his wife Sheila had just told him. Their son, Bobby, had been sent home from school again, the second time in two weeks. On this occasion, according to Sheila, he'd refused to answer a question from one of his teachers, then had become totally silent and stubborn. Nobody could get a word out of him, not even the astonished headmaster, Dr. Robertson, to whom Bobby had finally been sent by his teacher. Dr. Robertson personally called Sheila, because Bobby was such an outstanding boy, and he was really concerned about him.

Derek was normally a relaxed, easy-going sort of person, and it took a lot to get his full attention, let alone get him excited. But now he felt really concerned. For several weeks, Sheila had been saying that something was the matter with Bobby, but as usual, Derek had paid little attention to her complaints. Bobby seemed all right to him; about the correct height and weight for a thirteen-year-old, active, alert, like all the other kids.

Two days before, Sheila had been ominously silent throughout dinner. After Bobby had gone upstairs, and Derek had picked up the paper, Sheila said grimly "Derek, there's something the matter with Bobby." Derek didn't answer, and her voice rose. "Derek! Listen to what I'm saying! He doesn't talk to me, and he's off his food. Haven't you even noticed? He was always so close to you, and now he avoids even you."

Resignedly, Derek put the paper down and listened, half his mind still on the football scores. Sheila was still attractive, blonde and big-bosomed, not that he paid much attention to how she looked nowadays. He did notice that the corners of her mouth had turned down in a dissatisfied pout he'd learned to detest.

Derek shrugged, knowing the effect that had on her.

"All that's quite natural for a boy his age," he replied, picking up the newspaper again. "Bobby's fine. He's captain of the football team, he's at the top of his class. He has lots of friends. What more do you want? He'll be coming up to puberty soon, and that's going to be a big change "

Sheila's lips tightened. "Derek Sutherland, I don't think you're listening to me at all."

He sighed and put down the paper with a martyred expression. "All right, then," he said, "I'm listening."

"I really think Bobby is ill," said Sheila, pulling a strand of blonde hair out of her face. She emphasized the word "ill" and stared at Derek out of her big, pale grey eyes. "You know that girl Moira who lives on Cairn Street, the red-haired one who came to his last birthday party?"

Derek looked blank, and tried to remember.

"Well, she was diagnosed with leukemia a few weeks

ago, but all the neighbors knew that she'd been looking pale and thin for weeks before that. Only nobody paid any attention, including her parents, just like you're not paying attention to Bobby." Sheila angrily wiped a tear from her cheek with the back of her hand.

"All right," Derek said resignedly. "Tell him to come downstairs and I'll take a look at him."

Sheila brought Bobby down to the living room, and Derek examined him with some care, but found nothing untoward. Bobby was an extremely good-looking boy, well-developed for his age. Derek looked in his mouth, found it was clean, there was no enlargement of his neck glands. Depressing Bobby's tongue with the back of a spoon, he found that his tonsils and adenoids were not inflamed. Finally, and getting more annoyed by the minute. Derek listened to his son's chest. It sounded perfectly normal. Finally he checked Bobby's muscle tone and reflexes. Again, all was normal. The only unusual finding was that Bobby was a bit pale.

Derek then sent the boy back upstairs, and curtly told Sheila that there was nothing wrong with him, and that it was all in her own imagination. If that kid Moira she'd been going on about hadn't had leukemia, he told her, it wouldn't have occurred to her that anything was the matter with Bobby.

Not satisfied with Derek's conclusions, Sheila had insisted on a blood test, and they both waited for a week in some trepidation for the results, but to his smug relief, and to Sheila's annoyed surprise, these turned out to be entirely normal.

At the bottom of the hill, Derek turned the car toward South Street and the bridge. He really resented being forced to think about unpleasant or uncomfortable things, and normally Sheila paid the bills, argued with tradesmen when necessary, and endured the occasional uncomfortable interviews with the bank manager when the overdraft reached higher than usual levels. And of course Sheila took care of Bobby, his schoolwozk, everything except some occasional and infrequent cricket practice on the Inch. Derek had been a good bowler in his day, and occasionally they would go down to the Inch for some practice. Bobby preferred soccer, but was a good enough cricketer and they ran and caught and batted and bowled and generally had a good time.

Derek was, in his careless kind of way, inordinately proud of Bobby, and would talk about his son's accomplishments to the theater nurses, to the other doctors, to anyone who would listen. In his wallet, he carried a set of photos of Bobby as a baby, Bobby at the beach, Bobby scoring a goal, Bobby getting the scholar's cup at school. If Sheila and Derek went on a plane trip or a bus ride, just the two of them, she would count the minutes before Derek would start talking to whoever was sitting beside them, and then he'd have the pictures of Bobby out of his wallet in a jiffy.

And now, Bobby had been sent home from school because he wouldn't reply to a question. Derek wrinkled his brow. What a strange thing. He wondered for a moment what question could have elicited such a negative response. Then his mind went back to the hospital, to Lois Munday. Derek realized that his exit from the recovery room had been rather precipitous. Luckily the nurses up there were very capable, and they'd know how to take care of any problems. Lois had been a bit slow coming around, and at the end of the operation Derek had realized that he'd given her a bit more halothane than he'd meant to. Oh well, he thought, luckily there's a big margin of error there, and anyway nobody would ever know.

He waited at the traffic lights, then crossed the old bridge. There wasn't much traffic, and the weather was fine, with some high clouds to his right above Kinnoull hill. The sun shone intermittently on the car, and Derek pulled the sun visor down. To his left the big trees around the North Inch spread their wide, leafy branches over the grass at the side of the playing fields, and a couple of golfers headed toward the golf course, making practice swings as they walked. Under the bridge, the peat-colored river Tay rolled brown, wide and silent toward the harbor, and the sunlight sparkled up at him from the eddies.

The sight of the golfers made him think that maybe he'd have time for a quick round before going back to check on the patients who'd been operated on that day. Maybe he'd take Bobby with him. He turned right up Kincaid Crescent. His house was half-way up the hill, a semi-detached brown sandstone house with a small garden in front and a bigger one behind, where Sheila grew vegetables and some flowers. Derek didn't know much about gardening, and anyway by tacit agreement all that agricultural stuff was Sheila's affair. She usually took good care of the garden; earlier in the year, she had put in some smaller flowers around the rose bushes; pink, red, and yellow blooms that she seemed to have slackened off recently. The grass was too long, and weeds were springing up around the roses. Derek parked the car outside the low wall bordering the garden.

Inside the house, all was quiet. Sheila appeared from the kitchen, wiping her hands on her apron.

"He's upstairs," she said, her eyes cold. "He just went up to his room and wouldn't say anything. He's locked the door."

Derek sighed, and went slowly upstairs to talk to his son.

A few minutes later, he came down again. "He doesn't want to talk to me," he said to Sheila. "Maybe you should go up. I think he's crying. And I'm off. I'll be at the golf course the next hour or so."

It wasn't until some time later that Sheila found out the question Bobby's teacher had asked him at school, the question he had refused to answer. It was a simple enough one, it seemed. In fact, the teacher had asked the same question to all the other children in the class, and until she reached Bobby, they had all answered, one way or the other. The girls had been asked, "Would you like to grow up to be like your mother?" and the boys were asked the same question about their fathers.